RAMPAGE OF THE
MOUNTAIN MAN

RAMPAGE OF THE MOUNTAIN MAN

William W. Johnstone
with J. A. Johnstone

PINNACLE BOOKS
Kensington Publishing Corp.
www.kensingtonbooks.com

PINNACLE BOOKS are published by

Kensington Publishing Corp.
119 West 40th Street
New York, NY 10018

PUBLISHER'S NOTE
Following the death of William W. Johnstone, the Johnstone family is
working with a carefully selected writer to organize and complete
Mr. Johnstone's outlines and many unfinished manuscripts to
create additional novels in all of his series like The Last Gunfighter,
Mountain Man, and Eagles, among others. This novel was inspired by
Mr. Johnstone's superb storytelling.

All Kensington titles, imprints, and distributed lines are available at
special quantity discounts for bulk purchases for sales promotions,
premiums, fund-raising, educational, or institutional use. Special
book excerpts or customized printings can also be created to fit spe-
cific needs. For details, write or phone the office of the Kensington
special sales manager: Kensington Publishing Corp., 119 West 40th
Street, New York, NY 10018, attn: Special Sales Department; phone
1-800-221-2647.

PINNACLE BOOKS and the Pinnacle logo are Reg. U.S. Pat. &
TM Off.
The WWJ steer head logo is a trademark of Kensington Publishing Corp.

ISBN-13: 978-0-7860-4640-9
ISBN-10: 0-7860-4640-6

First printing: December 2007
Eighth printing: May 2013

16 15 14 13 12 11

Printed in the United States of America

Chapter One

A heavy, booming thunder rolled over the breaks, and gray veils of rain hung down from ominous, black clouds that crowded the hills. Though it had not yet reached him, the storm was moving quickly, and Smoke Jensen took a poncho from his saddlebag and slipped it on to be prepared for the impending downpour.

Smoke was on his way to Denver, and he was butt-sore from riding. Looking to hunker down from the approaching storm, he saw the little town of Willow Creek rising before him. The town had no more than half-a-dozen commercial buildings, and about three dozen houses.

Smoke leaned forward and patted his horse on the neck.

"What do you say that we find us a place to ride this storm out?" Smoke asked his horse. Often on long, lonely rides, Smoke wanted to hear a human voice, even if it was his own. Talking to his horse provided him with an excuse for talking aloud, without really talking to himself.

"A livery for you, and maybe supper and a beer for me," he continued in his one-sided conversation.

The first few drops of rain had just started when Smoke rode in through the big open door of the Jim Bob Corral. His nostrils were assailed with the pungent but familiar smell of hay, horseflesh, and horse manure. To a city person the odor might be unpleasant, but to Smoke, the aroma was almost comforting. Smoke took off his poncho and rolled it up. He had just finished tying it back onto his saddle when a boy of about sixteen appeared, having come from somewhere deep in the shadows of the barn.

"You wantin' to board your horse here, mister?" the boy asked.

"Yes," Smoke answered. "Find a dry place for him, rub him down, and give him oats." Smoke gave the boy a dollar.

"How long?" the boy asked.

"Just tonight."

"Then it's only a quarter," the boy said. "I'll get your change."

"You keep the change," Smoke said. "Just take extra care of my horse."

A broad smile spread across the boy's face. "Mister, the folks stayin' over to the Dunn Hotel won't be gettin' no better treatment than this here horse."

"I appreciate that," Smoke said.

Smoke looked across the street at the saloon.

"Do they serve food in the saloon?" he asked.

"Yes, sir, and it's good food too," the boy said. "My ma cooks there."

Smoke smiled. "Then I know I will enjoy it."

The rain was coming down pretty steadily now as Smoke hurried across the street for the saloon. Stepping inside, he took off his hat, then poured water from the crown as he looked around. For a town so small, the saloon was surprisingly full. It even had a piano, at which a piano player was grinding away in the back.

More than half the patrons in the saloon turned to look at him, and as they realized he was not a local, even more turned to see who the stranger was in their midst.

The barkeep moved toward him when Smoke stepped up to the bar.

"Hope you ain't put out none by ever'one lookin' at you, but we don't get a lot of visitors here, especially on a night like this."

"A night like this is what drove me here," Smoke replied.

The bartender chuckled. "Yes, sir, I see what you mean. What's your pleasure?"

"I'd like a beer."

"Yes, sir, one beer comin' up."

A moment later, the bartender put a mug of golden beer with a frothy head in front of Smoke. Smoke blew off some of the head, then took a long swallow. After a full day of riding, the beer tasted very good to him and he took another deep drink before he turned his back to the bar to have a look around the place that called itself The Gilded Lily.

A card game was going on in the corner and Smoke watched it for a few minutes while he drank his beer.

Smoke's peripheral vision caught someone coming in through the back door, and turning, he saw a tall, broad-shouldered man, wearing a badge. Because he had just come in from the rain, water was dripping from the lawman's sweeping mustache.

"I'm lookin' for a man named Emerson Pardeen," the man said.

One of the cardplayers stood up slowly, then turned to face the man with the badge.

"I'm Emerson Pardeen. Who the hell are you?"

"The name is Buck Wheeler. *Marshal* Buck Wheeler," he added, coming down hard on the word "Marshal."

"Yeah? Well, what do you want with me?"

"I'm taking you back to Dodge City to stand trial for the murder of Jason Tibbs."

"Dodge City is in Kansas, this is Colorado. You got no jurisdiction here."

"Maybe I should've told you I'm a United States marshal," Wheeler added. "I've got jurisdiction everywhere."

"Yeah? Well, Mr. United States Marshal Buck Wheeler, I ain't goin' back to Dodge City with you," Pardeen said.

"Oh, you're going back all right," Wheeler said. "Either sitting in your saddle, or belly-down over it."

Realizing that a gunfight was very likely, the others who had been sitting at the table jumped up and moved out of the way, a couple of them moving so quickly that their chairs fell over.

The marshal pulled his gun and pointed it at

Pardeen. "Now, shuck out of that gunbelt, slow and easy-like," he ordered.

Pardeen shook his head. "No, I don't think so. I think maybe I'm just goin' to call you on this one."

"Whatever you say, Pardeen. Whatever you say," the marshal replied.

Smoke, like the others, was watching the drama unfold, when he heard a soft squeaking sound as if weight were being put down on a loose board. The sound caused him to look up toward the top of the stairs. When he did so, he saw a man standing there, aiming a shotgun at the back of the marshal.

"Marshal, there's a gun at your back!" Smoke shouted. Concurrent with Smoke's warning, the man wielding the shotgun turned it toward Smoke.

"You sorry son of a bitch!" he shouted.

Smoke had no choice then. He dropped his beer and pulled his pistol, firing just as the man at the top of the stairs squeezed his own trigger. The shotgun boomed loudly. The heavy charge of buckshot tore a large hole in the top and side of the bar, right where Smoke had been standing. Some of the shot hit the whiskey bottles in front of the mirror, and one of the nude statues behind the bar. Like shrapnel from an exploding bomb, pieces of glass flew everywhere. The mirror fell except for a few jagged shards, which hung in place where the mirror had been, reflecting distorted images of the dramatic scene playing out before it.

Smoke's single shot had not missed, and the man with the shotgun dropped his weapon. His eyes rolled up in his head and he fell, twisting around so that he slid down the stairs on his back and headfirst, following his clattering shotgun to the ground floor. The wielder of the shotgun lay at the foot of the stairs, with his head on the floor and his legs splayed apart stretching back up the bottom four steps. His sightless eyes were open and staring up toward the ceiling.

The sound of the two gunshots had riveted everyone's attention on that exchange, and while their attention was diverted from him, Pardeen took the opportunity to go for his own gun. Suddenly, the saloon was filled with the roar of another gunshot as Pardeen fired at the marshal who had confronted him.

Marshal Wheeler had made the fatal mistake of being diverted by the gunplay between Smoke and the shotgun shooter. Pardeen's bullet struck the marshal in the forehead and the impact of it knocked him back on a nearby table. The marshal lay belly-up on the table with his head hanging down on the far side while blood dripped from the hole in his forehead to form a puddle below him. His gun fell from his lifeless hand and clattered to the floor. Pardeen then swung his pistol toward Smoke.

"Mister, this isn't my fight," Smoke said. "We can end it here and now." Smoke put his pistol back in its holster.

As he realized that he now had the advantage, a big smile spread across Pardeen's face. "Oh, it's goin' to end all right," Pardeen said. "'Cause I aim to end it right now." Pardeen cocked his pistol.

Those who were looking on in morbid fascination were surprised by what happened next, because even as Pardeen was cocking his pistol, Smoke drew and fired.

His bullet caught Pardeen in the center of his chest and Pardeen went down. He sat up, then clutched his hand over the wound as blood spilled between his fingers.

"How the hell did you do that?" he asked. He coughed once—then he fell back dead.

"What's goin' on in here?" a voice asked. "What's all the shootin'?"

When Smoke turned toward the sound of the voice, he saw a man dripping water onto the floor as he stood just inside the open door. Because the man was standing in the shadows, Smoke couldn't quite make out his features.

"Step into the light so I can see you," Smoke said.

"Mister, do you know who you are talking to?" the man in the door asked.

Smoke pulled the hammer back, and his pistol made a deadly metallic click as the sear engaged the cylinder. "Doesn't much matter who I'm talking to. In about one second you'll be dead if you don't step into the light."

This time the man moved as ordered. Doing so enabled Smoke to see the badge on the man's shirt, and he let the hammer down on his pistol, then dropped it back into his holster.

"Sorry, Sheriff," Smoke said. "I didn't know you were the law."

"What happened here?"

"I'll tell you what happened," one of the other card-players said.

"Who are you?"

"The name is Corbett." Corbett pointed to Smoke.

"This here fella just kilt three men. He kilt the marshal, Eddie Phillips, and Emerson Pardeen."

The sheriff made a grunting sound. "Now you tell me, Corbett, just why would this fella kill the marshal *and* Pardeen? Marshal Wheeler stopped by my office not ten minutes ago to tell me he was here to arrest Pardeen, so I know it isn't very likely that Marshal Wheeler and Pardeen would be on the same side in this fracas."

"Hell, Sheriff, I don't know why he done it. Maybe you need to ask him."

"All right, I'll ask him," the sheriff said. "Did you kill all three of these men, mister?"

"No. I only killed two of them," Smoke replied.

Inexplicably, the sheriff chuckled. "I see. You just killed two of them. So that makes you what? One-third innocent?"

"One-hundred-percent innocent," Smoke replied. "I only killed the ones who were trying to kill me. And in my book that is self-defense."

"He's lyin', Sheriff," Corbett said. "He kilt Phillips and Pardeen in cold blood."

"Oh, so now you are saying he only killed two of them?"

"In cold blood, yes," Corbett said.

"Corbett is the one who is lyin', Sheriff," the bartender said. "This fella is telling the truth. Eddie Phillips shot first. He was standin' up there at the head of the stairs holdin' a scattergun pointed at the marshal's back. This fella shouted a warnin' to the marshal, and Phillips turned the gun on him. Take a look at the bar here, and you'll see what I'm talkin' about. Hell, it was a wonder I wasn't kilt my ownself. Then Pardeen kilt Marshal Wheeler and swung his gun around toward this fella, tellin' him he was fixin' to kill him too. And what happened then, you ain't goin' to believe."

"Try me," the sheriff said.

"Well, sir, this here fella had already put his gun away. Pardeen had the drop on him, and was pullin' back the hammer when this fella drew and shot him. Damn'dest thing I ever seen."

The sheriff stroked his chin as he looked at Smoke. "Is what he saying true?"

Smoke nodded. "It's like the barkeep said. Pardeen was about to shoot me."

"Pardeen wasn't about to shoot him," Corbett said. "He was just goin' to hold him for killin' Phillips and the marshal."

"Hold him?"

"Yeah, Pardeen was goin' to hold him until you got here," Corbett said.

Several in the saloon laughed then.

"Tell you what, Sheriff. You arrest him, I'll testify against him at his trial."

"Corbett," the sheriff said. "I'm not aware that there is any paper out on you, but that might be because I haven't looked hard enough."

Corbett's eyes narrowed. "You ain't goin' to find any paper on me, Sheriff. The one you should arrest is this fella."

The sheriff looked around the saloon at the other patrons, who were still watching the drama.

"Anyone in here back up what Corbett is saying?" the sheriff asked.

Several responded at once.

"He ain't tellin' it the way I seen it," one of the other customers said. "I seen it the same way the bartender told it."

"That's the way it looked to me, too," another said.

"Yeah, ever' word the bartender said is the gospel."

The sheriff held up his hand. "So what I'm hearin' is, nobody backs up Corbett's version of the story?"

Everyone was quiet, and the sheriff looked at Corbett. "Looks like a clear case of self-defense to me," he said.

Corbett looked at Smoke. "Pardeen was my friend," he said. "I don't like the way you shot him down like that. Maybe I'll just settle the score myself."

"No!" the sheriff said. "There's been enough killin' for one night."

"What's your name, mister?" Corbett asked.

"Jensen. Kirby Jensen. But most folks just call me Smoke."

There was a collective gasp from everyone in the saloon.

"Smoke Jensen," one unidentified speaker said. "No wonder he could do what he done. Ain't nobody nowhere no faster'n Smoke Jensen."

"Are you the Smoke Jensen from over by Big Rock?" the sheriff asked. "That Smoke Jensen?"

"I have a ranch just outside Big Rock, yes," Smoke replied. He knew that the sheriff was trying to determine if he was *the* Smoke Jensen, but humility prevented him from elaborating.

"I'll be damned," the sheriff said. "What are you doing in Willow Creek?"

"I'm just passing through, on my way to Denver," Smoke said.

The sheriff looked over at Corbett, who had also recognized the name.

"Corbett, you still want to settle accounts with this fella?"

Corbett stroked his chin nervously. "Uh, no, Sheriff, it's like you said, there's been enough killin' for one night."

Corbett pointed at Smoke. "But I think maybe you ought to know that Pardeen has a brother named Quince. He ain't goin' to like it that you kilt Emerson, and one of these days you'n him are goin' to run across each other." Corbett smiled, a dry, humorless smile. "And when you two do run into each other, well, I would like to be there to see it."

"That wouldn't be a threat now, would it, Corbett?" the sheriff asked.

"No threat," Corbett said. "Just a friendly warnin', so to speak."

"There ain't nothin' about you friendly," the sheriff said. "If I was you, Corbett, I'd leave town right now."

"In case you ain't noticed, Sheriff, there's a storm goin' on out there," Corbett said.

"Because I'm going to go back to my office and look for a dodger on you," the sheriff continued, as if he had not even heard Corbett. "And if I can't find one, I may just come back and arrest you anyway."

Corbett glared at Smoke and the sheriff for a

moment longer. Then he picked up his hat and started toward the door. "I'll be goin' now."

"Wait!" the sheriff called after him.

Corbett stopped and looked back.

"What about your pards?" The sheriff asked, pointing at Pardeen and Phillips.

"What about 'em?" Corbett replied.

"Are you just goin' to walk out and leave them layin' here? Aren't you going to wait until the undertaker comes so you can make burial arrangements?" the sheriff asked.

"Hell, they ain't either one of 'em my kin. That means they ain't my responsibility," Corbett said. "Just put 'em anywhere."

"I see. Friendship don't mean that much to you, does it?" the sheriff asked.

"They was my friends when they was alive. They're dead," Corbett said as if, somehow, that justified his indifference to them. He pushed through the batwing doors and walked out into the pouring rain.

"Are you planning on staying in town for long, Mr. Jensen?" the sheriff asked.

"The name's Smoke, Sheriff," Smoke said in a friendly tone. "I had only planned to stay the night, just long enough to ride out the storm. But I reckon I can stay a bit longer if you think that's necessary."

The sheriff looked at the bodies still lying on the saloon floor. "No," he said, shaking his head. "There are enough witnesses here to verify what happened. I see no need for getting a judge to come this far just for an inquest that we know how it's going to turn out."

"If you do need me for anything, just get in touch with Sheriff Carson in Big Rock."

"I'm sure there won't be a need for that," the sheriff replied. "Oh, but Smoke, there's one thing Corbett said that you should take to heart."

"What's that?"

"Quince Pardeen. Do you know him?"

Smoke shook his head. "I've heard his name, but I can't say that I know him."

"He's good with a gun, but that ain't the thing that makes him so dangerous. What makes him dangerous is the fact that he is a killer, and he don't particular care how he kills. You look out for him."

"I will, Sheriff," Smoke replied. "And thanks for the warning."

Chapter Two

Denver wasn't the largest city Smoke had ever seen, but it was the largest city in Colorado and as Smoke rode down Wynkoop Street, he had to maneuver his horse from side to side in order to negotiate his way through the heavy traffic of coaches, carriages, and wagons.

There was a large banner stretched across the street, and looking up, Smoke smiled when he saw the name on it.

COLORADO HONORS MATT JENSEN

This was a proud moment for Smoke, having Matt honored by the State of Colorado.

As a young boy, Matt Cavanaugh had run away from an orphanage, and would have died had Smoke not found him shivering in a snowbank in the mountains. Smoke took him to his cabin and nursed him back to health.

It had been Smoke's intention to keep the boy

around only until he had recovered, but Matt wound up staying with Smoke until he reached manhood. During the time Matt lived with Smoke, he became Smoke's student, learning everything from Smoke that Smoke had learned from Preacher many years earlier, including the most important lesson of all, how to be a man of honor.

By the time Matt reached the age of eighteen, he was skilled in everything from the use of weapons to fighting to tracking, hunting, and camping. Feeling that the time was right, he left to go on his own. Smoke did not have the slightest hesitancy over letting him leave because Matt had become one of the most capable young men Smoke had ever seen.

Just before Matt left, he surprised Smoke by asking permission to take Smoke's last name as his own. Smoke was not only honored by the request, he was touched, and to this day there was a bond between them that was as close as any familial bond could be.*

Smoke and Matt had shared their time together long before Smoke married Sally, and long before his two most loyal hands, Pearlie and Cal, had come to work at Sugarloaf. But Sally understood the bond between Smoke and Matt, and it was she who suggested that Smoke go to Denver for the ceremony.

After getting a room at the hotel, Smoke took a bath and put on a suit, then went downstairs and walked

*The Last Mountain Man

through the lobby to a large ballroom that was being used as a reception hall. Through the open door of the room, he could see several well-dressed men and women standing around, laughing and talking.

A large man was standing near the open door, looking out into the lobby. By the man's demeanor and by the expression on his face, Smoke could see that he was not a guest of the reception, but was a guard. The guard came toward Smoke, shaking his head and with his hand extended.

"Sir, this is a closed reception," the guard said.

"That's good," Smoke said. "It shouldn't be open for just anyone. Why, there's no telling what kind of disreputable figure might try to come in."

"You don't understand, sir," the guard said. "I'm talking about you. You can't come in here."

"Wait a minute. Are you calling me a disreputable figure?"

"No, sir, I'm just telling you that this is a closed reception and unless you have a personal invitation from the governor, you cannot come in."

"Well, the gentleman being honored and I are old friends," Smoke said.

"Do you have an invitation?"

"No."

The guard smiled triumphantly. "Well, if you were old friends, you would have an invitation now, wouldn't you? I'm sorry, sir, but you can't come in. I'm going to have to ask you to leave."

"Why don't we just ask the man being honored?" Smoke suggested. He started into the room.

"Sir, if you don't leave now, I am going to personally throw you out of here!"

Smoke looked at the guard. The guard was a big man and it was obvious that he could handle himself. But at the same time Smoke was looking the guard over, the guard was taking stock of Smoke, and Smoke could see by the expression on his face that he wasn't looking forward to any encounter with someone Smoke's size.

Smoke sighed. The guard was just doing his job.

"All right," Smoke said. "I don't want to cause any trouble." He pointed to the lobby. "I'll wait out here. I would appreciate it, though, if you would tell Matt Jensen that Smoke is here."

At that moment, the governor happened to glance over toward the door and saw Smoke standing in the door. Breaking into a wide smile, the governor came over to extend a personal greeting.

"Smoke Jensen," Governor John Long Routt said, extending his hand. "How good to see you."

"Hello, John," Smoke replied, returning the smile.

"Governor, this man doesn't have an invitation," the guard said.

"Really? Well, don't worry about it, Mitchell," the governor said. "Mr. Jensen and I are old friends."

"Oh. Mr. Jensen, I'm sorry I didn't know. I hope you don't take offense."

"Don't be sorry, my friend," Smoke said. "You were just doing your job. And, if I may say so, you were doing it quite well."

"Uh, yes, sir. Thank you, sir. But you should'a said you were a friend of the governor. You said you were a friend of the man being honored."

"Indeed he is, Mitchell," Governor Routt said. "In fact, he is much more than a friend. Perhaps you didn't catch his last name. It is Jensen."

"Jensen? Oh, you mean like Matt Jensen, the man getting the award tonight?"

"Yes," Governor Routt said. "Come with me, Smoke, I'm sure Matt is looking for you."

Smoke shook his head. "I doubt it," he said. "I didn't tell him I was coming. I wanted to surprise him."

"Oh. Well, that is even better. Come along."

Smoke followed the governor through a cloud of aromatic tobacco and pipe smoke. He saw Matt before Matt saw him. It was easy to pick Matt out from the crowd. His young protégé stood over six feet tall with broad shoulders and narrow hips. His blond hair seemed even more yellow than Smoke remembered.

Matt didn't see Smoke right away, because he had his back turned and he was surrounded by almost half-a-dozen very beautiful women, each woman vying for his attention. As Smoke approached, the women broke out into laughter over some story Matt was telling.

"You always were able to spin a good yarn," Smoke said.

Recognizing Smoke's voice, Matt turned toward his mentor with a broad smile on his face.

"Smoke! What are you doing here?"

"You are getting an award from the governor, aren't you?" Smoke replied. "I had to be here."

Matt took Smoke's hand in his and the two shook hands and clasped each other on the shoulder.

"Ladies, this is Smoke Jensen," Matt said.

"Did you say Jensen?" one of the women asked.

"I sure did."

"Is he your brother?" another asked.

Matt nodded. "Yes, indeed," Matt said. "Smoke is my brother."

There was a dinner after the reception, and though Smoke offered to leave, he was persuaded to stay when he learned that the governor had made special arrangements for him at the head table. When all were seated, Governor Routt tapped his spoon on the crystal goblet. The clear ringing sound could be heard above all the laughter and conversation, and it had the desired effect of silencing the guests.

"Ladies and gentlemen, it is my distinct honor and privilege tonight to host this banquet in honor of Matthew Jensen, one of Colorado's leading citizens.

"Last winter during an attempted train robbery, some bandits killed both the engineer and the fireman of the Midnight Flyer. Now, the dead man's throttle is supposed to stop the train anytime the engineer is incapacitated, but it failed, and rather than stopping the train as the bandits planned, their action caused a runaway train. Matt Jensen was a passenger on that train. And while he knew nothing about the attempted holdup, he did realize, rather quickly, that the train was in great danger. He knew also that, somehow, he would have to get to the engine.

"The only way for him to get to the engine, was to crawl along the top of the swaying, ice-covered cars on a train that was speeding through the dark at sixty miles per hour. Matt finally managed to reach the engine and stop the train, just before it rounded a sharp turn. Had he not succeeded, the speed they were traveling would have sent the train, and all one hundred thirty-one passengers, over the side of a mountain to a sure and certain death."

The governor paused in his speech long enough to enable the crowd to react with exclamations of awe and wonder at Matt's skill and bravery. The crowd did just as he expected, and the governor waited until it was quiet again before he continued with his proclamation.

"And now, as governor of the State of Colorado, I hereby issue this proclamation declaring this day to be officially entered into the state historical records as Matthew Jensen Day."

The presentation was greeted with applause and cheers for Matt, who despite the shouts of "Speech!" managed only to mumble his thanks.

Following the reception and dinner, Smoke was surprised by the number of people who, after congratulating Matt, came to shake *his* hand.

At breakfast the next morning, Smoke commented on his surprise over the number of people who had made a special effort to greet him.

"You shouldn't be surprised," Matt replied. "Surely you know that you are one of the best-known men in the entire state of Colorado. Why, if you ran for governor today, I've no doubt but that you would be elected."

Smoke chuckled. "Don't tell John that," he said. "Though he has no need to worry. I have no intention of ever entering politics. But maybe you should. You are getting quite an enviable reputation yourself, and you are still young enough—why, you could have a very successful political career."

"Thanks, but no, thanks," Matt replied, clearly uncomfortable with any such suggestion. Clearing his throat, he changed the subject. "How is Sally?"

"Sally sends her love."

"You tell her that I send mine as well," Matt said.

"I'll do that," Smoke said, putting some money on the table as he stood.

"No," Matt said resolutely. He picked the money up and gave it back. "I'm buying breakfast."

Smoke pocketed the money and laughed. "All right," he said. "But don't you think for one moment that a measly breakfast is going to pay me back for all the meals I furnished you when you were a snot-nosed kid."

Matt laughed as well and walked to the door with his friend. It was always like this when the two encountered each other. Matt had never made an effort to dissuade Smoke from going, nor had he ever put forth an offer to join him. Each man was supremely confident in his own life, and in the absolute certainty that their friendship would remain strong despite lengthy and distant separation.

"Smoke?" Matt called as Smoke mounted his horse.

Smoke swung into the saddle, then patted his horse on the neck before he responded.

"Yes?"

"You take care, you hear? You're the only family I have."

Smoke touched the brim of his hat and nodded. "I'll do that, Matt," he replied.

As Smoke reached the outskirts of Denver, he had to stop at the railroad tracks to wait for a train to pass. He sat in his saddle and watched the windows slide by, nodding at a couple of the passengers who had nodded at him.

One of the passengers on the train was Trent Williams, and though Williams did not acknowledge the cowboy who sat on his horse alongside the track, he did see him. Then, just after they passed the cowboy, Williams heard the hiss and squeal of the brakes. As the train started to slow, Williams took an envelope from his inside jacket pocket and pulled a well-read letter from the envelope, opened it, then read it again.

Dear Mr. Williams,

Your offer to buy fifty-one per cent of the Miners Bank and Trust has been received, and our board asks that you come to Denver to present your proposal in person.

We are in agreement that we would like to have you run our bank, but there is some concern as to whether we should turn over absolute control to one man, as would be the case if you were to acquire fifty-one per cent of the stock. We look forward to meeting you, and to discussing at length the details of the sale. Please advise us when you will arrive. I will meet you at the depot to take you to the bank, where the board meeting will take place. In

order that you may recognize me, I will be wearing a red
feather in the band of my hat.

> *Sincerely,*
> *Vernon Bess*

Williams put the letter away as the train screeched to
a halt. When he stepped out onto the platform, he saw
a man wearing a hat with a red feather in the band.

"Mr. Bess?" he asked.

The man smiled and extended his hand. "Yes, you
are Mr. Williams, I presume?"

"I am."

"I have a carriage here," Bess said. "The board meeting will be held at ten o'clock this morning. Do you
have luggage?"

"I do, yes."

Bess made a motion toward the driver of the carriage,
and the driver went to retrieve Williams's luggage.

"I think you will have no trouble with the board. As
president of the Bank of Salcedo in Wyoming, you have
just the kind of experience that can make a success of
our bank. Although I must say that at first the board
members were a little put off by your insistence on
owning fifty-one percent. I think you will have to ex-
plain why you feel that is necessary."

"It is absolutely necessary if I am to make a success
of the bank," Williams said.

"I'm sure you will be able to make your case satisfac-
torily," Bess replied.

The board, which was made up of investors and
businessmen from Denver, had gathered at the bank

for the meeting and they greeted Vernon Bess when he arrived.

"Gentlemen of the board, it is my pleasure to introduce Mr. Trent Williams. As you know, Mr. Williams is president of the Bank of Salcedo. I have done research on that bank and find that it is one of the most successful and fiscally sound banks in all of Wyoming. I believe him to be just the man we are looking for."

Williams acknowledged the introduction, then spoke to the board for a few minutes about his plans for the bank. Then he asked if there were any questions.

"Mr. Williams, why do you insist on buying fifty-one percent of our bank?" one of the board members asked.

"If I am going to make this bank successful, I must have total freedom of operation," Williams explained. "With fifty-one percent, I will not have to be bound by any restrictions placed on me by the board."

"So, what you are saying is that you want to make us irrelevant."

"Well, I wouldn't put it quite that way," Williams replied. "I will, of course, be open to any suggestions the board might have."

"I don't know if I can go along with that. After all, I have a lot of money invested in this bank. What if you are wrong and the bank fails?"

"I will have a lot more money invested than you," Williams said. "That means I have even more incentive than you to make the bank succeed."

"Elmer, think about it," Bess said to the hesitant board member. "He's not going to invest fifty thousand dollars, then let the bank fail."

"I agree," one of the other board members said. "If

Mr. Williams needs freedom of action to save the bank, I say let's give it to him. God knows we haven't been doing very well ourselves. And this way, we'll be able to recoup some of our money while still maintaining an investment. If he succeeds in making the bank successful, we will congratulate ourselves for having made such a sound decision."

"All right," said Elmer. "I just wanted to ask the question, that's all. How soon can we expect the fifty thousand dollars?" he asked Williams.

"I will have to return to Salcedo and put my affairs in order there," Williams said. "It would not be fair to my employers to leave without giving adequate notice."

"An honorable thing for you to do," Bess said. "All the more reason I believe we should accept the proposal. I now call for a vote."

The board voted to accept the proposal, with even Elmer voting "aye." Williams accepted the congratulations of the board, then left the bank to walk down to the hotel. Before getting a room at the hotel, he stopped at the Western Union Office to send a telegram.

UNDERSTAND YOU HAVE NEED FOR CATTLE STOP
PLEASE ADVISE ME OF BEST PRICE PER HEAD
STOP REPLY TRENT WILLIAMS SALCEDO WYOMING
TERRITORY STOP

Chapter Three

Smoke had been home for two weeks when he was awakened one morning by the aroma of breakfast cooking. When he got dressed and went into the kitchen, he saw that Sally was preparing a veritable feast: eggs, bacon, biscuits, gravy, and fresh-baked bear claws. Pearlie and Cal were already in the dining room, drinking coffee and looking on hungrily.

"You boys are up early," Smoke said, speaking to his two longtime and most loyal hands.

"How could I sleep with Pealie's stomach growlin' so?" Cal asked.

"Oh? Was your stomach growling, Pearlie?" Smoke teased.

"How could it not be?" Pearlie replied. "There I was, sleepin' out there in the bunkhouse all peaceful like, when all of a sudden I started smellin' the most wonderful smells. You doggone right my stomach started growlin'."

"So, me'n Pearlie come in here and seen Miz Sally just cookin' away," Cal said.

"So, Miz Sally, ain't it about ready?" Pearlie asked. "All them smells got me so hungry I can't hardly stand it."

Sally sighed. "Pearlie, I swear, your grammar is so atrocious that it makes me cringe."

"Well, yes'm, I mean bein' as you was a schoolmarm 'n all a'fore you and Smoke married up, well, I reckon it'd be only natural that you wouldn't think I talk all that good," Pearlie said.

Sally put her hands over her ears. "Ahhh!" she said. "Smoke, shoot him! Shoot him right now before he says another word!"

"No, ma'am!" Pearlie said. "Leastwise, not till I've et some of this here breakfast."

Sally laughed, and shook her head. "You are incorrigible," she said.

"Yes'm, I reckon I am," Pearlie said. "I'm hungry too."

"Go sit at the table, all of you. I'll bring it to you."

After the huge breakfast, when Smoke finished his coffee, Sally jumped up from the table and refilled his cup.

"You're being awfully nice, Sally," Smoke said.

"Can't I be nice to my husband if I feel like it?" Sally replied with a sweet smile.

"You'll get no argument from me," Smoke said, returning the smile.

"I swear, Miz Sally, if this ain't about the best breakfast I done ever et anywhere," Pearlie said.

"Ha!" Cal said. "It's come to my mind, Pearlie, that anything you eat is the best thing you ever ate."

"Well, yeah, I do like to eat, there ain't no denyin' that. But this here breakfast is particular good."

Cal nodded. "I'll have to agree with you on that. Why the big feed, Miz Sally?"

"No particular reason," Sally answered.

Smoke stared at his wife over the rim of his coffee cup. Seeing his intense stare, Sally looked away.

"Another bear claw, darling?" she asked.

"What is it, Sally?" Smoke asked. "What is going on?"

"What makes you think something is going on?"

"Because I know you, Sally. We're married, remember?"

"All right, I'll tell you," Sally replied.

Sally poured herself a cup of coffee, then sat back down before she went on.

"Do you remember the big winter freeze we had a couple of years ago? We lost over eighty percent of our herd. Do you remember that?"

"Of course I remember that," Smoke said. "We not only lost our herd, we almost lost Sugarloaf."

Sally reached back to the sideboard and got a small book, which she slid across the table to Smoke.

"What is that?" Smoke asked.

"It's the *Farmer's Almanac,*" Sally said. "According to the *Almanac,* this winter is going to be as bad as that one was."

"Oh, that's bad," Pearlie said. "That's really bad."

"And that's why the big breakfast?" Smoke asked. "We are celebrating the fact that we are going to have another bad winter?"

Sally shook her head. "No, we are celebrating the

fact that a bad winter isn't going to be as big a problem for us this year."

Smoke drummed his fingers on the table. "What makes you think it won't be a problem?"

"After that last big freeze, you built shelter areas, remember?"

"Of course I remember. But we can only shelter about half of our herd."

"That's all we'll need to shelter," Sally said.

"Sally, it won't put Sugarloaf in danger like the last freeze-up, but do you have any idea how much money it would cost us to lose three thousand head."

"Just over one hundred thousand dollars," Sally said easily.

"What?"

"It would cost us just over one hundred thousand dollars to lose three thousand head. But we won't lose them if we sell them," Sally said.

Smoke shook his head. "You might be right, but if everyone is in the same situation, we won't be able to sell them."

"I know where we can sell them," Sally said.

"Where?"

"We can sell them to Mr. Colin Abernathy."

Smoke shook his head in confusion. "I don't know anyone named Colin Abernathy. He's not a local rancher. Is he an absentee owner?"

"Mr. Abernathy is the Indian agent for all the Cheyenne in Wyoming Territory. He needs the beef to get the Indians through the winter."

"Wait a minute. Did you say all the Cheyenne in Wyoming?"

"Yes, and to be honest, that is the fly in the ointment," Sally said. "Mr. Abernathy will only pay for them when they are delivered to the procurement center. That means we'll have to drive three thousand head to Sorento, where we will deliver them to Cephus Malone."

"I thought you said Colin Abernathy. Who is Cephus Malone?"

"Malone works for Abernathy."

"I see. And where is Sorento?"

"It's in Wyoming Territory, near the town of Laramie."

"Whoa, that's almost five hundred miles. You are proposing that we drive three thousand head five hundred miles? Sally, darlin', I know you mean well, but think about it. It would take us a month to get there, and you say that it is just a fly in the ointment. That's a pretty big fly, don't you think?"

"It is, I suppose," Sally said. "But when you think about it, we will have a pretty big fly swat." Sally smiled sweetly at her husband.

"What do you mean, we'll have a pretty big fly swat?"

"Mr. Abernathy is paying thirty-five dollars a head at delivery."

"Thirty-five dollars a head?" Smoke said in surprise. "Why, that's . . . ."

"That's one hundred and five thousand dollars," Sally said, finishing Smoke's sentence.

Pearlie dropped his fork and stared across the table at Sally. Cal laughed out loud.

"Pearlie, that's the first time I ever seen anything stop you eatin' in mid-chew," Cal said.

"Miz Sally, did you . . ." Pearlie began, then remembering that his mouth was full, finished chewing and swallowed before he returned to his question. "Did you just say one hunnert'n five thousand dollars?"

"I did say that," Sally said. She smiled at Smoke. "That's why I was able to answer your question as to how much it would cost us to lose three thousand head."

"Lord, I've never seen that much money. I ain't never even heard of that much money," Cal said.

"You haven't said anything, Smoke," Sally said. She took a sip of coffee and stared at her husband over the rim of the cup. "What's the matter? Has the cat got your tongue?"

"That's a lot of money," Smoke said. "And you are right, that is one big fly swat. Something like that would be worth going all the way to Sorento."

"Smoke, do you really think we can drive that many cows all the way to Sorento?" Pearlie asked.

"Looks like we don't have any choice," Smoke said, smiling at Sally. "The boss has spoken."

"Lord, just us?" Cal asked.

Smoke chuckled. "What's the matter, Cal? Don't you think we can do it?"

"I—I reckon so, if you say we can," Cal said, though it was obvious he was unconvinced.

Smoke laughed again. "Don't worry, we'll get some men to help us: drovers, a blacksmith, a cook."

"You won't need a cook," Sally said.

"No cook? Miz Sally, you don't aim for us to make a drive like that on nothin' but beef jerky, do you?" Pearlie asked.

"No, I expect you to make the drive on bacon and

beans, biscuits and cornbread, ham and fried potatoes, some roast beef, steak from time to time, apple
pie, and . . . maybe a few bear claws."

"Lord a'mercy, you're goin' with us?"

"No," Smoke said.

"Yes," Sally said at the same time.

"Sally, this isn't some picnic in the country," Smoke
said. "I'm not going to let you go."

Sally stared at Smoke with here eyes flashing.
"Smoke Jensen. Did you just say what I thought you
said? Did you say you aren't going to *let* me go?"

"I, uh . . ." Smoke began, but he stammered to a
stop in mid-sentence.

"Cal, if you would be so kind as to hitch up the
team, I'll take a wagon into town and pick up all the
possibles we're going to need for the drive," Sally said.

Cal looked at Smoke.

Smoke smiled, and shook his head. "Well, do what
the lady says," he said. "Maybe a few bear claws would
taste good out on the trail."

"Yes, sir!" Cal said with pleasure.

"I'll help you with the team," Pearlie said, following
Cal outside.

"I thought you might see it my way," Sally said after
the two young men were gone.

"I haven't seen it your way," Smoke said.

"Oh? Kirby Jensen, are you telling me you are going
to stop me from going?"

Sally used Smoke's real name, a sign that she meant
business.

"No, hold on now," Smoke said, raising his hands in

defense. "I said I haven't seen it your way. I didn't say you weren't going."

Sally smiled. "I didn't think you would actually try to stop me."

"I won't do that," Smoke said. "But if there comes a gully-gusher and you're trying to drive the chuck wagon hub-deep through water and mud, I don't want to hear the slightest complaint from you."

Sally leaned into Smoke and looked flirtatiously into his eyes.

"Why, Smoke, darling," she said. "Do I ever complain?"

Chapter Four

Even as Pearlie and Cal were hitching up the wagon for Sally to drive into town, several hundred miles north, in the little town of Salcedo in Wyoming Territory, Trent Williams was awakened from a sound sleep by a loud knock on his hotel room door.

"Mr. Williams? Mr. Williams, sir?"

"Yes?" Williams answered in a voice that was groggy with sleep.

"It is seven o'clock, Mr. Williams. You left word with the desk that you were to be awakened at seven sharp."

"All right, all right, I'm awake," Williams said. "Quit pounding on the door."

"Yes, sir," the chagrined voice said from outside Williams's hotel room.

Trent Williams lived in the hotel. As president of the Bank of Salcedo, Williams could afford to live anywhere he wanted, but he preferred a hotel room to a house or an apartment in a boardinghouse. Life was just simpler living in a hotel.

A slight morning breeze filled the muslin curtains

and lifted them out over the wide-planked floor. Getting out of bed, Williams padded barefoot over to the window and looked down on the town, which was just beginning to awaken. The morning's enterprise had already begun. Water was being heated behind the laundry and boxes were being stacked behind the grocery store. A team of four big horses pulled a fully loaded freight wagon down the main street.

From somewhere, Williams could smell bacon frying and his stomach growled, reminding him that he was hungry. He splashed some water in the basin, washed his face and hands, then got dressed and went downstairs. There were a couple of people in the lobby, one napping in one of the chairs, the other reading a newspaper. Neither of them paid any attention to Williams as he left the hotel.

The morning sun was bright, but not yet hot. The sky was clear and the air was clean, and as he walked toward the café he could hear the sounds of commerce: the ring of a blacksmith's hammer, a carpenter's saw, and the rattle of working wagons. That was in contrast to last night's sounds of breaking liquor bottles, out-of-tune pianos, loud laughter, and boisterous conversations. How different the tenor of a town was during the business of morning and the play of evening.

Several of the town's citizens doffed their hats in respect to Williams as he passed them on the street. Williams nodded in return, but because of his station in the town, he did not doff his own hat.

"Good morning, Mr. Williams," the owner of the café said as Williams stepped inside. Eric Jordan held a folded newspaper out toward Williams. "Your table is ready for you, sir, and the coffee is hot."

Williams grunted in reply, then took the paper and walked over to his table. Even as he was sitting down, a waiter appeared and poured the coffee for him.

"Your usual, Mr. Williams?" the waiter asked.

"Of course my usual. Bacon, eggs, fried potatoes, biscuits and gravy," Williams replied. "Have I ever varied my order?"

"No, sir."

"Then don't waste my time asking foolish questions," Williams said. "Just get my breakfast out here."

"Right away, sir," the waiter answered.

Half an hour later, Williams was just finishing his breakfast when a man stepped up to his table. The man needed a shave and a bath. His clothes hung in rags from his body.

"You are in my light," Williams said. "Move."

Obligingly, the man stepped to one side. "Sorry, Mr. Williams. Didn't mean no offense," the man said.

"What do you want, Percy?"

Williams asked the question without so much as looking at the man, concentrating instead on his breakfast.

Percy ran his hand across the stubble of his beard. "Well, sir, Mr. Williams, you said I was to bring you a telegram if it come."

"That's right."

"Well, sir, it's come," Percy said. "It come this mornin'."

Williams stuck his hand out.

"Yes, sir, it come this mornin' and I got it first thing

and brung it over to you," Percy said, making no effort to hand over the telegram.

Williams grunted, then reached into his pocket and pulled out a quarter. He gave it Percy. "Will this compensate you for your trouble?"

"Yes, sir!" Percy said brightly. "Thank you, Mr. Williams."

"The telegram?"

"Oh, yes, sir. Here it is," Percy said, handing the little envelope to Williams. "You want me to hang around so's you can answer it?"

"No," Williams replied. "That won't be necessary."

"If you need me to run any more errands for you, I'll be glad to do it, Mr. Williams. Whatever you want, why, you just let me know and I'll do it for you," Percy said.

"What I want is for you to go away, Percy," Williams said, making a motion with his hand. "You smell and you are disturbing my breakfast."

"Yes, sir," Percy said, turning toward the door. "But if you need any more errands run, well, you know where I'll be."

"Yes, I know where you will be," Williams replied. "Like as not you'll be passed out on the floor of Duffy's saloon."

The smile left Percy's face, to be replaced by an expression of hurt. "There's no need for you to talk to me like that," Percy said. "Just 'cause I got no money or no place to live, that don't mean I ain't a person."

Williams opened the envelope without answering and, realizing that Williams was no longer paying any attention to him, Percy turned and walked away.

Williams read the telegram.

PER YOUR INQUIRY INDIAN AGENCY DOES REQUIRE
BEEF STOP WILL PAY THIRTY-FIVE DOLLARS PER HEAD
PAYABLE ON DELIVERY TO SORENTO STOP

Williams folded the telegram and put it away, then, smiling, began drumming his fingers on the table.

"Good news, sir?" the proprietor of the café asked.

"Yes, Mr. Jordan, it is very good news."

"About the bank?"

"Uh, in a manner of speaking, I suppose you could say that it is about the bank," Williams said. "Although I do have a life other than as president of the bank," he added.

"Yes, sir, I'm sure that you do," Jordan replied. "But you are a very conscientious man, Mr. Williams. All the stockholders insist that the bank has prospered because of you. The bank is very fortunate to have you. Indeed the town of Salcedo is fortunate to have you."

"Well, thank you, Mr. Jordan," Williams said. "I appreciate that."

"More coffee?"

"No, I'll just finish this cup, then be on my way."

"Very good, sir," Jordan said. "Just call me if you need anything."

Williams nodded, then took a swallow of his coffee and looked once more at the telegram. Jordan had asked if this news concerned the bank. It did concern a bank, just not this bank. If everything worked out right—and he saw no reason why it would not—he would soon own his own bank.

When Williams read in the paper that all the Indians had been ordered onto reservations, he realized that feeding them would become the responsibility of the U.S. government. He also realized that that would require a lot of beef, and the moment he realized that, he knew that he had found the way to pay for the bank he wanted to buy. All someone had to do in order to make a lot of money was be in position to make that beef available to the U.S. government.

Williams was not a rancher, but that didn't mean he couldn't come up with enough cattle to negotiate a profitable deal with the U.S. government. Last month he had bought a demand mortgage from the bank. That mortgage, for one thousand dollars, was due two weeks from today.

Twice before, Jason Adams, owner of Backtrail Ranch, had arranged an extension on his loan. No doubt he would attempt to do so again, but this time it would not be the bank he was dealing with. By buying the note, which was a perfectly legitimate business arrangement, Williams would be able to force Adams to deal directly with him.

What made the deal particularly attractive as far as Williams was concerned was that he would not have to deal with the board of directors. He could, and he would, make his own arrangements with regard to the note. And those arrangements could be quite lucrative.

Williams had Adams over a barrel. If Adams wanted to save his ranch, he was going to have to pay off the note. And the only way he could pay off the note would be by forfeiting his two thousand head of cattle. Williams chuckled as he did the math. By settling the loan, he would be paying one thousand dollars for two thousand head of cattle. That came out to fifty cents a head. He would then sell those same cows at thirty-five dollars a head. That would be a pure profit of sixty-nine thousand dollars. That was more than enough to buy the Miners Bank. Yes, sir, the arrangements would be quite lucrative indeed.

As Williams walked from the restaurant to the bank, he stopped at the barbershop for his weekly tonsorial appointment. The barber, Earl Cook, was sitting in his chair reading the newspaper when Williams walked in. Hopping up quickly, he made a point of brushing out the chair before holding his arm out in invitation.

"Good morning, Mr. Williams," Cook said. "Here it is, nine o'clock on Tuesday morning, and you are here, punctual as usual."

"I consider punctuality to be the hallmark of any businessman," Williams said as he sat in the chair. "I only wish the bank customers were as punctual in the payment of their debts."

"Indeed, indeed," Cook said as he draped the cover over Williams. "You will want a shave, I suppose?"

"Yes," Williams said, leaning back as Cook lowered the back of the chair.

Cook made lather, then began applying it to Williams's chin. "Jason Adams was in here earlier this morning."

"Adams was here? What for?"

"Why, for a shave and a haircut," Cook replied. Cook chuckled. "Wearing a suit, he is, and with a fresh shave and a haircut, he is quite dapper-looking if I do say so."

"Hmmph," Williams said. "You'd think he would have better things to do with his money."

"I expect he'll be dropping in to see you later today," Cook said. He began applying lather to the lower part of Williams's face. "I expect he just wanted to make a good impression."

"He could have saved his time and his money," Williams replied. "I'm afraid I won't be able to extend his loan any longer. I wish I could do something for him, I truly do. But he has already had two extensions, and I am running a business."

"I understand," Cook said as he drew the razor across Williams's face. "It's just that Jason and his wife, Millie, are such good people, pillars of the church, always first to volunteer to help someone when help is needed."

"Now, Mr. Cook, if I ran the bank with my heart instead of my head, where would we be? You are a stockholder, are you not?"

Cook chuckled. "You've got me there, Mr. Williams. As I told you, we are very lucky to have a man with your business sense. And you are right, you can't run a bank with your heart."

Williams sighed. "Well, I must confess that I am being disingenuous with you. I too have been worried about Jason Adams, so I have done something that I might regret."

"What is that?"

"I bought his note from the bank," Williams said.

Cook raised up to look at him. "You bought Jason's note? Why would you do that?"

"Because in all good conscience, I cannot allow the bank to extend his note any longer. However, as the personal holder of his note, I believe I can work out some way with Mr. Adams that will allow him to keep his ranch. That is, if he is willing to work with me."

"You are a good man, Mr. Williams," Cook said as he resumed shaving the banker. "Yes, sir, you are a good man."

"Of course, Jason may not like what I am offering him," Williams said. "It's going to be harsh, but it's the only way he will be able to save his ranch. And after all, it is better to swallow a bitter pill than to lose the entire ranch."

"That's true all right," Cook said as he continued to cut the hair. "Sometimes a fella just has to bite the bullet."

Half an hour later, Williams was in his office in the back of the bank when Ron Gilbert, his head teller, knocked on the door.

"Yes, Gilbert, what is it?"

"Mr. Williams, Mr. Jason Adams is here to see you," Gilbert said.

"Is he here to pay his note, or to ask for an extension?"

"From the expression on his face, he is here to ask for an extension, I believe," Gilbert said.

"That is a shame," Williams said. Williams projected an image of concern and compassion, though in truth he could scarcely contain his joy over the fact that everything was going exactly as he had planned.

"Send him in," Williams said.

Adams came in and stood nervously just inside the door. He was, as Cook had described, wearing a suit and was freshly shaved and trimmed. It was obvious that he was going all out to make as positive an appearance as he possibly could.

"Good morning, Jason," Williams said, smiling at the rancher. "Please, come in, have a seat. How is Millie?"

"My wife is fine, thank you for your concern," Adams replied nervously.

"And your two boys? They must be a head taller than they were the last time I saw them."

Adams nodded. "Yes, sir, they've grown quite a bit."

"Well, I hope everything is fine with you. What brings you to town, Jason? What can I do for you?"

"I'm here to talk about my loan."

"You are a little early, aren't you? Your loan isn't due for a couple of weeks."

Adams looked surprised. "You can remember when my loan is due?"

Williams cleared his throat. It wouldn't be good to show that he was taking a particular interest in Jason Adams's loan.

"Well, when I heard you were in town today, I thought it might have something to do with your loan," Williams said. He forced a laugh. "I didn't think you would stop by just to pass the time of day."

"Oh, no, sir, no, sir," Adams said. "I would never waste your time like that."

Williams rubbed his hands together.

"So, you want to pay your loan off, do you?" Williams asked cheerfully. He knew that Jason had no intention of paying off the loan. In fact, he didn't want him to pay off the loan.

Adams's lips drew into a tight line. "Uh, no, sir, I'm

afraid I can't do that," he said. "I'm going to have to ask for another extension."

"Oh," Williams said. "Oh, that's too bad. Yes, sir, that is too bad." Williams shook his head. "Is there any chance you will be able to pay it off by the time it is due?"

"No, sir," Adams said. "I'm sorry, Mr. Williams, I truly am. But I'm not going to be able to pay the loan off."

"Mr. Adams, for your sake, and for the sake of your family, I was really hoping that this time you would be able to pay the note off," Williams said as he stroked his chin. "You see, I'm afraid that it isn't going to be possible to give you another extension."

"Not—not possible?" Adams asked, obviously crestfallen by the information. "Are you saying you won't extend the note?"

"I'm really sorry, Mr. Adams," Williams said. "I wish I could extend your loan again, I really do. But my hands are tied. I have an obligation, not only to the stockholders of this bank, but also the depositors."

"I see," Adams said. "What—what is going to happen now?"

"Well, I'm afraid that you are going to lose your ranch."

Adams shook his head. "No, you can't take the ranch away from me," he said. "You can't! That's my home. That's the only place me'n Millie has ever lived. Both our kids was born there. Please, there must be some other way out of this rather than forcin' me to lose my ranch."

"I'm sorry, I wish I could help you," Williams said. "But I'm afraid there's nothing I can do. Please try to understand, my hands are tied."

"What . . . what am I going to tell Millie?" Adams asked, barely managing to keep control of his emotions.

Williams drummed his fingers on the table as if in deep thought. Then he ran his hands through his hair. "There is—one—way," Williams said. "I'm not sure you will want to go along with it."

"What do you mean I won't want to go along with it? If there is a way, any way . . ." Adams's desperate plea trailed off.

"After all, I suppose that, for you, the most important thing would be to save your ranch, am I right? I mean, it is your home."

"Yes. I'd do anything to save it."

"Then I do have an idea. It isn't something that I want to do, but under the circumstances, I'll do it for you," Williams said. "I'll buy the note from the bank. Then you would owe me, and not the bank."

"And you would give me an extension?"

Williams chuckled and held out his hands. "No, no, don't misunderstand. There is no way I could afford to do something like that," Williams said. "But what I will do is mark the note paid in full in exchange for your cattle."

"My cattle? How many of my cattle?"

"All of them."

"What? No, I couldn't do that. Why, I have two thousand head," Adams said. "I couldn't possibly let you have two thousand head of cattle for one thousand dollars."

"Consider this, Mr. Adams," Williams said. "The note you signed with the bank was for your ranch and all livestock and improvements. So you are faced with this choice. Let the bank foreclose and lose everything, including your cattle, or settle with me for your cattle, and keep your ranch."

"I couldn't possibly do that," Adams said. Suddenly, he smiled. "But I could sell enough of my cattle to pay the note."

"No, you can't do that," Williams said.

"What do you mean I can't do that? Of course I can. I don't know why I didn't think of it earlier."

"If you sell those cattle, Mr. Adams, you will go to jail."

"What are you talking about? Why would I go to jail?"

"Remember, your loan note was for the ranch, livestock, and all accoutrements," Williams said. "That means you have your cattle mortgaged, and there is a law against selling mortgaged property."

"I—I didn't know that," Adams said in a defeated tone.

"Now you do know. So the choice is this, Mr. Adams. Either turn over all your cattle to me, in exchange for a release from debt, or I will be forced to foreclose on your ranch and your cattle." Gone was the silken, cajoling demeanor in Williams's voice. He was now speaking in a cold, clipped, and demanding voice.

"I—I suppose when you put it that way, I really have no choice," Adams said.

Sensing victory, Williams eased up a bit. "Mr. Adams, the truth is, I've gone way out on a limb for you on this. I probably shouldn't have done so, but I've already bought the note. It was the only way I could think of to save your ranch."

"I see," Adams said.

Williams opened the drawer of his desk and pulled out a paper.

"We can take care of this right now if you want to," he said. "Sign this paper turning your cattle over to me, and I'll release the lien on your ranch."

Williams slid the paper across to Adams, then handed him a pen. Adams held the pen poised over the line for his signature for a moment, but he didn't sign.

"What's wrong?"

"I've got two more weeks," he said.

Williams chuckled. "Mr. Adams, you've had two years to settle this debt and you've been unable to do so. What makes you think you can do it in two more weeks?"

"I can't settle in two more weeks," he said. "But before I do something like this, I need to discuss it with Millie."

"I see," Williams said. "And your wife makes all your decisions for you, does she?"

"No, sir. But we do make them together," Adams replied.

Williams sighed. "All right, Mr. Adams, discuss this with your wife if you must. But make certain she understands all the ramifications of it. Because if you don't accept this offer before the two weeks are up, the deal will be taken off the table. I'm afraid then that I will be forced to exercise every clause of the loan agreement. And that means, Mr. Adams, that you will not only forfeit your cattle, you will lose your ranch as well."

"Yes, sir, I understand," Adams said. "And I appreciate what you are doing for me, Mr. Williams, really I do. It's just that I'm going to have to bring my wife around."

"Very well. Give her my best," Williams said.

"I will. And thank you again, sir."

After Adams left, Williams walked over to his window to watch as the rancher climbed up into his buckboard, then drove away. Two thousand head at fifty cents a head, for which he would get thirty-five dollars a head. Yes, sir, this was going to work out just fine.

Chapter Five

Big Rock, Colorado

As the two cowboys dismounted in front of a saddle store, one of them rubbed his behind.

"Damn, that's the hardest, most uncomfortable saddle I ever sat in," he said. "I'll be glad to get mine back."

Don't know why you brung it in to get repaired anyway," the other cowboy said as they tied off their horses at the hitching rail. "As far as I could see, there wasn't that much wrong with it."

"The fender was tore."

"Well, hell, it don't hurt nothin' to have a tore fender. All a fender does is make a saddle look good. Don't have nothin' to do with the way it sits."

"Maybe it don't mean nothin' to somebody like you. But I'm particular about my saddle. You can ask anyone and they'll tell you that LeRoy Butrum is particular about his saddle."

"Yeah, if you ask me, you're old-maid particular," the other cowboy said.

"And you don't never care what yours is like. I

swear, Hank, if I hadn't been around when you was born, I wouldn't even believe you was my brother."

The two men stepped up onto the porch, then pushed the door open to go inside. The store smelled of leather, saddle soap, and neat's-foot oil. There was one particularly handsome saddle on display.

"Lookie here," LeRoy said, rubbing his hand over the saddle. "He's got my saddle out here for the whole world to see."

"Did he fix the fender?" Hank asked.

LeRoy put his hand on the piece of leather that was attached to the stirrup strap.

"Yep, here it is, as good as new," he said.

The proprietor came up front then and, seeing the two cowboys standing by the saddle, nodded at them.

"Boys," he said.

"Mr. Pogue," Hank replied.

"Tell me, Mr. Pogue, why you got my saddle out front like this?" LeRoy asked. Then he smiled. "Prob'ly 'cause it's the prettiest saddle in town, huh?"

"Not exactly," Pogue said. "I had it out here to sell it."

"To sell it?" LeRoy responded loudly. "What the hell do you mean you had it out here to sell it? Mister, this here ain't your saddle to sell."

"You said you would pick it up within a week," Pogue replied. "It's been a month."

"Yeah, well, I didn't have the money then. But I'm here to pick it up now."

"Good, that will make both of us happy," Pogue said.

LeRoy gave Pogue a five-dollar bill. Pogue just stared at it for a moment.

"What is this for?" he asked.

"What do you mean, what is this for? This here is for the work you done on the saddle."

"That will be twenty-five dollars," Pogue said.

"What?" LeRoy and Hank shouted as one.

"The cost of the repair to your saddle is twenty-five dollars."

"The hell you say!" LeRoy replied. "Mister, you can get a brand-new saddle for twenty-five dollars."

"Not like this one."

"Well, you didn't make this one, and I already paid for it once. All you done was put on a new fender."

"And I'm chargin' you twenty-five dollars for that," Pogue said.

"You can charge all you want, I ain't payin' it," LeRoy said angrily. "Just take the damn thing off."

"That'll be ten dollars," Pogue said.

"Ten dollars? What for? I told you to just take it off. I don't want it," LeRoy said.

"The ten dollars is for the aggravation," Pogue said.

"I ain't payin' you no ten dollars for nothin'," LeRoy said. He jerked the fancy leatherwork fender off the stirrup strap and tossed it toward Pogue. "There, I done the work for you. Come on, Hank, let's go."

LeRoy put the saddle up onto his shoulder and started toward the door.

"Stop!" Pogue called at them. "You're stealing that saddle."

"You can't steal what's already yours," LeRoy said without looking back toward Pogue.

Fortunately, Hank was looking toward Pogue, because he saw the saddle-shop proprietor hurry toward the counter and reach for a shotgun. Quickly, Hank's pistol was in his hand, pointing toward Pogue.

"Don't you try nothin' dumb now, Mr. Pogue," Hank cautioned.

"You are stealing that saddle."

"We ain't stealin' it," LeRoy said. "Soon's I get ten dollars, I'll come back and pay you, even though I don't think I ought to have to."

"Help! Someone, help!" Pogue started shouting. "I'm being robbed!"

LeRoy put the saddle down while he started removing the old saddle from the horse he had ridden.

"Help! Sheriff! Help!" Pogue continued to shout.

"Will you shut up?" Hank yelled at Pogue.

Both men were stopped then by the sound of a pistol being cocked. Turning, they saw one of the deputies standing out in the road, pointing his gun at them.

"What's going on here?" the deputy asked.

"Thank God someone answered my call," Pogue said. He pointed at the Butrum brothers. "These men are stealing this saddle."

"I ain't stealin' it," LeRoy said. "This here saddle belongs to me."

"You brought it in for repair, and you did not pay for the repair," Pogue said. "According to the law, until you pay for the repair, the saddle belongs to me."

"I undid the repair," LeRoy said.

"That doesn't matter. I already did the work."

"I think you two boys better come with me," the deputy said.

"Come on, Deputy, this here is just a misunderstandin', that's all," LeRoy said. He reached for his saddle.

"No, leave the saddle and come with me. Both of you."

Pogue waited until the deputy had them halfway to the jail before he stepped outside to retrieve the saddle.

"Will you lookie there?" LeRoy muttered. "That son of a bitch got my saddle."

"It isn't your saddle until you have satisfied the debt owed against it," the deputy said.

Neither Sally, Pearlie, nor Cal were aware of the drama that had just played out at the saddle shop when they rolled into town later that morning. Big Rock was a busy place with two trains at the depot, one passenger and one freight. The passenger train was taking on passengers for its run to the east, and even though the engineer was at rest, the fireman wasn't. He was working hard, stoking the fire to keep the steam pressure up.

In contrast to the fireman's toil, the engineer was leaning out the window of the highly polished green and brass locomotive, smoking a curved-stem pipe as he watched the activity on the depot platform. He was serene in the power and prestige of his position.

Passenger trains were called "varnish" by railroad people because, unlike the roughly painted freight cars, the passenger cars were generally beautifully finished. The conductor stood beside the string of varnished cars, keeping a close check of the time. The freight train was sitting over on the sidetrack, its hissing relief valve opening and closing as the steam pressure was maintained. The "varnish" had priority over the main line, and not until it departed would the freight be allowed to move back onto the high iron in order to continue its travel west.

Two stagecoaches and half-a-dozen carriages were also sitting at the depot, either having just delivered or waiting for train passengers. Out in the street behind the depot, a horse-drawn streetcar rumbled by.

This was what greeted Sally, Pearlie, and Cal as the three came into town to buy supplies. Sally was driving a large wagon and Pearlie and Cal were mounted, but riding slowly to keep pace with the wagon.

"Whoo-ee, this sure is a busy place this morning," Cal said as he saw three loaded freight wagons rumbling by.

"It always gets busy when a train is here," Sally said.

"Miz Sally, you know what we ought to do?" Pearlie asked. "We ought to make arrangements with the railroad to carry the cattle up to Sorento. That way we wouldn't have to drive 'em none."

"My goodness, Pearlie, do you have any idea how many cars it would take to move three thousand cattle?" Sally asked.

"No, I don't."

"Well, if you could get thirty cows to a car, it would take a hundred cars," Sally said. "That would be at least five trains. And because there is no track direct from here to Sorento, the trains would have to go almost a thousand miles to get there. That means it would take nearly as long to ship them up by train as it would to drive them . . . and the shipping cost would eat up about a quarter of the gross."

"How'd you come up with all that?" Pearlie asked. "You're awfully smart to figure all that out."

Cal laughed. "Maybe if you would think about something other than eatin' all the time, you would be able to come up with things like that too."

"What are you talkin' about?" Pearlie replied. "You didn't know none of that stuff neither."

"Yes, I did."

"Did not."

"Did too."

Sally stopped the wagon and the two young cowboys halted their horses. They sat in the middle of the street while traffic passed back and forth around them, paying little attention to them.

"Boys," Sally said, scolding them. "Would you please stop arguing? I've got business to attend to, and you do as well. Remember, Smoke wanted you to find some drovers who are willing to make the drive with us. You do understand that, don't you?"

Pearlie and Cal looked at each other for a moment. Pearlie was the first to speak.

"Yes, ma'am, we understand. It's just that we were wonderin' . . ." He let the sentence hang.

"You were wondering what?" Sally asked. "What's wrong?"

"Miz Sally, that seems to me like an awful big responsibility for me'n Cal to handle," Pearlie said. "I mean, they're goin' to be workin' for Smoke. Seems like he should be hirin' 'em. What if we don't get the right kind of men?"

"Pearlie, you are going to be the foreman, and Cal, you are going to be right under him. Everyone we hire will be working for the two of you, just like they are working for Smoke and me. You've been around

Sugarloaf for a long time now. You know what kind of men will be good for the job."

"But . . ." Pearlie began.

"But nothing," Sally said. "Smoke has every confidence in the world in the two of you, and so do I. Now, go hire us some good men. You can do that, can't you?"

Pearlie nodded. "Yes, ma'am," he said. "Yes, ma'am, I reckon we can do that. Right, Cal?"

Cal nodded solemnly. "Yes," he agreed. "We'll get men you'n Smoke will be proud of."

"I know you will," Sally said. She slapped the reins against the backs of the team and the mules strained into the harness, pulling the wagon forward.

"When you've hired the men, come down to the general store," Sally called back over her shoulder as she drove away. "I should have the wagon loaded by then."

"Yes, ma'am," Pearlie replied. "Come on, Cal, let's me'n you go get us some cowboys."

"You got 'ny idea where we should start?" Cal asked.

"Not directly. But town's a busy place today. I'm sure we'll run into someone, somewhere," Pearlie replied.

Chapter Six

As the two cowboys rode down to the opposite end of town, they saw a fistfight in progress in the street in front of the livery. One of the combatants was a soldier in uniform. He was wearing sergeant's stripes on his sleeves.

The other combatant was a civilian. The civilian was much younger than the soldier, but he was nearly as big, and he was more than holding his own.

As the cowboys got closer, they saw that the civilian was Mike Kennedy. Kennedy worked for the livery stable as a hostler and as an apprentice blacksmith. Mike was about the same age as Cal, and, in fact, the two were good friends. Mike was younger and smaller than the sergeant, but he was strong and whatever it was that started the fight had filled him with resolve. At first there had been a sly smirk on the sergeant's face.

"Boy, I'm goin' to play with you for a bit," the sergeant said. "Then I'm going to hurt you, and I'm going to hurt you bad."

But Mike was proving to be a little more than the sergeant expected. The sergeant swung hard with a roundhouse right, but Mike, who was quick and agile, ducked under the swing, then countered with a left jab to the sergeant's nose. It was considerably more than a light jab, because the soldier's nose went flat, then almost immediately begin to swell. The sergeant let out a bellow of pain as a trickle of blood started down across his mustache.

"Why, you snot-nosed kid!" the sergeant shouted. "I'm going to knock your block off!" He swung with another roundhouse right, missing again, and this time Mike caught him with a right hook to the chin. The hook rocked the sergeant back, but it didn't knock him down.

By now a rather substantial crowd had gathered to watch the fight, and everyone was rooting for their champion. To the surprise of both Cal and Pearlie, there seemed to be about as many soldiers cheering for Mike as there were supporting the soldier.

Mike scored with two more sharp jabs, and it was now obvious that the sergeant was on his last legs. He was stumbling about, barely able to stay on his feet. Mike had set him up for the finishing blow when one of the soldiers who had been supporting the sergeant suddenly grabbed the boy from behind. With his arms pinned, Mike was an easy target for the roundhouse right that, until now, had missed.

The sergeant connected and Mike's knees buckled, but he didn't go down. Pearlie slid down from his horse and before the sergeant could throw another punch, Pearlie brought the butt of his pistol down on the head of the man who had grabbed Mike. The man collapsed like a sack of potatoes and, though Pearlie and Cal were prepared to have to defend the action if need be,

Pearlie found himself cheered by the crowd, civilian and soldier alike.

With his arms now free, Mike was able to finish the fight with two more blows, setting his man up with a hard left jab, then dropping him with an even harder right cross.

With the fight over and nothing to hold the spectators' interest, the crowd broke up. Several of the soldiers dragged their beaten comrade away with them, leaving Mike standing in the middle of the street, breathing hard from the exertion.

It wasn't until that moment that Pearlie realized the fight hadn't been as one-sided as he had thought. Mike had a cut lip and a swollen eye. The boy walked over to the watering trough and dipped his handkerchief into the water.

"Here, let me do that," Cal said, taking Mike's handkerchief and dabbing lightly at his lip.

"Thanks, Cal," Mike said.

"What was the fight about?"

"The soldier took some oats from Mr. Lambert's livery. When I told him he had to pay for them, he called me a liar. One thing led to another and the next thing you know, we was fightin'."

"Kennedy, you're fired!" a man said, coming up to them then.

"Mr. Lambert, that soldier was stealin' oats from you."

"He said he wasn't," Lambert said.

"He was, I seen him do it."

Lambert shook his head. "Well, that don't matter none anyway," he said. "What's a nickel's worth of oats? You get the army mad, we won't get none of their business. All for a nickel's worth of oats? It just ain't good business, boy," Lambert said. "'Bout the only way I can make up for it now is to fire you."

"But Mr. Lambert, I need the job," Mike said.

"Sorry, boy, but business is business. Besides, this ain't the first time you've got into a fight. And I told you last time I wasn't goin' to put up with no more of it. You're fired."

A couple of the soldiers overheard the conversation, and they came back up to talk to the livery owner.

"Mr. Lambert, don't take it out on the boy," one of the soldiers said. "I don't know whether Sergeant Caviness stole any oats or not, but I do know that Caviness is a hothead, and he hit the boy first."

Lambert waved his hand. "Well, he wouldn't have hit Kennedy if the boy hadn't done somethin' to provoke him. He's fired, and that's it."

Lambert turned and started striding purposefully back to the livery.

"I'm sorry," one of the soldiers said. "It ain't right that you get fired for somethin' Caviness done."

"Ahh, don't worry about it," Mike said. "Truth is, I think Mr. Lambert was lookin' for an excuse to fire me anyway. I know he's been complainin' about how much it costs to keep me on."

"Yeah, well at least you taught Sergeant Caviness a lesson," the other of the two soldiers said. "He's a bully who hides behind his stripes. He knows that none of the soldiers he picks on can fight back without windin' up in the stockade. That's why there was so many of 'em cheerin' for you."

"I welcome the support," Mike said. "But I still lost the job."

"Pearlie, what do you think?" Cal asked.

Pearlie nodded. "I think yes," he said.

"What are you two talking about?" Mike asked.

"You're goin' to be lookin' for another job, right?" Pearlie asked.

"Yeah, I reckon I will be," Mike answered.

"How'd you like to come work for the Sugarloaf?"

"What?" Mike asked, brightening considerably at the offer. "Are you serious?"

"Yes, I'm serious."

"Do you think Mr. Jensen would hire me?"

"We're hirin' you," Pearlie said.

"You?"

Cal nodded. "We're fixin' to drive a herd of cows up to Wyoming," he said. "Smoke sent us into town to hire some men. If you want the job, it's yours."

"Yes, sir, I want the job!" Mike said excitedly. "You better believe I want it."

"Good. Now we just need to find five more men."

"Three," one of the soldiers said.

"What do you mean I only need three more?" Pearlie asked.

"My name is Andy Wilson," the soldier said. He pointed to the other soldier. "This here is Dooley Thomas. We'd be happy to come work for you if you'll have us."

Pearlie shook his head. "Huh-uh," he said. "I'm afraid not."

"Why not? We're good workers," Andy replied.

"You're also in the army. I ain't goin' to hire no deserters, and I know Smoke won't."

Andy smiled broadly. "Well if that's the only problem, then it ain't a problem," he said.

"And why isn't it a problem?"

"'Cause we ain't deserters," Andy said. "Get your paper out, Dooley," Andy said to his friend. As Dooley pulled out a piece of paper from his back pocket, Andy did the same. He showed the paper to Pearlie.

"What is this?"

"These here is our discharge papers," Andy said. "Me'n Dooley has done served our time, and we got ourselves mustered out this mornin'. We're still wearin' uniforms 'cause we ain't got us no civilian clothes yet."

Pearlie read both papers, then he looked at Andy. "According to this paper you're from Cincinnati, and Dooley here is from Boston."

"Yes, sir, that's right."

"What did you do before you come into the army?" Pearlie asked.

"Well, sir, I worked down on the river docks, loadin' and unloadin' boats," Andy said.

"I worked in a factory making bricks," Dooley said.

"A dockworker and a brick maker," Pearlie said. "There won't be much call for loadin' boats or makin' bricks during this drive."

"Wasn't much call for loadin' boats or makin' bricks in the army either," Andy said. "But we both learned to soldier."

"I need cowboys. Do either of you know anything about cows?"

"They give milk," Dooley said.

"Horses can give milk," Cal said.

"Well, I can tell the difference between a cow and a horse," Dooley said.

Pearlie looked surprised for a moment; then he laughed out loud.

"Well, I'll give you credit for honesty," he said. He stroked his chin. "I reckon anyone who can learn how to soldier can learn how to cowboy. All right, you two go with Mike. Mike, get your tack and go down to the general store. Miz Sally is down there getting supplies. You can help her load the wagon."

"Who is Miz Sally?" Dooley asked. "How will we recognize her?"

"She's the boss's wife," Mike said. "And don't you be worryin' none about recognizing her. She'll be about the prettiest woman in town. I know what she looks like."

Chapter Seven

Pearlie and Cal watched as the three men walked down toward the general store.

"You think they'll work out all right?" Cal asked.

"I don't know why not. Like I said, they learned how to soldier. And I like the way they took up for Mike like that."

"Yeah," Cal said. "I liked that, too."

A couple of minutes later, Pearlie and Cal tied their horses off in front of the Longmont Saloon, then stepped inside.

"Pearlie, Cal," Louis Longmont called to them from behind the bar. "It's good to see you boys. Is Smoke with you today?"

"No, sir, Mr. Longmont, he's still out at the ranch," Pearlie answered.

Longmont smiled. "Well, that's all right. You boys are always welcome, with or without Smoke. What'll it be?"

"Two beers," Pearlie said.

"And I'll have the same," Cal added.

Longmont chuckled as he drew four mugs, then set

them in front of the two boys. "Cal, wasn't that long ago you wasn't old enough to drink beer. I remember Miz Sally tellin' me what she'd do to me if she caught me servin' you one."

"I'm old enough now," Cal said.

"Yeah, that's why I put them in front of you. No way I'd go against Miz Sally otherwise. So, how are things goin' out at Sugarloaf?"

"We're lookin' to hire three good men," Pearlie said.

Longmont looked surprised. "Really? It's mid-fall. Most ranches lay off at the end of summer. What are you doin' out at Sugarloaf that you need more men?"

"We're drivin' a herd up into Wyoming," Cal said.

"Oh, I see. So you're lookin' to hire someone next spring," Longmont said.

"No, not in the spring—we want someone now," Pearlie said.

"Why would you want someone now? Why not wait until you actually drive the herd?"

"'Cause we're driving the herd up now," Cal said.

"What? This late in the year? Why, that's crazy. Why would Smoke do somethin' like that?"

"'Cause Miz Sally has got it in her mind that we're goin' to have another winter kind'a like that one we had a couple years back when there was that big freeze-out," Cal said. "So, we're sellin' off half the herd to the U.S. government so's they can provide beef for the Indians. Only, the government won't pay for the beef until we deliver it to them."

Longmont nodded. "Yeah, I guess I can see why you would want to drive a herd north. I guess my question now is, can you do it?"

"I think we can if we have good men with us," Pearlie said. "You said a lot of cowboys have been laid off for the winter, right?"

"Yes."

"What about Billy Cantrell? He was riding for the Double Tree. He's a good man with cattle. I'd like to have him. Do you know if he was laid off?"

Longmont laughed. "He was laid off all right. But I don't think he'll be making any trail drives with you."

"Why not? Me'n Billy's always got along. And I know that Smoke will match whatever he was getting' over at the Double Tree," Pearlie said.

"Yeah, well, Billy is in jail, and he's likely to be there until spring."

"Why is that?"

"Seems Billy got upset with a drummer from Denver. He didn't like the way the drummer was actin' around Chris Candy."

"What do you mean the way he was actin' around Chris Candy? Chris Candy's a whore," Pearlie said. "Billy can't get upset with ever' man who has anything to do with her. That's her job."

"Well, it ain't her job to get her eye blackened, and that's what the drummer did."

"Oh," Pearlie said.

"So Billy blackened both the drummer's eyes, and he broke the drummer's nose. If Sheriff Carson hadn't pulled him off when he did, why, like as not Billy would've broken both the drummer's hands as well."

"How long is he in jail for?" Cal asked.

"Well, the judge gave him thirty days or thirty dollars. Since Billy didn't have thirty dollars, he's servin' the thirty days."

"Do you think Sheriff Carson would turn him over to us if we paid his fine?" Cal asked.

Longmont nodded.

"I reckon he would," he said. "Especially if he knew that Billy was going to be out of town and out of his hair for a while."

"Then Smoke will pay his fine."

"Hold on now, Pearlie," Cal said. "Hadn't we better take that up with Smoke first?"

"Didn't he say he would trust us to get good men?" Pearlie replied.

"Yes, but . . ."

"But nothin'. Billy's one of the best cowboys around. Everyone knows that. He's well worth paying off his fine to have him with us."

"All right, if you think so," Cal said, though the "all right" was somewhat reluctant.

"If Smoke don't like it, I'll take all the responsibility," Pearlie said. "And I'll pay the fine myself."

Cal shook his head. "No need for that," he said. I'll back you on it with Smoke, and I'll pay half the fine."

"Good," Pearlie said. He took another drink of his beer. "Now we only need two."

"You don't need to go nowhere else," Billy said when Pearlie and Cal came down to the jail to hire him. Billy pointed to the two men in the cell next to him. "These here is the Butrum boys, LeRoy and Hank. Hire them and you'll have everyone you need."

"I can't just hire anybody," Pearlie said. "They need to have some skills."

"I've punched cows with these boys for most of the past year," Billy said. "They're good hands, both of 'em."

"Why are they in jail?" Pearlie asked.

"Well, because they . . ." Billy began, then stopped. "Truth to tell, I don't know why they're in jail. They was already here when Sheriff Carson brung me in. Hey, LeRoy," he called.

Both Butrums were asleep, or appeared to be, as they were lying on their bunks with their hats pulled down over their eyes.

"LeRoy," Billy called again.

"What do you want?" LeRoy answered from under his hat.

"What for are you and Hank in jail?"

"For stealin' back what was our'n," LeRoy answered. He had still not removed his hat.

"What do you mean, stealing back what was yours?"

LeRoy finally removed his hat and sat up on his bunk. "Do you know that low-assed pipsqueak named Josiah Pogue?"

"Yes, he owns the leather-goods shop," Pearlie said. "I don't know him well, but I know who he is."

"He done some work for me, then he tried to charge too much. When I couldn't pay it, he took my saddle," LeRoy said.

"Well, that's not stealin', that's legal," Pearlie said.

"Yeah, well, what he done was put a fender on. When I couldn't pay for the fender, I took it off and give it back to him, but that wasn't good enough. He wanted my whole saddle. So me'n Hank took the saddle anyway."

"Which is when the deputy showed up, and that's how we wound up in here," Hank said, finishing the story.

"If me'n Cal can get this cleared up, would you two boys agree to work for Sugarloaf?"

Hank nodded. "Yeah, we'll come work for Sugarloaf, won't we, LeRoy?"

"Sure. It's better than bein' in here."

A little bell rang as the door to Pogue's leather-goods store was opened.

"I'll be right with you," a reed-thin voice called from the back of the store.

A moment later a small, bald-headed man appeared. He was wearing an apron, and it was apparent he had been doing some leatherwork in the shop behind the store. Examples of his work were on display about the store, and Cal had to admit that the man was an artisan.

"Yes, sir, can I help you gentlemen?" Pogue asked. Then, recognizing them, he smiled. "You two men work for Mr. Smoke Jensen, don't you?"

"Yes," Pearlie said.

"He's a fine man. Are you perhaps looking for something for him?"

Cal was looking at a belt, holding it up to examine the intricate scrolling in the leather.

"That is a fine belt, if I do say so myself," Pogue said.

"Yes, sir, it is pretty all right," Cal agreed.

"I can make you a very good price for it."

"Uh, no, sir, we ain't here to buy nothin'," Pearlie said.

The smile left Pogue's face.

"Then why are you here?" he asked.

"We want to talk to you about the Butrum brothers."

"Oh, them," Pogue said. "They are brutish men, the two of them. I hope the sheriff sends them to prison. They need to learn that they can't just come in here and take what doesn't belong to them."

"But the saddle did belong to them, didn't it? It was LeRoy's saddle, I believe."

"In a manner of speaking, it was his saddle," Pogue agreed. "But I had a legitimate lien against it. And until that lien is satisfied, the saddle belongs to me."

"Would it square things with you if the lien was paid off?" Pearlie asked.

"As far as not makin' a claim on the saddle, yes, it would," Pogue said. "But I would still like to see them punished."

"Why?"

"Why? Because they need to know that they can't just run roughshod over decent citizens. Besides, I'm a little frightened of them," Pogue added.

"Suppose you were paid off the ten dollars, and the Butrums left town so there would be no possibility of them causing you any more trouble. Would that satisfy you?"

Pogue studied Pearlie for a moment. "Why are you so interested in what happens to the Butrums?"

"Because Smoke is going to drive a herd of cows north, and we want to hire the Butrum boys to help us. But we can't as long as they are in jail."

"How far north?"

"All the way to Wyoming."

Pogue whistled quietly. "That's a long way to drive cattle."

"Yes. And it should certainly be far enough to keep the boys out of your hair," Pearlie said.

"What hair?" Cal asked, laughing out loud.

For a moment, the expression on Pogue's face was one of irritation over the allusion to his lack of hair. Then, he began to laugh, and he rubbed his hand across his bald head.

"Yes, what hair indeed?" he replied. "All right, boys. If you see to it that I get my ten dollars, I'll inform Sheriff Carson that I don't intend to press charges."

"Thank you," Pearlie said. He pulled out his billfold, then extracted ten dollars and gave it to Pogue.

"Thanks," Pogue said, taking the money. He took a pencil and piece of paper from behind the shelf, then wrote out:

I, Josiah Pogue, having been duly satisfied as to the debt owed me by the Butrum brothers, do hereby free them of any further financial obligations toward me, and relinquish any claim to the saddle belonging to LeRoy Butrum. I also withdraw the charges I filed against them.

"Are you sure you want to do this? I mean, have you really thought about what you are doing?" Sheriff Carson asked a few minutes later as he released Billy, Hank, and LeRoy to Pearlie and Cal.

"I'm sure," Pearlie answered. "I know Billy to be a good hand, and if he vouches for the other two, that's good enough for me."

Sheriff Carson chuckled. "I'm not talkin' about

that," he said. "I know all three of those boys and they probably will make you good hands. I'm talkin' about this foolishness of trying to drive a herd that far north at this time of year."

"You know Smoke as well as anyone, Sheriff," Cal said. "If he says he can do it, I believe he can do it."

"Well, I'll give you this," Sheriff Carson said. "If any man alive can take a herd of—how many cows did you say it was?"

"Three thousand head," Cal answered.

Sheriff Carson gave a low whistle. "Three thousand head," he repeated. "Well, like I was about to say, if any man alive can take a herd of three thousand head all the way to Wyoming this late in the season, Smoke Jensen is that man. But I certainly don't envy any of you."

"Hold it," LeRoy said. "What are you talking about? What do you mean taking three thousand head of cattle to Wyoming? I thought you said we was comin' to work at Sugarloaf."

"That's right," Pearlie said. "And the work you're goin' to be doin' is takin' a herd to Wyoming."

"When?"

"Now," Pearlie said.

"Now! Are you crazy? It's damn near winter."

"Yes, that's why we need to get started right away," Pearlie said.

LeRoy shook his head. "Huh-uh," he said. "You didn't say nothin' about drivin' no herd north when you hired us. All you said was that you was lookin' for some more hands."

"If you don't want to go, I'm sure we can arrange

for you to stay here in jail," Pearlie said. "I can always get someone else."

"Yeah? Well, you just . . ." LeRoy began, but Hank interrupted him in mid-sentence.

"No!" he said. "You don't need anyone else. Don't pay my brother no never-mind. Me'n LeRoy will do it."

The wagon was about half-loaded by the time Pearlie, Cal, Billy, Hank, and LeRoy arrived. Mike, Billy, and the Butrums already knew each other, but Andy and Dooley had to introduce themselves. Pearlie noticed that both former soldiers were now wearing new jeans and plaid shirts.

"Yeah," Andy said. "Don't they look nice? Miz Sally bought 'em for us. First time I've had 'nything other'n an army uniform on in four years."

"Come on, boys," Pearlie said, picking up a bundle. "Let's get the wagon loaded so we can get back to the ranch in time for supper."

Chapter Eight

The Cheyenne village of Red Eagle

The village was typical of all the villages of the Plains Indians. The tepees were erected in a series of concentric circles with the openings facing east. They were pitched alongside a fast-flowing stream, which provided not only water for drinking, cooking, and washing, but also fresh fish. Although there were no addresses as such, everyone knew where everyone else lived by their position within the circles.

Fall had already come and the bright yellow aspen trees stood out from the dark green conifers interspersed with a spattering of red and brown from the willow, oak, and maple that climbed the nearby mountainsides. Smoke curled from the tops of the lodges as the women prepared meals while the men watched over the herd of horses, or worked at cleaning their rifles or making bows and arrows. Children played beside the water.

The chief of the village was a man named Red Eagle. Red Eagle was once the great warrior chief of a proud people, but now he was a chief in name only. In compliance with a treaty signed with the soldiers, Red Eagle had moved his people onto a reservation.

The reservation guaranteed peace with the soldiers, but it stripped his people of all identity and pride. Now, they were totally dependent upon the white man for their very survival. They were not allowed to hunt buffalo, for to do so would require them to leave their designated area. But there were few buffalo anyway, the herds having been greatly diminished by the white men who had hunted to supply meat for the work crews that were building the railroads, or worse, the buffers who took only the hides and left the prairie strewn with rotting meat and bleaching bones.

Red Eagle's people were dispirited. Without the buffalo, there was little to eat. They had been promised a ration of beef by the agency, but the promised beef had not materialized. Even if it had, it was a poor substitute for the buffalo. Red Eagle did not care much for beef, and he knew that his people felt as he did. But if it was a choice of beef or starvation, they would take beef.

Not everyone agreed with Red Eagle. There were some who wanted to leave the reservation, to be free to hunt what buffalo remained. But Red Eagle had no wish to see his village subjected to the kind of murderous attack he and his wife had lived through at White Antelope's village at Sand Creek, so he counseled his people to stay on the reservation.

Sand Creek proved, however, that even obedience to the white man's law would not always protect you. There, Colonel John M. Chivington and his Colorado militia had murdered men, women, and children, even as the terrified Indians were gathering around a tepee flying the American flag.

White Antelope, the head of the Sand Creek village, was Red Eagle's very good friend. An old man of seventy-one, White Antelope was convinced that the soldiers were attacking because they didn't understand that his people were a peaceful band. In order to prove that his village was friendly, he raised the American flag over his tepee. Then, in order to reinforce his declaration of peace, he started walking toward Colonel Chivington carrying a white flag.

Despite White Antelope's efforts to show the soldiers that neither he nor his people represented a danger to the soldiers, he was shot down. Red Eagle had screamed out in anger and grief at seeing his friend murdered.

That had been many years ago, but sometimes Red Eagle still believed he could still hear the old chief singing the Cheyenne death song as he lay dying.

"There is not a thing that lives forever
   Except the earth and the mountains."

Red Eagle realized then that if he stayed, he would be killed, despite the protection of the American flag and the flag of surrender. He grabbed his wife by the hand and they darted down a ravine, miraculously escaping Chivington's band.

Now, Red Eagle was the leader of his own village, and he was determined not to let his people be slaughtered as had been the villagers under White Antelope's protection. If the soldiers demanded that Red Eagle keep his people on the reservation, then that is exactly what he would do. And if Walking Bear and the band of young firebrands who followed him wanted to make trouble off the reservation, then they would have to deal with the soldiers themselves, because he would not make council on their behalf.

As the shadows of evening pushed away the last vestiges of color in the west, Red Eagle came out into the village circle to sit near the fire. The village circle acted as a community center for the village. It was an area of dry grass, smooth logs, and gentle rises making it a very good sitting place. Every night that weather permitted, men, women, and children from the village would gather around the fire's light and talk of the events of the day.

The village circle was a place where problems were discussed, group decisions made, and young men and young women could court under the watchful eyes of the village. It was also a place of entertainment, sometimes consisting of dancing, but often a place where stories were told.

One of the reasons Red Eagle was a leader of the village was because he was an old man who had lived through many winters, and had experienced a lot of adventures. That made him a particularly good storyteller when he was in the mood, and tonight he was in just such a mood. Besides, he thought, a good story would lift his people's spirits so that they would not think of the hunger that was gnawing at their bellies.

"Listen," Red Eagle said, "and I will tell you a story."

Those who were around him, the men of the council,

the warriors, and those who would be warriors, drew closer to hear his words. The women and children grew quiet, not only because it was forbidden to make noise while stories were being told around the campfires, but also because they knew it would be a good story and it filled them with excitement to hear it.

As the fire burned, it cast an orange light upon Red Eagle, making his skin glow and his eyes gleam. A small gas pocket in one of the burning logs popped, and it sent a shower of sparks climbing into the sky, red stars among the blue. Red Eagle held his hand up and crooked his finger as he began to talk.

"Once there was a time before the people, before Kiowa, before Arapaho, before Commanche, before Lakota, even before Cheyenne."

"What time was this, Grandfather?" one of the children asked. Red Eagle was not the young questioner's biological grandfather, but he was the spiritual grandfather of them all, and so the child's innocent question reflected that.

"This was the time before time," Red Eagle replied. "This was in the time of the beginning, before the winter-count, before there was dry land. Then, there was only water and the Great Spirit, who floated on the water. With him were only things that could swim, like the fish and the swan, the goose, and the duck.

"The Great Spirit wanted to have people, but to do that, had to make land to walk upon. So he asked someone to dive to the bottom. 'Let me try,' a little duck said.

"The swan laughed at the little duck. 'You are much too small. I am a mighty swan, the most noble of all creatures. I will dive to the bottom and find earth.'

"So the swan dove down through the water to try and find the earth. But when he came up, his bill was empty.

"'The water is much too deep,' the swan said. 'I could not find the bottom.'

"'Let me try and find the bottom,' the little duck said.

"But the goose laughed at the duck. 'You are much too little and too weak to find the bottom. I am a goose. I am big and strong. I will find the bottom.'

"So the goose took a deep breath and dove very deep, but he couldn't reach the bottom either. He came up, gasping for breath, and he said, 'Great Spirit, I think you are playing tricks with us. I think there is no bottom.'

"'Please, let me try,' the little duck said again.

"Both the swan and the goose laughed. 'Foolish little duck,' they said. 'If we could not find the bottom, what makes you think you can?'"

"'I believe I can do it,' the little duck said again.

"'You may try,' the Great Spirit said.

"The little duck took a deep breath and plunged down through the water. He was underwater for a long time, and everyone thought that the little duck had drowned and they were very sad. 'You should not have let him try,' they said to the Great Spirit, but the Great Spirit told them to have patience.

"Then, when it seemed that all was lost, the little duck came back up with a bit of mud in its bill.

"'How could he do that when we could not?' the swan asked. 'He is small and we are big.'

"'He is small, but his heart is big and his soul is

good. That gives him very strong medicine, and that is why he succeeded where you failed,' the Great Spirit said.

"Then, taking the mud from the bill of the little duck, the Great Spirit worked it in his hands until it was dry, and with it, he made little piles of land on the water surface. That land grew and grew until it made solid land everywhere." Red Eagle held his arm out and took in all the land around him. "And that is what we see today."

"And then did our people come to live on the land?" one of the children asked.

"Yes," Red Eagle said. "Two young men and two young women who were looking for food walked for eight days and eight nights without eating, or drinking, or sleeping. They saw a high peak and decided to go to it to die, for it would be a marker to show their burying place. But when they got there, they saw a yellow-haired woman who showed them the buffalo. The men hunted the buffalo and got food to eat, and the women bore many sons. The sons took many wives and bore more children. I am the child of one of those children, just as you are the children of my children. And thus we are all Cheyenne."

Once Red Eagle finished his story, others began to tell stories as well. If the story was to be a tale of bravery in battle, the one who spoke would walk over to the lodge pole and strike it with his coup stick. Then everyone would know that he was going to tell a story of an enemy killed in battle. In such stories the enemy warriors were always brave and skilled, because that made the warrior's own exploits all the greater.

Not all stories were of enemies killed in battle. Some of the stories were of hunting exploits, and some told of things that had happened in the time of their father's father's father that had been handed down through the generations to be preserved as part of their history.

One of those who spoke little, but of whom many tales were told, was Walking Bear. A few days earlier, Walking Bear had led a war party against a small establishment that consisted of a military stockade, stagecoach station, and telegraph office. The stockade was manned by about fifty soldiers, and when Walking Bear tried a frontal attack against the soldiers, he was driven back by cannon fire and by the long-range fire of the soldier's rifles. As the soldiers were protected by the heavy timbers of the stockade, Walking Bear was unable to dislodge them, even though he had superior numbers.

Walking Bear tried a few ploys. He sent ten warriors down toward the soldiers to act as decoys, but they were unable to draw the soldiers out. The next morning he sent twenty, and this time the soldiers came out as far as the bridge, but would come no farther.

Some suggested the warriors should slip down at night and set fire to the stockade, but Walking Bear insisted that only cowards fight in such a way. They finally decided that they would try another frontal assault the next day, massing all their numbers. Before they could launch their attack, though, they were surprised to see an entire platoon of cavalrymen ride out of the fort, cross the bridge, then head westward at a trot. The soldiers had come out of the fort to provide an escort for an approaching wagon train.

Elated at their good fortune, Walking Bear mounted all his warriors and they swarmed down on the wagons and the escorting soldiers.

The soldiers reached the wagons, then, in a classic formation, circled the wagons and dug in. The soldiers fought bravely, and Walking Bear's own brother was killed in the first few minutes of fighting. Angered and grieving, Walking Bear led the Cheyenne into ever-decreasing circles around the wagons, lashing their ponies to make them go faster and faster. Walking Bear was wearing his medicine bonnet and carrying his sacred shield, so he knew that no bullets would strike him.

As the circle tightened closer to the wagons, the soldiers continued their firing until, finally, all the soldiers were out of ammunition. When the soldiers stopped firing, the Cheyenne charged straight for the wagons and killed all the soldiers. They fell upon the wagons in eager anticipation, but were very disappointed by what they found. Though they had hoped for weapons and ammunition, there was nothing in the wagons but bedding and mess chests.

When Walking Bear returned, he told the others in the council that the white men had been taught a lesson and would now obey the treaty they had signed.

"No," Red Eagle said. "I fear that all you have done is anger the white man so that we will get no beef."

"You want beef?" Walking Bear retorted, angry that Red Eagle did not respect his story of bravery in battle. "I will get beef for you. I will get all the beef you can eat."

"How will you do such a thing?" Red Eagle asked.

"Are you an old man that you have forgotten the way of our people? I will get beef the way Cheyenne have always gotten food. I will find it, and I will bring it back. I will not wait for the white man to give it to us, as if we are children, pawing and mewing to suckle at the teat."

Walking Bear's words were angry and disrespectful of an old man who had, long ago, earned the respect of all his people. As a result, many who heard the words gasped.

Red Eagle stood up, and pulled his robe about him. He pointed. "Go," he said. "Leave our village before you bring evil to us."

"And if I say I do not wish to go, what can you do?" Walking Bear asked. He laughed, a disrespectful, guttural laugh. "You can do nothing, old man," he taunted. "You are old and weak, and you have no medicine."

Red Eagle said nothing, but he raised his hand into the air, then made a circular motion with his fingers. Then, there was the whirring sound of wind through feathers. A large eagle suddenly appeared swooping down out of the darkness. He made a pass at Walking Bear's head, legs extended, claws bared. The eagle raked his claws across Walking Bear's face, leaving three, parallel, bleeding gashes on his cheek. Then, with a graceful but powerful beat of his wings, the eagle soared back up to disappear in the darkness.

Those who watched the incident gasped and called out in shock and fear, but no one was more shocked or more frightened by what had just happened than Walking Bear himself.

Walking Bear put his hand to his cheek, ran the fingers across the cuts, then held them out to look at the blood, shining darkly in the firelight.

"How . . . ?" Walking Bear started to ask, but he never finished his question.

"Leave," Red Eagle said again, this time speaking very quietly, but with great authority.

"I will go," Walking Bear replied. "I am not going because you have ordered me to, but because I can no longer live with men who fear to walk the path of a warrior. Who will come with me?" he asked loudly.

About two dozen young men stood up, standing silently in the night, their eyes shining red from the light of the fire.

Red Eagle looked at all of the young men, then nodded.

"Do you see that the bravest of our people have joined me?" Walking Bear asked.

"Go," Red Eagle said. "Take your women and your children with you. You are no longer a part of this village."

"Eeeyahhhh!!!!" Walking Bear shouted, and those who had stood to go returned the shout.

As Walking Bear and those who followed him left the village, their departure was greeted with silence, partly in stunned disbelief over what they were witnessing and partly in grief at losing members of their village.

Red Eagle spoke to the village. "I will say for the last time the name of Walking Bear. I tell you now to speak the names of those who left us. Then, after this day, do not say their names again, for they are no more."

The villagers shouted the names of the warriors, and of the women and children of the warriors who left with them; then they began singing the lament of the dead for, as far as they were concerned, those who left the village that day were dead.

As Walking Bear and his warriors and their families moved away from Red Eagle's village, he could hear the sounds of the death songs. He could also hear the sound of weeping from the women and children of his band as they mourned those who were left behind.

"Warriors!" he called. "Be of stout heart! We ride the path of the brave! Eeeyaaah!!!!"

The other warriors with him joined in the yell, as much to buck up their own spirits as to shut out the mournful sounds from the village.

Chapter Nine

Puxico, Wyoming Territory

"Oyez, oyez, oyez, this here court is about to convene, the Honorable Judge Spenser Clark presidin'," the bailiff shouted.

"Ha, this ain't no court! This here's a saloon," someone shouted. His shout was met with laughter from others who were present.

"Crawford, one more outburst like that, and you'll spend thirty days in the jail," the bailiff said, pointing to the offending customer/spectator. "This here saloon is a court whenever His Honor decides to make it a court, and that's what he's done. Now, everybody stand up'n make sure you ain't wearin' no hat or nothin' like that while the judge comes in. And McCall, you better not let me catch you servin' no liquor durin' the trial."

"I know the rules, George. I ain't served nary a drop since the judge ordered the saloon closed," McCall replied.

The Honorable Spenser Clark came out of the back room of the saloon and took a seat at his "bench," which was the best table in the saloon. The table sat upon a raised platform that had been built just for this purpose.

The saloon was used as a court because it was the largest building in town. An ancillary reason for holding court in the saloon was because it was always crowded, thus making it easy for the judge to empanel a jury by rounding up twelve sober men, good and true. If it was sometimes difficult to find twelve sober men, then the judge could stretch the definition of sobriety enough to meet the needs of the court. The "good and true," however, had to be taken upon faith.

Quince Pardeen was being charged with the murder of Sheriff John Logan. There was no question that he had killed Sheriff Logan, because he had done so on the main street of the town in front of no fewer than thirty witnesses.

There was some question, however, as to whether or not it could actually be considered murder. That was because it was clear that Sheriff Logan drew his pistol first. Prosecution contended that the sheriff did so in the line of duty while attempting to arrest a man for whom there were wanted posters in obvious circulation.

The city of Puxico had only two lawyers, David Varner and Bailey Gilmore, neither of whom was a prosecuting attorney. Because of that, Judge Clark brought the two men into his hotel room prior to the trial.

"I don't suppose Pardeen has hired either of you to represent him, has he?" he asked.

"It is my understanding he is going to ask that a lawyer be appointed," Varner replied.

Judge Clark sighed. "Do either of you volunteer for defense?"

Varner and Gilmore looked at each other, but neither spoke.

"Very well, we'll flip a coin," the judge said, pulling a nickel from his pocket.

Varner called heads, it came up heads, and he asked to prosecute. That made Gilmore Pardeen's defense attorney.

Gilmore was conscientious enough to believe in providing the best defense possible, regardless of the heinousness of the crime, and he sat out to do just that. He made a very strong argument that Pardeen saw only the draw, and perceiving that his life was in danger, reacted as anyone would.

"Pardeen might be a wanted man," Gilmore said in his closing argument. "But even wanted men do not surrender their right to self-preservation.

"I lament the fact that Sheriff Logan was killed, and for that, his dear widow has our sincerest sympathy." Gilmore glanced over at Mrs. Logan, who, still wearing widows weeds, lifted her black veil to dab at her eyes with a silk handkerchief.

"Indeed," Gilmore continued, "the entire town of Puxico has our sympathy, for Sheriff Logan was known far and wide as a good and decent man."

"What the hell are you doin', lawyer?" Pardeen yelled angrily from the defense table. "Whose side are you on anyhow?"

"Mr. Pardeen, one more outburst like that and I'll have you bound and gagged," Judge Clark warned. "You may continue with your argument, Counselor."

The defense attorney nodded, then brought his closing argument to its conclusion. "Gentlemen of the jury, any way you look at this fracas, no matter how good and decent a man Logan was, if you are fair and honest in your deliberation, you will agree that Mr. Pardeen acted in self-defense."

Varner waited until Gilmore had taken his seat before he rose to address the jury. Before he said a word he made a sarcastic show of applauding, clapping his hands together so quietly that they could not be heard.

"I applaud the esteemed counselor for the defense," he said. "He is a good man who believes that anyone— even a person as evil and as obviously guilty as Quince Pardeen—deserves a good defense. He chose, of course, the only option open to him. He chose to make his plea, one of self-defense. But despite my esteemed colleague's most sincere attempt, the truth is"—Varner paused and looked directly at Pardeen— "Mr. Gilmore's noble effort was an exercise in futility. Quince Pardeen is a cold-blooded murderer. Many a good man has fallen before his gun—none finer than our own sheriff. By his lifetime of evil, Pardeen has forfeited forever any claim to self-defense."

After Varner sat down, Judge Clark instructed the jury and they withdrew to a room at the back of the saloon to make their decision. After only five minutes of deliberation, the jury sent word that they had reached a verdict.

After retaking his seat at the "bench," Judge Clark put on his glasses, slipping the end pieces over one ear at a time. Then he blew his nose and cleared his throat.

"Are counsel and defendant present?" He pronounced the word as "defend-ant."

"Counsel and defendant are both present at the table," Gilmore replied.

"Is the prosecutor present?"

"Hell, Judge, you can see him right in front of your face," one of the spectators shouted. "Get this over so we can get back to our drinkin'."

There was some nervous laughter, terminated by the rap of the judge's gavel. "Mr. Matthews, that little outburst just cost you twenty dollars," Clark said.

"Wait a minute, I ain't the only one who—" Matthews began, but he was interrupted by the judge.

"Now it's twenty-five dollars. Do you want to open your mouth again?"

This time Matthews's reply was a silent shaking of his head.

"I thought you might come to your senses," Judge Clark said. "Now, would the bailiff please summon the jury?"

The bailiff, who was leaning against the bar with his arms folded across his chest, spit a quid of tobacco into the brass spittoon, then walked over to a door, opened it, and called inside.

"The judge has called for the jury," he said.

At the bailiff's call, the twelve men shuffled from the room where they had conducted their deliberations, and out onto the main floor of the saloon, to the chairs that had been set out for them in two lines of six. They took their seats, then waited for further instructions from the judge.

"Mr. Foreman of the Jury, have you reached a verdict?" the judge asked.

"We have, Judge."

"Your Honor," the bailiff said.

"Say what?"

"When addressing His Honor the judge, you will say Your Honor," the bailiff directed.

"Oh, yeah, I'm sorry, I forgot about that. We have reached a verdict, Your Honor."

"Please publish the verdict."

"Do what?"

Judge Clark sighed. "Tell the court what the jury has found."

"Oh. Well, sir, Your Honor, we have found this guilty son of bitch guilty," the foreman said.

"You goddamn well better have!" someone shouted from the court.

The judge banged his gavel on the table.

"Order!" he called. "I will have order in my court." He looked over at the foreman. "So say you all?" he asked.

"So say we all," the foreman replied.

The judge took off his glasses and began polishing them.

"Bailiff, escort the defendant to the bench, please," the judge said.

Pardeen was handcuffed, and he had shackles on his ankles. He shuffled up to stand in front of the judge.

Pardeen was not a very large man. In a normal world, any belligerency on the part of a man as small as Pardeen would have been regarded as unimportant, or at least manageable. But this was not an ordinary world because Pardeen's small stature was offset by the fact that he possessed extraordinary skill with a handgun. But even more important than his skill with a pistol was the diabolical disregard of human life that would allow him to use that skill. It was said of Pardeen that he could kill a human being with no more thought than stepping on a bug.

Pardeen's hair was dark and his eyes were brown. One of his eyes was what people called "lazy," and it had a tendency to give the illusion that he was looking at two things at once.

"Quince Pardeen, it is said that you have killed fifteen men, and that you may be one of the deadliest gunmen in the West. I could not try you for all those killings—I could only try you for killing Sheriff Logan, and that I have done. You have been tried by a jury of your peers and you have been found guilty of the crime of murder," he said. "Before this court passes sentence, have you anything to say?"

"Nah, I ain't got nothin' to say," Pardeen said.

"Then draw near for sentencing," the judge said solemnly. "It is the sentence of this court that you be taken from this place and put in jail long enough to witness one more night pass from this mortal coil. At dawn's light on the morrow, you are to be taken from jail and transported to a place where you will be hanged."

"Your Honor, we can't hang 'im in the mornin'. We ain't built no gallows yet," the deputy who was now acting sheriff said.

Judge Clark held up his hand to silence the deputy, indicating that he had already taken that into consideration. "This court authorizes the use of a tree, a lamppost, a hay-loading stanchion, or any other device, fixture, apparatus, contrivance, agent, or means as may be sufficient to suspend Mr. Pardeen's carcass above the ground, bringing about the effect of breaking his neck, collapsing his windpipe and, in any and all ways, squeezing the last breath of life from his worthless, vile, and miserable body."

The gallery broke into loud applause and cheers and shouts.

"Hey, Pardeen, how does it feel? You'll be in hell this time tomorrow!" someone shouted.

"Hell is too good for you!" another said.

Judge Clark banged his gavel a few times, then realizing the futility of it, looked at the deputy.

"Get his sorry carcass out of here," he said.

Acting Sheriff Lewis Baker had been napping at his desk when something awakened him. Opening his eyes, he looked around the inside of the sheriff's office. The room was dimly lit by a low-burning kerosene lantern. A breath of wind moved softly through the open window, causing the wanted posters to flutter on the bulletin board.

A pot of coffee sat on a small, wood-burning stove filling the room with its rich armoa. The Regulator clock on the wall swept its pendulum back and forth in a measured "tick-tock," the hands on the face pointing to ten minutes after two. The acting sheriff rubbed his eyes, then stood up and stretched. Stepping over to the stove, he used his hat as a heat pad and grabbed the metal handle to pour himself a cup of coffee. Taking a sip of his coffee, he glanced over toward the jail cell. He was surprised to see that Pardeen wasn't asleep, but was sitting up on his bunk.

Baker chuckled. "What's the matter, Pardeen?" he asked. He took another slurping drink of his coffee. "Can't sleep?"

"No," Pardeen growled.

"Well, I don't know as I blame you none," the acting sheriff said. "I mean, you're goin' to die in about four more hours, so you may as well stay awake and enjoy what little time you got left on this earth." He took another swallow of his coffee.

"Ahhh," he said. "Coffee is one of the sweetest pleasures of life, don't you think? But then, life itself is sweet, ain't it?" He laughed again, then turned away from the cell.

He gasped in surprise when he saw someone standing between himself and his desk. He had not heard the man come in.

"Who the hell are you?" Baker asked gruffly. "And what the hell are you doing in here? You aren't supposed to be in here."

"My name is Corbett. I've come to visit Mr. Pardeen."

"There ain't no visitors authorized right now," Baker said.

"I've got some sad news for him."

"Sad news?"

"Yeah, his brother was killed."

Unexpectedly, Baker chuckled. "Is that a fact? His brother was killed, was he? Well, now, I wouldn't want to keep our prisoner from getting any sad news," he said. He made a motion toward the cell. "You just go ahead and tell Pardeen about his brother. The son of a bitch is going to be dead in four more hours. I'd like to do everything in my power to make his last hours as unpleasant as I can." Baker laughed again.

Corbett nodded, then walked over to the cell. "Pardeen, I hate to be the one to tell you this, but your brother Emerson got hisself kilt last week."

"Who killed him?"

"A fella by the name of Smoke Jensen. You ever hear of him?"

"Yeah, I've heard of him. How'd it happen?"

"Damn'dest thing you ever saw. Emerson had his gun drawed already, and he was comin' back on the hammer when Smoke Jensen drawed his gun and shot him."

"You seen this, did you?" Pardeen asked.

"Yeah, I seen it."

"He must be pretty fast."

"He is fast. He's faster'n anyone I ever seen."

"Yeah, well, I don't care how fast he is. I'm goin' to kill him."

Acting Sheriff Baker laughed so hard that he sprayed coffee. "You're going to kill him? And how are you going to do that? Come sunrise, you're goin' to be hangin' by your neck." He put his fist by his neck, then make a rasping sound with his voice and tilted his head in a pantomime of hanging.

"Give me your gun," Pardeen said quietly.

Nodding, Corbett drew his pistol and passed it through the bars to Pardeen.

"Sheriff, you want to step over here for a moment?" Pardeen called.

"What do you want?" the acting sheriff asked. Then, shocked at seeing a pistol in Pardeen's hand, he threw up his arms. "No!" he shouted in fear.

Without so much as another word, Pardeen shot the deputy.

"When you get to hell, tell my brother hello for me," Pardeen said.

"Where are the keys?" Corbett asked.

"They're over there, hanging on a hook behind the desk," Pardeen said, pointing.

Corbett stepped quickly over to the hook, took down the keys, then returned to unlock the cell door. "I've got a couple of horses in the alley," he said.

"I appreciate you doin' this for me."

"Well, your brother was my friend. I'd like to see the son of a bitch who killed him pay for it. And I figure you're the one who can make him do it."

The two men stepped out into the alley, but instead of going toward the two horses that were tied off in back, Pardeen turned and started walking up the dark alley.

"Hey, the horses is over here," Corbett called.

"I got somewhere else I'm goin' to first," Pardeen said with an impatient grunt.

"Where you got to go that's so important we can't ride outta here while we have the chance?" Corbett asked.

"The hotel."

"Why we goin' to the hotel?"

"You'll see when I get there," Pardeen replied. "That is, if you're a'comin' with me."

"Yeah," Corbett answered. "Yeah, I'm comin' with you."

The two men moved silently through the dark shadows of the alley until they reached the hotel. Slipping in through the front door, they could hear the snores of the night clerk who was on duty. Crossing the darkened lobby, Pardeen turned the registration book around so he could read the entries.

"What are you lookin' for?" Corbett whispered.

"Ain't lookin'. I found it," Pardeen replied, also in a whisper. He reached over behind the sleeping clerk and took a key down from a board filled with keys. Recrossing the lobby, Pardeen started up the stairs with Corbett, still unsure as to what they were doing, climbing the stairs behind him.

Reaching the second floor, the two men stopped for just a moment. A couple of candles that were set in wall sconces lit the hallway in a flickering orange light. The snoring of the various residents could be heard through the closed doors.

"He's down this way," Pardeen hissed.

"Who is?"

"The judge."

"We're lookin' for a judge? Why?"

"He's the son of a bitch that sentenced me to hang," Pardeen said. "I want to send a message to all the other judges so that if I ever get in this position again, they'll think twice before trying to hang me."

They walked quietly down the carpeted hallway until they found the door Pardeen was looking for. Slowly, he unlocked the door, then pushed it open.

The judge was snoring peacefully.

Pardeen pulled his gun and pointed it toward the

judge. Then, having second thoughts, he put the gun away.

"You got a knife?" he asked.

"Yeah, I got a knife," Corbett answered.

"Let me borrow it."

Corbett pulled his knife from its sheath and handed it to Pardeen. Pardeen raised the knife over the judge, paused for a moment, then pulled it back down.

"What is it? What's wrong?" Corbett hissed.

"I want the son of a bitch to wake up long enough to know what's happening to him, and and to see who is doing it."

Corbett nodded.

Pardeen reached down to cover the judge's mouth with his hand.

"Wake up, you son of a bitch," he said.

The judge snorted in mid-snore, then opened his eyes. For just a moment there was confusion in his eyes, but when he recognized Pardeen, the confusion turned to fear, then terror. He tried to speak, but couldn't because Pardeen's hand was clamped down over his mouth.

"Ha! Bet you never thought you'd see me again, did you?"

The judge tried to speak again, but it came out as a squeak.

"Oh, I guess you're wonderin' how I got here, huh? Well, I tell you, Judge. I just killed the deputy and broke jail, and now I've come to kill you. What was it you said in court? Something about finding a contrivance or means to suspend me from the ground long enough to break my neck?"

Pardeen laughed a guttural laugh that was without humor.

"Well, this here knife is all the contrivance I need, Judge."

Pardeen pulled his hand away from the judge's mouth. The judge tried to sit up, but before he could, Pardeen brought his knife across the judge's neck. The judge put his hands up to his throat, then, with a gurgling sound, fell back down onto the pillow. He flopped once or twice like a fish out of water, then lay still in a growing pool of blood.

"Is he dead?" Corbett asked.

"Yeah, he's dead."

Corbett went over to the window and tried to raise it.

"What are you doin'?"

"Killin' a judge like we done, maybe we ought to go out this way before somebody comes after us," Corbett said.

Pardeen laughed. "Who's goin' to come after us, Corbett? I killed the sheriff last week, the deputy and the judge tonight. They ain't nobody left to come after us."

Corbett thought for a moment, then laughed out loud.

"Yeah," he said. "Yeah, there ain't nobody left to come after us."

Chapter Ten

Sugarloaf Ranch

Smoke was surprised when he saw several head of cattle being pushed onto Sugarloaf. Riding out to see what was going on, he found a small, wiry young man, whistling and shouting as he drove the herd. He was riding one horse, and leading another.

When the young man saw Smoke, he rode toward him, touching the brim of his hat as he reached him. The hat was oversized, with a particularly high crown, almost as if the boy was trying to use it to make up for his small stature.

"You Smoke Jensen?" he asked.

"I am."

The boy smiled and stuck out his hand. "Mr. Jensen, I heard you was plannin' on makin' a big cattle drive up north."

"That's right."

"Well, these here is your cows that was way down on the south range. I reckon you would'a got around to 'em in time, but I thought I'd save you the trouble.

The name's Sanders. Jules Sanders. I come to join you on your drive, if you'll have me."

"Jules, don't get the wrong idea here, but how old are you?" Smoke asked.

"Tell me how old you want me to be and I'll accommodate you," Jules said.

Smoke chuckled. "That's not what I asked," he said. "I'll be honest with you, you don't look a day over fifteen."

Jules didn't answer. "Where you want me to put these cows?"

"You say you drove them up from the south range?" Smoke asked.

"Yes."

"That's twelve miles from here. You brought—how many are there?"

"Sixty-three head," Jules said.

"You brought sixty-three head up from the south range all by yourself?"

"Yes."

Smoke stroked his chin. "That's a pretty good drive for someone to make all by themselves, no matter how old they might be. You knew we'd be coming down there to get them, didn't you?"

"Yes, sir," Jules said. "I knew you'd be comin' for 'em."

"Then why didn't you just leave them there for us?"

"I wanted to impress you," Jules said.

"Well, I must confess, you did do that."

"Mr. Jensen, I need the job," Jules said.

"Jules, this is going to be one difficult drive. It's late in the year and we've got a long way to go. We'll be gone for some time. How would your mom and dad feel about that?"

"They're the reason I need to do it," Jules said. "My ma is bringin' in washin' and sech, all the while she's doin' for my dad. My dad is laid up with what the doc calls the cancer. I got to do somethin' to help out, Mr. Jensen."

Smoke was quiet for a moment, then he nodded. "All right, Jules. I reckon if you can bring this many head this far all by yourself, then you're man enough to do the job."

A big smile spread across Jules's face, and he stuck out his hand. "Thanks, Mr. Jensen," he said. "I can't tell you what this means to me."

Smoke shook Jules's hand. "One thing, though, Jules."

"Yes, sir, anything."

"We're sort of one big family here. I'm Smoke to all the men."

"Yes, sir, Mister—uh, Smoke," Jules said. He looked back at the cattle he had brought up. "Uh, what do I do with these critters?"

"Take 'em out to the north range, join them with the others you see there, then go on down to the house and see Sally."

"Sally?"

"My wife," Smoke said. "She's taking care of the business end of this. She'll make sure you're on the payroll. Uh, by the way, could you use a little advance to send back to your folks?"

Jules shook his head. "No, sir," he said. "I appreciate the offer, I purely do. But I don't want nothin' till I've earned it."

Smoke smiled, and nodded. "You're a good man, Jules," he said. "I don't care how old you are, you're a good man."

"Thanks."

"When's the last time you ate?"

"I had me some jerky back this mornin'," Jules said.

"Well, I know you don't want any money before you've earned it, but you wouldn't mind eatin' with us, would you?"

The broad smile returned. "No, sir, I wouldn't mind that," he said. "I wouldn't mind that none at all."

"When you get back to the house, tell Sally there'll be one more for supper."

"Yes, sir!" Jules said. He turned to the cattle he had brought up. "Get along, cows. They's grass for you and vittles for me."

Smoke watched Jules ride off, driving the cattle before him. He didn't really need another man, but there was something about this young man that reminded him of Matt, and there was no way he was going to turn him down.

Pearlie came riding up shortly after Jules rode off.

"Who was that?" Pearlie asked.

"Our new man."

"I thought we had everyone we needed."

"There's always room for one more," Smoke said.

Pearlie smiled. "Uh-huh," he said. "And if you particular like a person, why, I reckon you'd make room for him even if there weren't none."

"I made room for you once, didn't I?" Smoke asked.

Pearlie nodded. "Yes, sir, you done that all right," Pearlie said. They were referring to the fact that Pearlie, who had once been hired as a gunman to run Smoke off his ranch, had wound up joining the same man he was supposed to kill.

As a means of allowing everyone to get better acquainted with each other, Sally invited all the cowboys to have supper in the big house that night. She fixed roast beef, mashed potatoes with brown gravy, lima beans, and hot rolls.

"Do you folks eat like this all the time?" Jules asked.

"We sure do," Pearlie said.

"Ha!" Cal laughed. "Pearlie wishes we did."

"I figure that during the trail drive," said Sally, "there are bound to be times when you boys are going to get pretty frustrated by pushing a bunch of cows. So, if they start giving you too much trouble, maybe you can take some solace in having eaten their cousin tonight."

The others laughed.

"Say, Smoke, the county fair starts tomorrow," Cal said. "You reckon we could all go in for a bit? I mean, especially as we are going to be on the trail drive for so long."

"I don't see why not," Smoke said.

"You know what we ought to do? We ought to play a baseball game," Jules said.

"What?" Billy asked.

"We ought to play a baseball game," Jules said again. "We've got enough for a baseball team. There's Pearlie,

Cal, Andy, Dooley, Hank, LeRoy, Billy, Mike, and me. That's nine people."

"What about Smoke?" Billy asked.

"Smoke can be our manager."

"What's a manager?"

"A manager is someone who doesn't play, but sort of bosses the ones that do."

"Ha! That's Smoke all right," Cal said. "The bossin' part, I mean."

"Well, tell me just who we are goin' to play with this baseball team?" Pearlie asked.

"The St. Louis Unions."

"The what?"

"The St. Louis Unions," Jules repeated. "They are a professional baseball team and they go around play-ing local teams. If you beat them, they'll give you two hundred dollars."

"Two hundred dollars? That's a lot of money," LeRoy said.

"Yeah, that would be twenty dollars apiece," Dooley added.

"You can forget that," Pearlie said.

"What do you mean, we can forget it?" Jules asked. "It would be good to leave twenty dollars with my mom before we started on this trail drive."

"You can forget it, because we ain't likely to win."

"Well, come on, don't give up before we even try," Jules said.

"Didn't you say this St. Louis Unions was a bunch of professional baseball players?"

"Yes."

"Then that means that they play baseball all the

time. I prob'ly ain't played more'n two or three times in my entire life."

"Me'n Dooley have played a lot," Andy said. "We used to have baseball games out at the fort."

"Yeah, and Andy's real good at it," Dooley said.

"I've played a lot too," Jules said. "Come on, we can at least try."

"Jules, you're young so I don't hold it against you none that you ain't really got no sense," Pearlie said. "But this whole idea of playing a baseball game against a bunch of people who make a living playing baseball is a . . ."

"Great idea," Sally said, finishing Pearlie's sentence.

"What?" several of the others replied at the same time.

"I think Jules has a great idea," Sally said. "I think you should play a baseball game against these people."

"Sally, I tend to agree with Pearlie," Smoke said. "Why humiliate ourselves before our neighbors against a bunch of professionals?"

"We're going to be working together for the next several weeks, right?" Sally asked.

"Yes."

"Then what better way to learn to work together than to play a baseball game now? I think it will create a sense of cooperation and belonging."

"Even if we lose?" Cal asked.

"Yes, even if you lose," Sally said. "Win or lose, if you all play together, you are going to come out ahead. Go on, Smoke, sign them up to play a game."

Smoke chuckled and shook his head. "All right," he said, "I'll challenge the—what are they called?"

"The St. Louis Unions," Jules said.

"I'll challenge the St. Louis Unions. But if we are humiliated, it's on your shoulders."

"I can take it," Sally said.

As Smoke, Sally, and the contingent from Sugarloaf rode into town, they passed under a banner that was stretched across the street, tied up on one side at Andersons's Apothecary and on the other at Miller's Meat Market. In big red letters the sign read:

Welcome to County Fair

A series of exploding firecrackers made Billy's horse rear up, but Billy got it under control very quickly. The young boys who had set off the firecrackers laughed as they ran up the street.

Several vendors had set up booths in the street and were selling such things as taffy, roasted peanuts, fudge, and slices of pie. The city band, resplendent in their red and black uniforms, was seated on a temporary stage, playing a rousing march.

"Look, over there," Jules said, pointing to an open field. There, several men wearing identical straw hats, white shirts, and matching trousers were throwing a ball back and forth.

"Why are they all dressed alike?" Cal asked.

"They are in their uniforms," Jules answered.

"Uniforms? You mean like the suits the soldiers wear?"

"Sort of like that," Jules said. "They all wear the same uniform so you can tell who is on your side."

"Well, now, that don't make no sense a'tall," LeRoy said. "I mean, all you got to do is look at who the person is."

"It's probably for a little intimidation as well," Sally suggested.

"What does that mean?" Cal asked.

"It's just a way of giving them an edge," Sally explained.

"I see. Well, it ain't workin', whatever it's supposed to be doin'," Cal said.

"Shall we go over there and challenge them?" Smoke asked.

"Yeah," Pearlie said. "Let's do it."

"Really? You were one of the ones who thought it was such a crazy idea," Jules said.

"Yeah, but that was before I saw what a bunch of sissies these guys are. I think we won't have any trouble with them."

Smoke cut his horse over toward the field where the uniformed baseball players were throwing the ball around. Half-a-dozen kids were sitting on the top of a split-rail fence, watching the players.

"Who's in charge here?" Smoke called when he rode up.

At Smoke's call, one of the players threw a ball to another, put his glove in his back pocket, expectorated a wad of chewing tobacco, wiped his mouth with the back of his hand, then came over to talk to Smoke.

"I'm in charge here," he said. "What do you need?"

"Is it true that you will give two hundred dollars to any team that can beat you?" Smoke asked.

"Well, to a degree, that is true," the player said.

"What isn't true?"

"We don't just give the money away. You have to enter the contest. And enterin' the contest is goin' to cost you money."

"How much?"

"Fifty dollars."

"Fifty dollars?" Jules groaned. "Why does it cost fifty dollars?"

"Where do you think we get the money to pay those who beat us?" the player asked.

"Does anyone ever actually beat you?" Smoke asked.

"Not very often," the ballplayer admitted.

"When can we play?" Smoke asked.

"As soon as we get the fifty dollars."

"Smoke, I'm sorry," Jules said. "I didn't have no idea it was going to cost money to play."

"That's all right," Smoke said, taking out the money and giving it to the ballplayer. "Here's your money, mister," he said. "Let's play."

"Yes."

Chapter Eleven

Big Rock

Word spread quickly around town that there would
be a baseball match between the professional players
who called themselves the St. Louis Unions and an aggregate of players from in and around Big Rock. As a
result, nearly all the town gathered to watch the game.

Baseball was not unknown in Big Rock. There had
been games contested between men from Big Rock
and teams from nearby towns. But this was the first
time that a touring professional team had ever come
to town, so interest was high.

"Do you think our boys have a chance of winning?"
someone asked.

"Not a snowball's chance in hell," another answered.
"But that won't keep me from cheering them on."

"No, me neither. I'd like to see those St. Louis boys
get their comeuppance."

The Unions, dressed in their white uniforms, were
on the field giving a display of their skills by batting the
ball, scooping it up from the ground, and throwing it

sharply from base to base. After several minutes of such activity, the manager of the St. Louis Unions walked across the field to speak with Smoke.

"The game will commence in thirty minutes, and we will play by the Cartwright Rules," he said. He handed Smoke a booklet. "If you don't know the rules, they are in this book. Three strikes and you are out. Three outs and the other team comes to bat. When each team has made three outs, that will be an inning. We will play nine innings, unless the game is tied. Then we will continue to play until the tie is broken."

"We know the rules, mister," Pearlie said.

"Pearlie, Mr. Thayer is just extending a courtesy," Smoke said.

"I think he's trying to—to intimidate us," Pearlie said, recalling Sally's word. "But it ain't goin' to work, mister. It ain't goin' to work."

"I will tell my players to go easy on you," Thayer said as he turned to walk away."

"Oh, I'd love for us to give his team a good beating," Pearlie said.

"I wonder where Miss Sally is," Cal said. "I thought she would be here to watch us play."

"Maybe she don't want to see us lose," Mike said.

"Lose? We haven't played the first pitch yet and you are already talking about losing. Now, that's a fine way to look at it, don't you think?" Jules asked.

"Well, come on, Jules, look at them people. They got them fancy clothes they're a'wearin'. They got them fancy gloves."

"They've provided us with gloves," Jules said.

"Yeah, but they're nothin' like them fancy gloves they all got."

"Here comes Sally now," Smoke said. "I wonder what she's carrying."

Sally was carrying a bundle and as she approached them, she smiled broadly, then put the bundle down on a bench.

"What have you got there?" Smoke asked.

"Open it," Sally said. "The St. Louis Unions aren't the only ones with uniforms."

"You bought us uniforms?" Jules asked excitedly.

"I bought all of you matching red shirts," Sally said. "That, with your blue denim trousers, will make a uniform."

"Oh, yeah!" Jules said as he held up one of the shirts. "And these here is a lot better-lookin' than them white pajama-lookin' things those folks is wearin'."

Within minutes, every one of Smoke's men was smartly outfitted with the new red shirt and the result was dramatic. They took on the same aura as the uniformed St. Louis Unions.

Sheriff Carson agreed to be the umpire, and he walked out onto the ball field, leaned over to brush off the home plate, then stood up to bellow out as loud as he could:

"Play ball!"

They had played eight and a half innings of baseball and though the St. Louis Unions were leading, the score, at four to one, was much closer than anyone had thought possible. As it turned out, Jules was a very good baseball player, and Mike, Andy, and Leroy were also quite skilled. The others were good enough to keep the game from getting embarrassingly out of hand.

Now, in the last half of the ninth inning, with none out, Billy was walked, giving them a man on base. Cal singled, but Billy was held at third. Hank popped up and the ball was caught by the Unions' second baseman. LeRoy struck out, and that brought Jules to the plate.

"Come on, Jules, a home run would tie the game!" Pearlie shouted.

Jules nodded, then struck his bat against the plate a couple of times before looking at the pitcher.

"Boy," the catcher said from behind him. "I've been watching you. You're a pretty good ballplayer. What are you doing with this bunch of yokels? Why don't you leave them and come with us?"

"You really think I'm good enough to play with you fellas?" Jules asked.

"I sure do."

The pitcher fired the first ball to the plate. Jules swung, but missed.

"That didn't look all that good," Jules said to the catcher.

"Ah, don't worry about it. Tommy is a very good pitcher. You've hit him three times today, and not even the best batter can hit him every time. That's why if you strike out, nobody would ever suspect you did it on purpose."

"What do you mean, on purpose?" Jules asked.

"Well, we divide up the gate from every game. If anyone beats us and we have to pay two hundred dollars, it comes out of our pocket. Your pocket, if you join us. So, why don't you just strike out now and end this game? It'll be better for all of us if you do."

Jules swung and missed at the second pitch.

"Attaboy," the catcher said. "Miss this pitch and you'll be one of us."

Jules turned to look at the catcher.

"Mister, if I strike out, it ain't a'goin' to be on purpose," Jules said. "And I wouldn't want to play with people like you anyway."

The catcher chuckled. "Have it your way, kid," he said.

Then he called to the pitcher. "Quit playin' around with him, Tommy. Throw it past him!"

"No batter, no batter, no batter," the shortstop called.

"Throw it by him, Tommy. Let's collect our money and go have a few beers," the first baseman called.

The left fielder started whistling.

Jules scraped at the ground with his feet and watched as the pitcher wound up, then threw. Jules swung the bat, and had the satisfying feeling of making contact with the ball on the sweet spot of the bat. The ball flew high over the left fielder's head. Jules tossed the bat aside and started for first base.

Billy came home and Cal rounded second, headed for third, rounded third, and streaked home. Jules was right behind Billy, rounding second as Billy started home. Jules saw the left fielder run for the ball, then pick it up just before Jules reached third. Jules rounded third and started for home as the crowd cheered for him.

Then, to Jules's surprise, the left fielder made a tremendous throw, and Jules saw the ball fly into the catcher's mitt just before he reached home plate. Jules slid into home plate, but the catcher was waiting for him and he put the tag on him before he reached the plate.

"You're out!" the umpire called.

The cheers turned to groans.

"You should've took me up on my offer, boy," the catcher said. "You wound up being out anyway, and now you got nothing to show for it."

"Yeah, I've got something to show for it," Jules said and he stood up and wiped the dust from the seat of his pants. "I've got my honor."

The high, skirling sound of a fiddle could be heard from one end of the street to the other as the dancers dipped and whirled to the caller's patter:

"A right and left around the ring
    While the roosters crow and the birdies sing.
All join hands and circle wide,
    Spread right out like an old cow hide.
All jump up and never come down,
    Swing your pretty girl round and round."

Even though Smoke's baseball team had lost to the professionals of St. Louis, they had played so well that they were being heralded as heroes by the citizens of Big Rock. As a result, none of the boys had any difficulty in finding young girls who were willing to dance with them. In fact, several of the girls came up to the boys, hinting that they were thirsty, or suggesting that their dance card was empty for the next dance.

The only ones who were not having a good time at the dance were the ballplayers of the St. Louis Unions. When they saw that the girls were more interested in the young men of Smoke's baseball team, they began to get angry and they started taunting Smoke's men.

"Perhaps we should have lost the game. Then the girls would have taken pity on us, as they have these poor rubes," one of the players suggested.

"I think we should have played the girls," another player said. "They would have given us a better game."

One insult led into another, until finally one of the Unions reached out and tripped Jules as he was dancing. When Jules fell, all the Unions laughed loudly.

"What's the matter, boy? Are you so clumsy that you can't even keep your feet?" one of the players called out.

"You tripped me!" Jules shouted, jumping up and confronting the one who had done it.

The St. Louis player pushed Jules back, and another St. Louis player tripped him again.

"My word, they are as clumsy on the dance floor as they are on the baseball diamond."

This time when Jules jumped up, he came up swinging, connecting with a right jab to the chin of the one who was tormenting him. The player went down, but another player attacked Jules.

Within seconds, the rest of Smoke's men joined in the action and the entire dance came to a halt as the young men from both camps traded blows. The fight continued in a grand scale with tables and chairs turning over, punch bowls being spilled, and men and women shouting, some in alarm and some in encouragement.

The fight lasted for several minutes until, eventually, Smoke, Sheriff Carson, and two of his deputies managed to break it up. As the fight finally came to an end, it became obvious that Smoke's men had gotten much the better of the St. Louis Unions, all of whom were now nursing black eyes and bloody noses.

As the cowboys rode back out to Sugarloaf that night, they were laughing and singing.

"Well, they may have beaten us at baseball, but we sure gave 'em a licking where it counts," Cal said.

"We sure did," LeRoy said.

"You won on the baseball diamond as well," Smoke said.

"No, we lost, four to three," Jules said.

"Uh-huh," Smoke said. "Only their manager bet me two hundred dollars that they would win by at least five runs."

"They only beat us by one run," Jules said.

"That's right," Smoke said. He reached into his pocket and pulled out a wad of bills. "And that's why we won two hundred dollars. You fellas can divide it up exactly as you would have had we won the game."

"Then I can leave my mom twenty dollars before we leave," Jules said excitedly.

"Forty dollars," Pearlie said. "You can have my share."

"Sixty," Cal offered.

"I'd give you my money too, Jules, only I ain't had no work in near two months now," Billy said.

"Me neither," LeRoy echoed.

"I thank you, but Ma don't need no more money than this," Jules said. "This'll keep her till we get back." He looked at Pearlie and Cal. "Thanks to you two," he added.

"Ah," Pearlie said. "It wasn't nothin'."

"You didn't really make a bet with that baseball team, did you?" Sally asked that night as she lay in bed beside Smoke.

"What makes you think I didn't?"

"Because I was with you all day, remember? You couldn't have made such a bet without me knowing about it."

"Well, suppose I didn't."

Sally laughed. "Nothing, except you are a wonderfully generous man, Kirby Jensen."

"So are Pearlie and Cal. They gave their money to Jules."

"I know. You have been a wonderful influence on them."

"Ha!" Smoke said. "We all know who has been the real influence on them. No tellin' where those two would be now if it weren't for you."

Sally snuggled up against Smoke. "Let's face it," she said. "You and I make a wonderful team. That's why I know we are going to get there first."

Smoke lay quietly for just a second. Then he raised himself up on one elbow and looked down at Sally.

"What did you say?"

"I said we make a wonderful team."

"Yeah, I heard that part. I mean, what did you say after that? Something about getting there first?"

"Yes. I said that's why I know we are going to get there first."

"Get where first?"

"To Sorento."

"What does getting there first have to do with it? First before who?"

"First before anyone else," Sally said.

"Sally, darlin', you aren't making sense. Did you or did you not tell me that Mr. Abernathy will buy our cattle at thirty-five dollars a head?"

"Yes," Sally answered.

"Then what does getting there first have to do with it?"

"Well, actually what he said was, he will buy the first three thousand head of cattle delivered to him," Sally said. "I just assumed it would be us."

Smoke let out a sigh, then fell back on his pillow. "You just assumed?"

"Yes. Darling, I know we will get there first," Sally said.

"We damn well better get there first," Smoke said. "Otherwise, we'll be worse off than we are now. I'd hate to be somewhere on the trail, facing a winter like the one we faced before."

"It's a simple thing," Sally said.

"A simple thing?"

"Yes. Our cows are here, we want them in Sorento. All we have to do is take them there."

"Right, that's all we have to do."

Sally rolled into Smoke and kissed him, not a long-time married kiss, but a deep, lover's kiss.

"Oh," Smoke said when she pulled her lips from him. "That was quite a kiss."

"No matter what happens, Smoke, I know you will get us there. I have all the confidence in the world in you," Sally said.

"With trust like that, how can I let you down?" Smoke asked.

Chapter Twelve

The first pink fingers of dawn touched the sagebrush, and the light was soft and the air was cool. This was Smoke's favorite time of day and as he stood by the fire, drinking coffee, he watched his cowboys moving the herd together for the start of the drive.

Behind him he heard the sound of pots and pans being moved around, and he smelled the aroma of frying bacon and baking biscuits. He also caught a whiff of the sweet smell of Sally's patented bear claws. Turning, he saw Sally working at the chuck wagon.

Damn, he thought, he was one lucky man to have found someone like Sally. Sally was Smoke's second wife. After his first wife, Nicole, and their baby were killed, Smoke went on the blood trail, tracking down and killing the men who had so destroyed his life.

After that, Smoke didn't think he would ever be able to love again. But he met a beautiful and spirited young schoolteacher who changed his mind. This was not to say that he had forgotten Nicole; she would always have a place in his heart and Sally understood that. In fact, Sally was so confident in her own position that, though she had never met Nicole, she thought of Smoke's dead wife as a sister to her.

Smoke was so deep in concentration that, for a moment, he didn't realize Sally was staring at him with a bemused expression on her face.

"Good morning," Smoke said.

Sally chuckled. "Good morning," she replied. "If you want to call the boys in, breakfast is about ready."

Sally had gotten up even before sunrise to cook a full breakfast meal for eleven people. After breakfast, she would pack up the chuck wagon and leave, going out ahead of the herd. The men would lunch in the saddle with strips of jerky and cold biscuits. They wouldn't see Sally again until supper.

It was not only Sally's job to get into position in time to fix supper, it was also her job to find a place where the herd could bed down for the night. This was a very responsible job, but Smoke had absolutely no qualms about her ability to perform the tasks assigned.

Smoke walked over to the chuck wagon to see the breakfast she had prepared. She had scrambled eggs, fried potatoes, sausage, stewed apples, and biscuits and gravy.

Smoke whistled in amazement as he eyed the spread.

"Good Lord, Sally, I hope you don't feed them this big a breakfast every morning," he said. "My Lord, they'll get so fat they can't even ride."

Sally laughed.

"This is the first day," she said. "It's just my way of getting things started on the right foot."

"Yeah, well, I hope you don't spoil them into thinking that they are going to eat like this for every meal. I mean, you aren't going to feed them like this, are you?"

"Maybe not quite this well," Sally replied. "But don't forget, a well-fed cowboy is a happy cowboy."

"You didn't pack your china and silver, did you?" Smoke asked sarcastically.

"Oh, that's a good idea," Sally teased. "Maybe I will do that."

"Right," Smoke replied sarcastically.

Sally laughed. "Call the boys in, Smoke," she said. "I need to get going if I'm going to get ahead of the drive."

The drive had been out for four days and nights so far, and there had been no real problems except fatigue. Smoke was pleased with the job Pearlie and Cal had done in picking hands for the drive. Billy Cantrell and the Butrum brothers had proven to be great hands. Mike Kennedy had as well. Only the two former soldiers, Andy and Dooley, were inexperienced, but not even that was causing much of a problem. They were good workers and eager to learn from the more experienced of the outfit.

It was early in the morning of the fifth day, and the last morning star made a bright pinpoint of light over the purple mountains that lay in a ragged line far to the north and west. The coals from the campfire of the night before were still glowing, and Smoke watched as Pearlie threw chunks of wood onto them, then stirred the fire into crackling flames, which danced merrily against the bottom of the suspended coffeepot.

A rustle of wind through feathers caused Smoke to look up just in time to see a golden eagle diving on its prey. The eagle swooped back into the air carrying a tiny field mouse, which kicked fearfully in the eagle's claws. A rabbit bounded quickly into its hole, frightened by the sudden appearance of the eagle.

"Want some coffee, Smoke?" Pearlie called.

"Yes, thanks," Smoke answered.

Pearlie used his hat as a heat pad against the blue-iron handle and poured a cup, then brought it over to Smoke.

"Who's watching the herd?" Smoke asked.

"Billy and Mike ate their breakfast early and have gone out to relieve Cal and Andy."

"Cal and Andy were riding nighthawk?"

"Yes."

"Hmm, I didn't think Cal would have the nerve to be alone with Andy after that joke he pulled on him," Smoke said.

Smoke's comment referred to an incident on their first day out. Cal had told Andy that the feces from some cows were edible, and to prove his point, he went over to pick up a handful of cow manure and eat it.

While all the other cowboys laughed, Andy fought hard to keep from gagging. Then, feeling sorry for him, Pearlie explained that what Cal had eaten was actually a piece of Sally's gingerbread.

"Well, sir, Andy took it pretty good and I think Cal is sort of ashamed of himself for the joke, so they've been gettin' along just real good since then," Pearlie said.

"Speak of the devils, here they come," Smoke said,

nodding toward two riders who were coming into the camp then.

Both men dismounted, then went over and poured themselves cups of coffee. Andy walked over to a log and sat down with some of the others to wait for breakfast, while Cal came up to Smoke and Pearlie. Cal's coffee was black and steaming and he had to blow on it before he could suck it through his lips.

"Cows quiet through the night?" Smoke asked.

"Bedded down like they had blankets and pillows," Cal responded.

"That's good."

"You know what I'm beginnin' to think?" Cal asked. "I'm beginnin' to think we might just pull this off. I mean, look, we've been out for four full days now, and there ain't been no trouble of any kind."

Pearlie chuckled. "We've only been out for four days. Hell, we're barely off Sugarloaf, and you're already talkin' about how easy it's goin' to be."

"No," Cal responded quickly. "I'm not sayin' it's goin' to be easy. I'm just sayin' I believe we can do it."

Pearlie snorted. "I didn't know you ever doubted it."

Cal looked back toward the chuck wagon. "I tell you what, this coffee was good, but I'm gettin' a little hungry. I wouldn't mind havin' a biscuit or two."

"I seen Sally put some in the Dutch oven just a little while ago," Pearlie said. "I expect breakfast will be ready in a minute or two." He looked over at a couple of lumps on the ground. The lumps were actually bedrolls and right now, both were occupied by the men who had been on nighthawk from midnight until four. "I guess I'd better wake up Billy and Hank."

"No, let me do it," Cal said. "They seemed to take particular pleasure in waking me up this mornin' at four when it was time for me to take the watch. I am going to enjoy returning the favor."

"Be my guest," Pearlie invited.

Cal crept over very quietly until he was positioned exactly between the two sleeping men. He stood there for a moment, listening to their soft snoring as he smiled in anticipation of the moment. Then he yelled, at the top of his voice.

"All right you two, let's go! Get 'em up an' head 'em out! We can't wait around here till Christmas!"

Billy and Hank awoke with a start, Billy letting out a little shout of surprise as he did so.

"What is it? What's happening?" Billy asked.

Cal laughed.

Hank groaned. "Damn you, Cal, what do you mean a'wakin' me up like that. I was talkin' to the purtiest little lady you ever did see, in my dream. And iffen I had seen you in my dream doin' somethin' like what you just done, why, I would'a shot you down and that's a fact."

Cal laughed. "You'll dream her up again, I'm sure," he said. "'Cause, truth to tell, dreams are about the only place you'll ever be talkin' to a pretty girl anyway."

"Oh, yeah? Well, what about after that baseball game? I danced with lots of pretty girls."

"They wasn't dancin' with you," Cal said. "They was dancin' with a baseball player. Anyhow, what are we standin' here gabbin' for when Miz Sally has gone to all the trouble of cookin' up a good breakfast. I figured you'd want to eat the biscuits while they're still hot."

"I tell you what I would like to do with those biscuits while they're still hot," Billy grumbled. "And it ain't got nothin' to do with eatin'·'em."

Cal laughed. "Come on, boys, we're burnin' sunlight," he said more softly.

After breakfast, all the cowboys saddled their mounts, then rode out to get the herd moving again. Nearby, three thousand head of cattle, fully awake on this, a new day, milled around nervously. The animals, used to the freedom of the open range, were now forced together in one large, controlled herd. That made them acutely aware of different sights, sounds, smells, and sensations, and they were growing increasingly anxious over the change in what had been their normal routine. So far there had been no trouble, but Smoke knew that the least little thing could spook them: a wolf, a lightning flash, or a loud noise.

He listened with an analytical ear to the crying and bawling of cattle. He was also aware of the shouts and whistles of the wranglers as they started the herd moving.

Although Sally's job was to cook, sometimes in the morning she would saddle her own horse and help the others get the cattle moving. Smoke watched her dash forward to intercept three or four steers who had moved away from the herd. She stopped the stragglers and pushed them back into the herd. Smoke couldn't help but marvel at how well his wife could ride. It was almost as if she and the horse were sharing the same musculature and nerve endings.

Once the herd was actually under way, though, Sally returned to the chuck wagon. The vehicle was being drawn by a particularly fine-looking team of mules. Smoke had hitched up the team for her, and he was standing alongside the wagon as Sally approached.

"Maybe you should break those three steers up," Sally suggested, pointing toward the animals she had just pushed back into the herd. "I swear, this is the third day in a row I've had to deal with them. I believe if they were separated, we wouldn't have a problem."

"Or maybe we would have a problem three times as large," Smoke suggested. "How do you know each one of the cows wouldn't just recruit new cows to help them out? Then you'd have three eruptions instead of just one."

Sally nodded. "You may be right," she said. "I guess I can push them back in tomorrow, or every day as far as that goes, just as long as we're on the trail."

"That's my girl," Smoke said with a broad smile.

Sally walked up to the side of the chuck wagon and tied a knot in a hanging piece of rawhide cord. Each knot represented a day, while a double knot indicated a Sunday. As they knew what day they left, the strip of rawhide would serve as an effective calendar.

"How is the chuck wagon working out for you?" Smoke asked. "Is there anything we need to change?"

"Nothing needs to be changed," Sally said. "I have to hand it to you, Smoke. When you built this wagon, you did a great job."

"All I did was put it together," Smoke said. "You're the one that had it all laid out." Smoke ran his hand lightly across the chuck box, which was a shelf of honeycombs and cubbyholes.

"Well, I guess I'd better get going," Sally said. Kissing

him, she climbed up onto the wagon seat and, with a slap of the reins against the backs of the team, the wagon moved forward.

Smoke watched Sally move out at a rather brisk rate, going much faster than the herd. It was her job each day not only to find a spot that would be suitable to bed down the herd for the night, but also to have the camp established and the supper cooked. By the time the weary cowboys arrived with the herd, they would be ready to eat, then turn in, leaving Sally to clean up and roll out the bread dough for the next day.

Smoke watched Sally drive her wagon by the herd. Then he swung into the saddle and turned his attention to the task at hand, moving the herd another twenty miles.

Chapter Thirteen

The cowboys knew something was different one morning a few days later when Sally did not go ahead of them, but stayed with the herd as it started out. Then, at mid-morning, Smoke called a halt and gathered all the cowboys around him.

"Boys, just over that rise there is the little town of Braggadocio." He pointed to the east. "Sally says we're going to need a few more supplies, so I'm going to send some of you into town to pick them up."

"I'll go," LeRoy said quickly.

"Yeah, me too," Andy said.

"Heck, I want to go as well," Mike said.

"May I go?" Jules asked.

Smoke held up his hands. "You can't all go," he said. "I've got to keep some of you back to watch over the herd."

"I'll stay back," Pearlie offered.

Smoke shook his head. "No, I want you to go in with the others. Cal, you stay back."

"All right," Cal said.

"What about sending half of us in now, then we switch so the other half can go into town tomorrow?" Andy suggested.

Smoke shook his head. "I wish I could let you do that," he said. "But the truth is we can't take the time to spend two days here. So what I want is for those of you who do go into town to buy the groceries on Sally's list, then get back out here."

"Wait," LeRoy said. "You mean we can't even go into the saloon for a beer?"

Smoke chuckled. "I'm not that hard of a slave driver," he said. "You can spend a little time in the saloon, as long as you remember that I want you back here by nightfall."

"I'll keep an eye on them, Smoke," Pearlie said.

Sally chuckled. "You are going to keep an eye on them? Isn't that a little like setting the fox to watch the henhouse?"

"Oh, now, Miz Sally," Pearlie said. "Do you really think that?" He was obviously hurt by her insinuation.

Sally laughed out loud and reached out to touch him. "I was teasing you, Pearlie," she said. "I know you aren't going to get into any trouble."

Pearlie smiled as well. "I didn't think you meant nothin' by that," he said.

"All right, who is going and who is staying?" Smoke asked.

"You already told me I was stayin'," Cal said.

"Cal, if you want, I'll stay and you can go," Jules volunteered.

Cal chuckled. "Nah, you go ahead. I don't mind stayin'."

"I'll stay," Billy offered.

"I'll stay," Dooley said.

Finally, it was agreed that Cal, Hank, Dooley, and Billy would stay with the herd. Pearlie, Andy, LeRoy, Mike, and Jules would go into town.

Sally presented Pearlie with the shopping list and some money. "This is what I want," she said.

"I'll get ever'thing you got on that list, Miz Sally," Pearlie promised. "You can count on it."

"I know I can," Sally said.

"What are you boys waitin' around here for?" Smoke asked. "We're in the middle of fall and it's getting dark earlier every day. If you're going to be back by nightfall, you had better get going."

"Yahoo!" LeRoy shouted. "Come on, boys, let's go! I aim to spend me some of that baseball money."

"Jules?" Billy called.

Jules looked back toward Billy.

"Would you see if you can find me some horehound candy? I'm just real partial to that."

Jules smiled and nodded. "Sure thing, Billy, I'll bring you some back," he promised.

"Thanks," Billy said with a big smile.

After they bought the supplies, they walked out of the store and Pearlie tied the bag of groceries to his saddle horn.

"Let's find us a saloon," LeRoy suggested.

"I don't know, I think we should get on back," Pearlie said.

"Pearlie, come on, Smoke said we could stay in

town for a while. I plan on havin' a couple of drinks, and maybe eatin' in a place where I can sit in a chair at a table. What do you say?"

Pearlie stroked his chin as he considered it, but didn't say anything.

"Look, you're our boss," LeRoy said. "So if you say we got to go back, why, we'll all go back. I'm just tellin' you that Smoke did say we could stay for a while."

Pearlie sighed, then nodded. "All right," he said. "You can stay. But just remember what Smoke said about staying out of trouble. Oh, and be sure and get back before nightfall tonight."

"We will," LeRoy promised.

"Mike?" Pearlie said.

"I'll look after 'em," Mike promised.

Pearlie nodded again, then mounted his horse. "Before nightfall," he said again, and the others nodded at him.

The cowboys watched Pearlie ride off before they started looking for the saloon. Then, finding it, they tied up to the hitching rail out front, pushed through the batwing doors, and strode up to the bar, catching the bartender's eye.

"Jules, I don't want to embarrass you or anything in here, so, what'll it be? Beer or sarsaparilla?" Mike asked.

Jules thought for a moment. He had tried beer before, and he didn't particularly like the taste, whereas he did like the taste of sarsaparilla. On the other hand, he was now a working cowboy, doing the same job as the other cowboys. He decided he should drink as the others as well.

"I'll have a beer," he said.

"Good man," Mike replied.

After ordering beers for each of them, LeRoy asked the bartender where they might find a whorehouse.

"Ain't nothin' exactly like that in Braggadocio," the bartender replied. He pointed toward the stairs. "But we got a top floor here with private rooms and beds, and half-a-dozen whores that look as good as any you're goin' to find in some big city somewhere."

As the bartender was talking, he saw Jules take a sip of his beer, then make a face at its bitterness. The bartender looked at LeRoy as he pointed to Jules.

"Ain't this here boy kinda young to be runnin' with you fellas? Most especial if you are talkin' about whores and such."

Jules's eyes narrowed. "Mister, you got somethin' to say about me, you say it to me. Don't be talkin' around me."

"All right, I'm tellin' you, I think you are still a little too wet behind the ears to be in here."

Jules took another swallow of his beer, this time making certain not to react to the beer's bitter taste. "You know, I heard there was lots of young fellas no older'n me killin' and dyin' in the late war. If it was to come down to that again, do you think I would be old enough to go to war?"

"Well, I reckon you might be," the bartender admitted.

"So that means I'm old enough to die?" Jules asked.

"I suppose so."

"That makes me old enough."

The bartender had a puzzled look on his face. "How does that make you old enough?"

"Well, now, a fella doesn't get any older than dead, does he?" Jules asked.

Suddenly, the bartender laughed. "I reckon you got a point there, boy," he said. "Yes, sir, I reckon you got a point."

"Whereat is a good place to eat?" LeRoy asked.

"Jenny's Place, just next door," the bartender replied.

"Well, sir, me an' my friends is goin' over to this here Jenny's Place to get us somethin' to eat," LeRoy said. "Then we're goin' to come back for some serious drinking and to make a run on them whores. Don't you let them get away."

"Oh, don't worry none about that. They'll be here."

The cowboys left the saloon, then turned into Jenny's Place, which was next door. Their orders came quickly, but while Mike, Andy, and LeRoy wolfed down their meals, Jules merely picked at his food.

"You plannin' on eatin' the rest of them taters?" LeRoy asked Jules. When Jules shook his head, LeRoy took Jules's plate and shoveled the uneaten potatoes off onto his own.

LeRoy spent the rest of the meal instructing Jules on the proper techniques of whoring. "You're prob'ly thinkin' you should get yourself a real young whore, ain't you? Maybe someone about your own age?"

"I don't know," Jules replied in a mumble.

"Come on, boy, pay attention," LeRoy said. "I'm tryin' to learn you somethin' about whorin' here."

"LeRoy, leave the boy alone," Mike said.

"I ain't doin' nothin' wrong," LeRoy replied. "I'm just tryin' to learn the boy a few things. You got no trouble with that, do you, boy?"

"No," Jules said. "It's just that . . ."

"It's just what?"

"If Pearlie was still here, I don't think we'd be doin' this."

"Doin' what?"

"Talkin' about goin' with whores and such," Jules said.

"Yeah, well, Pearlie ain't here," LeRoy said. "And he didn't say don't go with no whores now, did he?"

"No."

"So that takes care of that. Now, how 'bout what I asked you a while ago? If you was to have your choice betwixt a young whore and a old whore, which one would you choose?"

"I'd choose the young whore, I reckon."

"Why?"

"Well, 'cause I'm young," Jules said.

"Uh-huh, and that's just where you'd be makin' a big mistake," LeRoy insisted.

"Why would that be a mistake?" Jules asked.

"Because if she's that young, she won't be a'knowin' a whole lot more about it than you, for all that she is a whore," LeRoy explained. "What you need is to find yourself the oldest one in the place. See, that way, there ain' no kind of way she ain' never been rode, an' no kind of man she ain't never throwed. Besides which, the older the whores get, the younger they like their men. An old whore would be a real good one for breakin' you in."

Mike laughed. "LeRoy, will you leave the boy alone? You're as full of shit as a Christmas goose, you know that? Don't go listening to him, Jules. He's just tryin' to make sure he gets the youngest and prettiest one for himself. By the way, you goin' to eat the rest of your steak?"

Without answering, Jules forked the rest of his steak off his plate and onto Mike's.

"That's where you're wrong," LeRoy said to Mike. "I for sure don't want the prettiest one. The prettiest ones think their good looks is all they need. The ugly ones, now, will do whatever you want 'cause they want to stay on your good side. Unless you get one that's ugly, but don't know that she's ugly." LeRoy laughed. "Them's the worst kind, 'cause they figure they're pretty enough for looks to get them by, and they don't try none at all. An ugly woman that thinks she's pretty and don't try . . . well, you sure don't want that kind of whore if you can help it."

Mike laughed. "I keep tellin' LeRoy he ought to write a book. I mean, as much as he knows about whorin' 'n all."

"That's a fact all right," LeRoy said. "I could write me a good book."

"If you could write," Mike said, and all around the table laughed.

"Boy, you're lookin' a little peekid," LeRoy said to Jules. "You feelin' all right?"

"Sure, I feel fine," Jules said.

Though he wouldn't tell the others, he had butterflies in his stomach just from thinking about being with a woman.

When they returned to the saloon after their meal, they found a table and sat there having a few drinks while they were waiting.

As they waited, Jules studied the women who were at the moment working the men for drinks. One seemed to have a softer smile and a gentler disposition than the others. Somehow she seemed less threatening to him.

"If we do this, that's the one I want," he said to the others, pointing to one of the women. It was the first comment he had made in several minutes.

"What do you mean 'if' we do this? Of course we are going to do this," LeRoy said. LeRoy turned to look. "Which one is it you're a'lookin' at?"

When Jules pointed her out, LeRoy shook his head. "No," he said. "That ain't the one you want. Give me a few minutes, I'll find the right one for you."

"I don't want you to find one for me," Jules insisted. "That's the one I want."

"Boy, you didn't listen to nothin' I said, did you?" LeRoy said.

"That's the one I want," Jules insisted.

Finally, LeRoy shook his head. "All right, but don't say I didn't warn you none."

Even as they were talking, one of the women came over to the table where the four men were sitting. Putting a hand on her hip and thrusting her hip out provocatively, she leaned over the table. "The bartender says you fellas want some company tonight."

"Company, yeah," LeRoy said.

The woman straightened up. "First, we must get the unpleasant business of money out of the way. Our company will cost you gentlemen a dollar each, or two dollars apiece for the whole night."

"We can't stay all night," LeRoy said. "Fact is, we

can't stay very long a'tall so we was wonderin', I mean, seein' as we can't none of us stay very long, we was wonderin' if maybe you'd give us a cheaper price."

"My, my, ain't you boys cheap? Sorry, boys, but we can't give it to you no cheaper'n a dollar. But if you are willin' to pay for it, why, we can sure show you a good time." The woman smiled. "My name's Tillie."

"Tillie, I'm layin' me a claim on you right now," LeRoy said. "And the young'un here"—LeRoy pointed to Jules—"wants that one over there." He pointed to the girl Jules had chosen.

"Have you ever been with a woman before, honey?" Tillie asked Jules.

Jules felt his cheeks burning in embarrassment. "No, ma'am," he answered, barely mumbling the words.

"Then you've made a wise choice," Tillie said. "Doney is just real good with young boys who're doing it for the first time. It's almost as if she has a calling for it."

Tillie signaled the other three whores, and they came over to the table to stand beside her. She made the introductions, ending with Doney.

"Doney, this little sweetheart is one of your specials, if you get my meaning," Tillie said.

"She means he ain't never done it before," LeRoy added, and Jules felt his cheeks flush again.

"Is that right?" Doney asked.

"Yes, ma'am," Jules replied in a quiet voice.

Doney reached out to take Jules's hand in hers.

"Don't you be worryin' none about it, honey," Doney said to Jules. "We're goin' to have us a fine time, you'll see."

"Well, shall we all go upstairs?" Tillie invited.

"I reckon so, unless you're wantin' to do it right down here on the table," LeRoy said. "And I'm that ready I'm about to bust."

"Well, we certainly don't want to see him bust, do we?" Tillie said, laughing. "Come on, ladies, I do believe these gentlemen are badly in need of our services."

As they all climbed the stairs, Jules was certain that everyone in the saloon was watching them. But as they reached the first landing, he happened to glance into the mirror hanging behind the bar, and it didn't appear that anyone in the saloon was paying the slightest bit of attention to him and his friends. He was surprised by that, but it did make him feel a bit less embarrassed.

Once he and Doney were in her room, Doney shut the door behind them, then lit a single candle. She turned and smiled at Jules as she began stripping off her clothes. Jules watched, spellbound, as the smooth skin of Doney's shoulders was exposed. Then she turned so that he saw only her back as she removed the rest of her clothes. Calling on all the tricks of her professional experience, she used a shadow here, a soft light there, and a movement to hold her body just so. As if by magic, she seemed to lose so many years in age and gain so much in mystery that she became as sensual a creature as anyone who had ever appeared in Jules's fantasies. Finally, raising the corner of the sheet, she managed to slip into bed using the shadows in such a way that he wasn't sure whether he had seen anything or not.

She looked at Jules and laughed.

"What is it?" he asked. "What's wrong?"

"Are you just going to stand there like that?"

"Like what?"

"Like that?" Doney said. She pointed. "Honey, you still have your clothes on. Do you plan to keep your clothes on?"

"Oh," Jules said.

Jules just stood there.

"Well?"

"Well what?"

Doney sighed. "Honey, are you going to undress or not?"

"Oh," Jules said again. "Uh—Doney, would you mind if we . . . ?"

Jules paused in mid-sentence.

"If we what?"

"If we—uh—didn't really do anything? I mean, you can keep the money. It's just that—well—I don't think my ma would approve."

Doney smiled and patted the bed. "Sit here beside me, honey," she said.

Jules sat down.

"Unless I miss my guess, your friends are waiting just outside the door."

"Waiting outside the door? Why would they be waiting outside the door?" Jules asked.

"To see if you really do anything," Doney said. "If they don't hear anything going on in here, they are going to tease you unmercifully."

"Oh."

Doney's smile broadened. "I tell you what. Let's give 'em a show."

"What do you mean?"

"Start bouncing up and down on the bed," Doney said.

Now, as he understood what Doney was suggesting, a broad smile spread across Jules's face.

Outside the door, LeRoy, Andy, Mike, and the three women with them were straining to hear what was going on inside.

"How come there ain't nothin' happenin'?" LeRoy asked.

"Give 'em time, honey," Tillie said. "The kid is green. Doney will have to work on him for a while."

Suddenly, from the other side of the door, they heard the bed squeaking. LeRoy grinned broadly.

"There they go!" he said. "Hot damn, they are at it now."

The squeaking of the bed became more pronounced; then the squeaking was joined by squeals and groans.

"Oh, honey, oh, honey!" Doney was saying. "Oh, honey, yes, you are wonderful! You are magnificent!"

"Damn!" Mike said. "What's that boy doin' that's so great?"

"Honey, that's not a boy," Tillie said. "Sounds to me like he's all man."

Inside the room, Jules and Doney continued to bounce on the bed. Then, as she held up her hand as a signal, Doney's squeal reached a climax.

"Yes, yes, yes, yes!" she shouted. With a cutting motion of her hand, she signaled for them to stop.

"Okay, honey," she whispered. "Wait a minute, then go on out. I promise you, you won't be teased."

"Thanks," Jules said.

"You're a sweet boy," Doney said. "Come back and see me in a couple of years."

The sun was setting as the four young cowboys returned to the encampment.

"Well," Smoke said. "All back in one piece, I see."

"Yes, sir, Smoke. You said get back a'fore sundown and that's just what we done," LeRoy said.

"Did you have a good time?"

"We had a fine time," LeRoy said. "But I don't reckon none of us had as fine a time as Jules here."

"Oh?"

"Yes, sir," LeRoy said. "He had him a fine time. Just ask him. Maybe he'll tell you about it. He won't say nothin' at all to us."

"Well, I'm glad you boys had a chance to enjoy yourselves. That means that by tomorrow, you'll all be bright-eyed, bushy-tailed, and ready to go."

"Yes, sir, we will at that," LeRoy said. "Come on, boys, let's get the horses into the remuda."

"Sally held some supper for you," Smoke called to them.

When the other cowboys left, Jules hung back for a moment.

"Uh, Smoke?" he said.

"Yes?"

"Uh, truth to tell, I didn't do nothin'. Me'n Doney just made 'em think I did. But, don't tell 'em, all right?"

Smoke smiled, then reached out to squeeze Jules's shoulder.

"Don't worry," he said. "Your secret is safe with me."

Chapter Fourteen

One morning, less than a week after their stop at Braggadocio, Smoke noticed that Billy Cantrell seemed a little detached. While the others laughed and joked over breakfast, visiting for the last few minutes before getting the herd under way, Billy was walking around the encampment, pulling stems of grass and sucking on the roots, snapping twigs and smelling them, and scooping up handfuls of dirt to examine them very closely.

Smoke had already done those same things, and he knew exactly what Billy was looking for. He walked over to talk to the young cowboy. Billy looked up at him, but before he could say anything, Smoke spoke up. "I know," he said.

"Do you?"

"Billy, I was sucking on grass roots before you were born. I know exactly what you are doing."

"What's the name of that river you say we'll be crossing next?"

"The Eagle River."

"How far do you make it from here?"

"I'd say another forty miles," Smoke said.

"They're going to be dry miles," Billy said.

"Yeah, I know," Smoke said. "From the looks of the sign, there hasn't been a rain here in quite a spell, which means that any narrow streams or watering holes between here and the Eagle will, more than likely, be dried up."

"Forty miles. That means what? Two more days without water?" Billy asked.

Smoke nodded grimly. "I'm afraid so," he said.

"You prob'ly know this country better'n I do, Smoke. You know of any year-round streams or creeks between here and Eagle River?"

"There aren't any."

"Damn," Billy said. "That means the herd is going to get awfully thirsty."

"Yeah, which means they will spook easily," Smoke said. "You boys will just have to be very careful when you are driving them. Don't make any sudden movements or noises. The least little thing, a sneeze or taking off your hat too fast, could spook them into a stampede."

"We'll have to tell the others," Billy said.

"Billy, have you ever seen a stampede?" Smoke asked.

"No, I haven't. Have you?"

"Yeah, but not one with this many cows. If this herd goes, I can promise you, we will have our hands full."

"You got any suggestions on the best way to handle 'em if they start?" Billy asked.

"Yeah, my suggestion would be to get the hell out of their way," Smoke replied.

Billy chuckled. "Most likely, that ain't somethin' we'll have to tell 'em. I reckon if anyone sees a whole herd of cows comin' down on 'em at a gallop, they'll just natural get out of the way."

Smoke laughed as well. "You may have a point there," he said. "Next thing after you get out of the way, is just to follow them, and when they run down a little so that you can turn them, try and head them back in the right direction. But the best thing to do is keep them from stampeding in the first place."

Over the next two days, they pushed the cows through the dry area as gingerly as if the animals were made of glass. They made no sudden moves, whether mounted or not, and when they spoke to each other, they spoke in whispers. Finally, when Cal rode ahead and returned to tell them that they were now only ten miles away from water, it looked as if they would make it through with no real trouble.

Smoke signaled to the others that they would camp by water that night, and the others responded with grateful waves as they continued to work around the perimeters, keeping the cows moving forward steadily and confidently. Despite what had to be a terrible thirst, the herd was well under control.

That all changed when Dooley Thomas's horse was spooked by a rattler. The horse whinnied loudly, then reared up on its back legs. The cows nearest the snake-spooked horse started running, and that spread through the rest of the herd. Then, like a wild prairie fire before a wind, it took only seconds for the entire herd to be out of control.

"Stampede! Stampede!" Billy shouted from the front, and his cry was carried in relay until everyone knew about it.

"Stampede!"

There was obvious fright in the voices that shouted the warning, but there was grim determination as well, for every man knew what was at stake, and moved quickly to do what he could to stop the stampede.

Smoke was riding on the left flank and, fortunately for him, when the stampede started, the herd veered away from him, toward the right, a living tidal wave of thundering hoofbeats, a million aggregate pounds of muscle and bone, horn and hair, red eyes, dry tongues, and running noses. Although the herd consisted of three thousand individual animals, they were moving as one entity, huge and ferocious. Their pounding hooves churned up a huge cloud of dust to hang in the air, leaving the air so thick that within moments Smoke could see nothing. It was as if he were caught in the thickest fog one could imagine, but this fog was brown, and it burned the eyes and clogged the nostrils and stung his face with its fury. And it was filled with thousands of pounding hooves and clacking, slashing horns.

Leaning forward in his saddle, Smoke urged his horse to its top speed, allowing him to overtake the herd. Then he rode on their right in a desperate attempt to turn them back into the proper direction. He, like the others, was shouting and whistling and waving his hat at the herd, trying to get them to respond.

Then, to Smoke's horror, he saw Dooley fall from his horse. The stampeding cows adjusted their direction toward the helpless rider, almost as if they were intentionally trying to do him harm. Dooley regained his feet, but without a horse, all he could do was try to outrun them on foot. It quickly became clear that he was going to lose the race. Smoke watched the young ex-soldier go down.

Smoke raced to Dooley, but even before he dismounted, he knew the young man was dead. The entire herd had passed over him, their slashing and pounding hooves leaving his body lying in the dirt behind them, battered and torn.

Looking up toward the herd, Smoke saw that the cattle had slowed their run to a brisk trot, and as they did, the rest of the wranglers were able to turn them back in the direction they were supposed to be going. The stampede had at last come to an end, brought under control by the courage and will of the young men who had been pushing the herd.

With the herd once more under control, Andy and Pearlie came riding back to where Smoke was standing.

"Dooley! Dooley!" Andy shouted anxiously as he rode up. He leaped from his saddle and knelt on the ground beside his friend. "Dooley," he repeated, then shook his head as tears began streaming down his cheeks.

Smoke reached down to put his hand on Andy's shoulder.

"I'm sorry," Smoke said.

"Me'n Dooley was together from the time we come into the army at Jefferson Barracks back in St. Louis," Andy explained. "We mucked stalls together, walked guard together, put up with sergeants that was the scum of the earth, and fought the Indians in a dozen or more campaigns, all with nary a scratch between us. And now this."

Cal came back then, leading Dooley's horse.

"Get him on the horse," Smoke said. "We'll bury him tonight."

Cal nodded, then got down and reached for Dooley.

"I'll put 'im up," Andy said. "He was my friend."

"He was a friend to us all," Cal said.

Andy nodded, then stepped back to allow Cal to help him. They put Dooley belly-down across his saddle.

Within another hour, the herd caught the scent of water as they approached the Eagle River. They began running again, not stampeding, but moving toward the water at a gait that brought them quickly to the water's edge.

The lead cows moved out into the river and for a moment, Smoke was afraid that the cows coming up from behind would push the front ranks into deep water where they would drown. Fortunately, the herd had approached the river where a huge sandbar formed a natural ford, and the cattle were able to spread out enough that all could drink their fill. Although they had only come twenty miles today, it had been an unusually rapid twenty miles, so rapid in fact that they had overtaken, then outpaced the chuck wagon. Smoke called a halt to the drive, declaring that they would spend the next twenty-four hours right there.

Ordinarily, arriving at water after such a long, dry spell would be cause for a celebration. But though everyone was thankful for the water, no one felt like celebrating.

As Cal came riding toward the chuck wagon, Sally recognized him by the way he sat his horse, even before she could make out his features. She smiled at him.

"I saw the herd go by," she said. "I expect they've all drunk their fill by now."

"Yes'm, I reckon so," Cal said. Something in the tone of his voice alerted Sally.

"Cal, what is it? What's wrong?" Sally asked. She felt a quick stab of fear go through her.

"We had an accident," Cal said.

"Oh, my God, no!" Sally gasped. "It's not Smoke?"

"No, no, Miz Sally!" Cal shouted quickly, holding up his hand. "It ain't Smoke, he's fine. I didn't mean to scare you like that. It was Dooley."

"Dooley," Sally said with a sigh, thankful that it wasn't Smoke.

"Yes'm. It was Dooley—and—the thing is, he got hisself kilt."

"Oh!" Sally said, feeling guilty now over her sense of relief in learning that it had been Dooley and not Smoke.

"Smoke sent me out to tell you, and to ride into camp with you."

"Thanks," Sally said. "I appreciate the company."

After supper that night, they buried Dooley on top of a small hill that overlooked the Eagle River. Andy asked if he could say a few words.

"Of course you can," Smoke replied.

Andy stood over the mound of fresh dirt, holding his hat in his hands as he spoke.

"Me'n Dooley was friends," Andy said. "Now, ever'-body has friends, but if you ain't never been in the army, then you don't know how important army friends is.

"You see, most of us in the army is a long ways from home, so Dooley was more'n a friend; he was my brother. Like the song says, we rode forty miles a day on beans and hay. Mosquitoes was worse than Indians, boredom was worse than fear, loneliness was worse than brutal sergeants. But we managed to come through it all, because we was friends."

Andy paused for a moment and looked at the bowed heads around him. "You was all good friends to the two of us, and I reckon I'll get through this all right because of friends like you. I thank you for letting me speak these words."

One by one the others came by to shake Andy's hand, and say a word or two of comfort to him. Sally embraced him, then all went to spread their bedrolls. Smoke let everyone sleep through the night, secure in the knowledge that the herd was not likely to wander away from water.

* * *

Over the next two days it turned cold, and by nightfall of the thirteenth day out, it was so cold that a constant fog of vapor hung over the herd and issued from the noses and mouths of horses and men alike. The campfire that night was as welcome for its heat as it was for the fact that it cooked their supper meal and furnished the light.

Smoke and Sally slept in the chuck wagon. The others spread out a canvas from the side of the wagon and, building the fire up for maximum warmth, spread their rolls out under the canvas.

During the night, unnoticed by Smoke, Sally, or the sleeping cowboys, huge, white flakes began drifting down from the sky. The snowfall was heavy, continuous, and silent.

Smoke and his cowboys slept peacefully, warm in their bedrolls, completely unaware of the silent snowfall. While they were sleeping, the world around them was changing. There was no grass, no dirt, no rocks. Even the trees and shrubbery had become unidentifiable lumps. The entire world had become one all-encompassing pall of white.

Because she had to prepare breakfast, Sally was always the first to awaken. When she opened the back flap of the wagon and looked outside, she was greeted by such a white, featureless landscape that, for a moment, she thought she might still be asleep. Then, with a gasp, she realized what she was seeing.

"No!" she said aloud.

"What is it, Sal?" Smoke's question was mumbled from the warmth of his blankets.

"Smoke, look at this."

There was a such a sense of dread and foreboding in Sally's voice that Smoke roused himself from the blankets, then crawled to the back of the wagon to look outside.

"Oh, damn," Smoke said.

"What will we do, Smoke?"

"We keep going," Smoke said.

"How? We have three thousand head of cattle, and snow that is at least two feet deep. How are we going to move?" Sally asked.

"I haven't figured that part out yet," Smoke said. "But we are going to move. We've got no choice. It's either move, or stay here and lose the entire herd."

After Smoke was dressed, he jumped down from the chuck wagon, then crawled up under the canvas to talk to the others. They were all awake and squatting on their heels, looking out at the snow.

"Mornin', boys," Smoke said.

"Damn, Smoke, I thought the whole reason for takin' the herd up to Wyoming was so we wouldn't have to go through this," Pearlie said.

"Yeah, it was. But you know what they say. Man proposes, God disposes," Smoke replied. "I reckon this is just His way of testing us."

"Some test," Pearlie said.

"What are we goin' to do?" Andy asked.

"We're goin' on," Smoke said.

"What do you mean we're goin' on?" LeRoy asked. He pointed to the snow-covered terrain. "In case you ain't noticed, there's more'n two feet of snow out there."

Smoke stared at him. "I'm goin' on," Smoke said.

"You can go on with me, or you can turn around and go back."

"Then I'm goin' back," LeRoy said.

"Go back to what?" Hank asked. "We don't have anything to go back to."

"I don't care whether we have anything to go back to or not," LeRoy said. "Anything is better'n this."

Hank shook his head. "You can go back if you want to, LeRoy, but I'm stayin'."

"Come on, Hank, stayin' to do what?" LeRoy asked. "You know damn well we can't drive cows through two feet of snow. Not if we got behind each and every one of them and pushed."

Hank pointed to Smoke. "This man got us out of jail and I gave my word that I would go to Wyoming with him," Hank said. "And I aim to keep that word. As long as he is willin' to keep goin', then I'm staying with him."

"Hank?" LeRoy said, questioning, without actually forming a question.

"I'll see you when I get back."

"If you get back," LeRoy said. He sighed, then looked over at Billy. "Billy, you got more sense than this, don't you?"

"Tell all the painted ladies back in Big Rock I said hello, will you?" Billy asked.

"And tell my mom I'm doin' fine," Jules added.

LeRoy looked over at Andy. "What about you?" he asked.

"Dooley died tryin' to get these cows up to Wyoming," Andy answered. "Seems to me like iffen I'd stop now, well, I'd sort of be lettin' him down. No, sir, I reckon I'll be stayin' with Mr. Jensen and the others."

"LeRoy, if you're goin', get all your good-byes said and be goin'," Smoke said. "We've got work today."

"Damnit! Damnit, damnit, damnit!" LeRoy said, hitting his hand into his fist. "I ain't goin'."

"What do you mean you ain't goin'?" Pearlie asked. "Why not?"

"'Cause I reckon when you get right down to it, I'm as crazy as all the rest of you," LeRoy said, laughing as he spoke.

The others laughed as well.

"I figured you were too good a man to just pull up and leave a job undone," Smoke said. "I'm glad to have you with us."

"But what I want to know now is, how the hell are we going to do this?" LeRoy asked. "How are we going to get out of here?"

"We're goin' to ride out," Smoke said.

"That's easy enough to say. A horse will break trail in snow. A cow won't."

Smoke smiled broadly and held up a finger. "Then we'll break a trail for them," he said.

Chapter Fifteen

All that day the silence of the white-covered scene was broken by the sound of sawing and the shouts of men as they went about their labors, cutting limbs from the trees, then tying them into place. By nightfall they were ready, but because it was too dark to proceed, they made plans to get under way the next morning.

Exhausted and cold, the men built a big fire, then huddled under the tarp to take advantage of what warmth the fire put out. Pearlie was the one who noticed it first.

"I'll be damn!" he said, smiling broadly. "I'll be damn!"

"What is it?" Mike asked.

"Can't you smell it?"

Several of the men sniffed the air. "I can't smell nothin' but cold," Andy said.

"That's 'cause you ain't never smelt Miz Sally's apple pie before. Nor ate none of it either."

Cal nodded. "He's right!" he said. "I smell it too."

Soon, the rich aroma of cinnamon and apple permeated the entire area and everyone could smell it.

Supper was biscuits and a satisfying stew, but everybody's thoughts were of the apple pies Sally had made. After supper, she brought them out, three of them, which she carved into very generous portions for everyone.

"I thought that, after a day like today, a big piece of apple pie and a hot cup of coffee might lift everyone's spirits," she said.

"Yes, ma'am," Jules said as he took a huge bite of his pie. "You thought right."

The men's spirits were lifted and as they ate their pie and drank their coffee, they exchanged stories. Sally and the men laughed at a story Andy told about how he and Dooley had put one over on the same sergeant Mike had gotten into a fight with.

"Say, Jules, where'd you learn to play baseball like that?" LeRoy asked. "You were purt' near as good as them boys in them white pajamas."

The others laughed at LeRoy's reference to the uniforms of the St. Louis Unions.

"Pretty near as good? He was a lot better'n any of 'em," Cal said.

"Yeah," Andy said. "Where did you learn to play like that?"

"I don't know," Jules said. "Seems like from the first time I ever saw the game, I could play. I think it would be great to play ball and get paid for it like them boys was."

"But you have too much honor," Smoke said.

"Honor? What do you mean he has too much honor?" Pearlie asked. "I mean, yeah, I think he's got honor and all, but what does that have to do with playing baseball?"

"It don't have nothin' to do with it really," Jules said self-consciously,

"That's not what Sheriff Carson says," Smoke said.

"Tell them, Smoke," Sally said. Smoke had obviously shared the story with Sally.

"Sheriff Carson? What does he have to do with it?" Billy asked.

"He was umpire, remember?" Smoke said.

"Yeah, I remember."

"Sheriff Carson said that our man Jules here was offered the chance to play for the Unions, and to get paid for playing. But they wanted him to strike out his last time at bat."

"Strike out? What? They tried to talk him into striking out?" Billy asked.

"They told him if he would strike out that he could play for them. And he would make a lot of money, more money than he can make being a cowboy."

"Why, those dirty bastards," Hank said. Then, quickly, he looked over toward Sally. "Beggin' your pardon, ma'am, for the cussin'," he said.

"That's quite all right," Sally said. "Anyone who would try and get someone to cheat is a bastard," she said. The others laughed.

"Why didn't you do it?" Mike asked Jules

"Mike, you aren't serious," Billy said.

"Well, I mean, think about it," Mike said. "This was just one game that didn't really mean nothin'. He could'a made a lot of money."

"It wouldn't of been right," Jules said. "And I don't think you would've done it either."

Mike thought for a minute, then smiled. "Well, I reckon not," he said. "Of course, the question never come up because I ain't a good enough baseball player. But if it had come up, I reckon I would'a done the same thing as you done. Though I might of stopped to think about it a little."

The others laughed at Mike's admission.

"Say, Smoke, why don't you tell us about Matt?" Pearlie asked.

"Who?" Andy asked.

"Smoke rode all the way to Denver just to see a fella get some kind of award from the governor," Pearlie explained. "A fella by the name of Matt Jensen."

"Matt Jensen?" Andy said. "I've heard of him. They say he's fast as lightnin' with a gun. Say, you've got the same name. Is he your kin?"

"He's not blood kin," Smoke said. "But I raised him from the time he was twelve. That's how he came to take my name."

"Tell us about when you found him," Pearlie said. Pearlie looked over at Andy, Mike, Billy, and the Butrum brothers. "This is a good story," he said. "You'll like it."

"Well, it started in weather just about like this," Smoke said. "I got caught up in a snowstorm and I needed to be on the other side of the mountain range before the snow closed the pass. So, although every ounce of me wanted to hole up somewhere long enough to ride the storm out, I pushed on through, fighting the cold, stinging snow in my face until I reached the top of the pass. I made it through, then started looking for a place to spend the night when I saw the boy."

"That's when you seen him? In the middle of a snowstorm?" Mike asked.

"Yes. I almost missed him. There was a big drift of snow so that only the boy's head and shoulders were sticking out. He was under an overhanging ledge, and his head was back and his eyes were closed, so I didn't know if he was sleeping or if he was dead.

"The boy's face and lips were blue, and there were ice crystals in his eyebrows and hair. The only protection he had against the cold was a blanket that he had wrapped around him, and that blanket was frozen stiff."

"Damn, what did you do?" Andy asked.

"I put my fingers on his neck. It was cold, but I could feel a pulse. But I knew that if he didn't get him back to my cabin soon, he would die. So I cut some limbs and built a travois. Then, stuffing moss in between a couple of blankets, I made an insulated bedroll, and tying the boy onto the bedroll, started down the other side of the mountain.

"The snow continued to fall and walking was hard. I knew it was going to be hard enough for the horse to move, even without pulling a travois, so I walked in front of the horse, holding onto his bridle.

"It was so cold that the air hurt my lungs as I sucked it down. And I didn't have any snowshoes so, often, I would sink nearly waist-deep into the drifts.

"Because of the clear air, the unbroken whiteness, and the way distance was contorted, it seemed like I was getting nowhere. I remember once, I had been working really hard for two hours, and yet when I looked back over my shoulder, it was almost as if I had just left—I could still see the rock overhang where I found the boy, and if it had not been for the fact that I knew exactly where I was, and how far I had to go, I would've been pretty disheartened. But I knew that I would be to the cabin before nightfall.

"I trudged on through the snow for at least another three hours until, finally, the little cabin came into view.

"I have to admit that the cabin I lived in then wasn't much to look at. But considering the alternative at the time, it looked better than finest mansion you could imagine.

"I picked the boy up from the travois and carried him inside, then deposited him on the bed. Then, after I took care of the horse, I came back in and fixed supper."

"Did you make him apple pie?" Pearlie asked.

"I'm afraid not," he said. "That was a little beyond my capability."

"What did you make him?" Billy asked.

"Beaver stew."

"Beaver stew? Hmm," Billy said. "I don't know as I've ever et any beaver stew."

Smoke laughed. "That's what the boy said."

"That he'd never et beaver stew before?"

"That's it," Smoke said. "He didn't ask who I was, or where he was, or what was going to happen to him. All he said was that he didn't think he had ever eaten beaver stew before. I figured then that if he couldn't be shaken by nearly freezing to death, then winding up in a total stranger's house eating something he had never eaten before, then he had to be a boy with gumption."

"From what I've heard of the fella, he's proved you right," Andy said.

"Yes," Smoke said. "Matt has made me very proud over the years."

Smoke stretched and yawned. "I don't know about you boys," he said. "But I worked hard today, and I figure I'll be working just as hard tomorrow, so I plan to get some sleep."

"Smoke, do we need nighthawks tonight?" Pearlie asked.

"I wouldn't think so," Smoke replied. "Where would the cattle go? No, you can let everyone sleep in tonight."

"Ha," Mike said. "That almost makes the snow worth it."

By daybreak the next day, Smoke and the others were in position. As part of the outfit, every man had two horses in the remuda so as to always have one that was fresh. But on this morning every one of them was using both horses paired as a team, for a total of ten teams. They had tied a log crossways behind each team. All nine teams were abreast, and in front of them was the chuck wagon, its wheels lashed to poles that were running parallel with the wagon. The poles had the effect of creating runners, so that the chuck wagon was converted to a sleigh. In addition to the team of mules that normally pulled the wagon, the two horses that would have belonged to Dooley had been put in harness with the mules.

"Smoke, maybe you ain't thought of it," Andy said. "But if all of us is up here, there ain't nobody ridin' to keep the herd goin' straight."

Billy laughed.

"What is it? What did I say that was so funny?" Andy asked.

"You ain't got to worry none about them cows goin' nowhere," Billy said. "They're goin' to follow the road we'll be makin' for 'em."

"Billy's right," Smoke said. "We'll be cutting a trail for them and they'll follow along behind like some old yellow dog."

Andy nodded, then smiled. "Yeah," he said. "Yeah, I can see that. Damn, that's smart. How'd you come up with that idea?"

"You don't have to worry none about how Smoke comes up with ideas," Cal said. "He's 'bout the smartest person I know. 'Cept maybe Miz Sally."

In good-natured fun, Smoke threw a snowball at Cal, and Sally, who was close enough to hear the conversation, laughed out loud.

"Sally, don't you be paying any attention to him now," Smoke teased. "He's just buttering you up for more pie."

Sally laughed. "Well, when's the last time *you* made him a pie?"

Smoke laughed as well. "I guess you have a point there," he said.

Smoke looked out at all the men. All were standing

on the ground behind their teams, holding the reins as if they were plowing a field.

"Is everyone ready?"

"We're ready at this end, Smoke," Pearlie called back.

"All ready on this end," Cal said.

"Then, let's move 'em out."

Smoke was an active participant for, like the others, he had a team hitched to one of the logs and he urged his horses forward.

To Smoke's relief, the horses appeared to be able to pull the logs without too much effort. From time to time a rather large mound of snow would pile up in front of a log and whoever was driving that team would have to clear the snow away before they could proceed.

They had gone no more than twenty-five yards when Smoke turned to look behind them. His plan was working. Not only was there a wide swath through the snow behind him—the cattle were following along.

They plowed their way through the snow for the rest of that day and halfway through the next, until they came to an area where the snow was so sparse that vegetation was showing through. By then the cows, hungry after two days of not being able to graze, began to feed.

That night the cowboys celebrated with some of Sally's bear claws.

"So, LeRoy," Billy said. "What do you think about drivin' cattle through snow now?"

"Ah," LeRoy said with a dismissive wave of his hand. "I knowed all along that we could do it."

Chapter Sixteen

Salcedo

It was nine o'clock on a Tuesday morning and Trent Williams was in the barbershop getting his weekly shave.

"Have you seen Jason Adams yet?" Cook asked as he applied the razor to Williams's face.

"No, not yet," Williams said. "But I expect to be seeing him today."

"Yes, sir, I expect you will," Cook said. "Jason is one happy man."

"Well, I'm glad he is taking it so well," Williams said. "When I first offered him the deal, he seemed a little hesitant. But as I explained to him, it is the only way he can save his ranch."

"Hesitant? Why would he be hesitant?" Cook asked.

"Well, let's face it. In order to keep from having his ranch go into foreclosure, he is going to have to give up his entire herd. That's quite a sacrifice to make, but at least it will save his ranch."

"Oh, he isn't going to have to give up his ranch,"

Cook said. He made another stroke across Williams's face. "He isn't going to have to give up anything. He's coming in to pay off the loan."

"What?" Williams shouted, sitting up so fast that Cook cut his face. "Damn it, man, you have cut me!"

"I'm sorry, sir!" Cook said, chagrined at his mistake. He began wiping off the lather to examine the cut. "You rose up so quickly that . . ."

"Here, give me that!" Williams shouted, grabbing the towel. He wiped off his face and examined the cut. It was very small and was barely bleeding.

"Fortunately, it doesn't look very bad," Cook said, reaching up to touch it.

"Just leave it alone," Williams said irritably. Williams treated his own cut for a moment; then, when it was obvious that it wasn't going to bleed anymore, he looked over at Cook.

"What do you mean Adams is going to pay off the loan? How the hell is he going to pay off his loan?"

"Well, after old Mr. Devaney died, Jason said it seemed like the right thing for him to do."

"Devaney? Abner Devaney?"

"Yes, sir, that's the one."

"What does Devaney dying have to do with whether or not Adams pays off his note?"

"Well, sir, as I'm sure you know, Mr. Devaney was Millie Adams's father. When he died, he left all his money to her."

"All his money?" Williams shook his head. "What are you talking about? That old fool didn't have any money."

Cook chuckled. "Oh, yes, sir, he did. Turns out he

had quite a bit of money. I'm surprised you didn't know that."

"But how could he have money? He didn't have as much as one dime in the bank."

"No, sir, he didn't, but that don't mean he didn't have no money. He said he didn't believe in banks. He always kept his money in a jar, buried out back of his place."

"How much money was it?"

"According to Jason, it was a little over three thousand dollars. I don't know how much he owes, but he says that's enough to pay off his note."

"Yes," Williams said in a low, growling type voice. "Yes, that is quite enough."

Cook smiled broadly. "Well, there you go then. I know you told me that you bought the note. You must be happy, knowing that you aren't going to be stuck with the note."

"Yes, very happy," Williams replied, though the expression on his face indicated that he was anything but happy. Where would he get his cows now?

With Walking Bear

Walking Bear stood on the rock and looked far down into the valley at the two wagons moving slowly along the road that paralleled Wind River. Four soldiers rode in front of the wagons and four soldiers rode behind. One who had stripes on his sleeves rode alongside. Walking Bear knew that a soldier who had stripes on his sleeves was a soldier chief, and that could only mean one thing. Something very valuable was being carried by the wagons.

Looking behind him, Walking Bear saw twenty mounted warriors awaiting his orders. He felt a swelling of pride because so many had left the camp of Red Eagle to follow him. Red Eagle was an old man whose time had passed. Walking Bear was young and strong and unafraid of the white man. Soon, all in Red Eagle's camp would follow him, and perhaps other camps as well. He would lead not twenty, but many times twenty, a mighty nation of warriors, and they would drive the white man away from the ancient land of the Cheyenne once and for all.

He came back down from the rock.

"What did you see, Walking Bear?" one of the warriors asked.

"Two wagons," Walking Bear reported. "They are heavy with things the white man values."

"Are there soldiers?"

"Yes, soldiers in front and in the back. A soldier chief rides alongside."

"Perhaps we should let the wagons pass," one of the others suggested.

"If you are a woman, too frightened to do battle, you may stay," Walking Bear said. He beat his fist against his chest. "I will attack the soldiers and take what is in the wagons. Brave hearts will go with me, cowards will stay behind."

The Indian who suggested that they should let the wagons pass was shamed by Walking Bear's words and, to redeem himself, he rode to the front, then turned to face the other warriors. He held his rifle over his head.

"I, Little Hawk, will ride by the side of Walking Bear when we attack the soldiers!" he shouted.

The others let out a shout of defiance and held their rifles aloft as well.

Walking Bear nodded in appreciation, then turned and started riding behind the ridgeline, approaching the wagons and soldiers in a way that kept the warriors out of sight.

When he reached the end of the valley, he led them up to the top of the ridgeline. As he had planned, the wagons were now beyond so that, as the warriors came down the hill, they would be approaching the wagons from the rear.

Lifting his rifle to his shoulder, Walking Bear aimed at the soldier riding at the end. He fired, and the soldier tumbled from the saddle.

"Eeeeeyaahhh!" Walking Bear yelled, and the shout was picked up by the other warriors.

"Indians!" one of the soldiers called, his voice cracking with fear.

The wagon drivers urged their teams into a gallop, but the wagons were too heavily laden and Walking Bear and his warriors overtook them easily. Walking Bear divided his men into two columns, sending one to one side of the wagons and the other to the other side. Recognizing the leader of the soldiers by the stripes on his sleeves, Walking Bear shot him.

With their leader down, the remaining soldiers seemed unsure of what to do. Half of them slowed their horses and attempted to give battle, but the others galloped away, abandoning their fellow soldiers and the wagons.

Little Hawk, perhaps in a attempt to make up for his earlier hesitancy, rode up close enough to leap from his horse into one of the wagons. He killed the driver with his war club, then, even as he was holding up his hands, whooping in victory, was shot. He tumbled from the wagon and was run over by the wheels.

The second wagon driver was killed. Then the two remaining soldiers, realizing that they were now alone, tried to flee, but they were both run down and killed.

The Indians overtook the lumbering wagons and brought them to a halt.

Walking Bear beamed with pride over the tremendous success of his adventure. Behind him in the road lay seven dead soldiers, including the soldier leader and the two drivers. Only four of the soldiers had gotten away, and they had not even attempted to give battle. As for the losses Walking Bear suffered, Little Hawk was the only warrior killed.

"Get the food from the wagons," Walking Bear said. "We will take it to the village of Red Eagle. Let us see him tell the people they cannot take food from us."

Several of his warriors leaped up onto the wagons and rolled back the tarpaulin cover. Both wagons were filled with boxes and the Indians proceeded to break into the boxes.

"Iron!" one of the Indians said in exasperation when he saw that the box contained nothing but large pieces of blued iron. "Why would they put iron in boxes?"

"No food, Walking Bear," one of the others said in disgust. "You said there would be food, but there is no food."

Walking Bear stared at the boxes, nearly all of

which had been opened now. There was white man's writing on the outside of the boxes, but he was unable to read it.

STOVE, HEATING
DISASSEMBLED

"Aaaarggghh!" Walking Bear shouted in anger and frustration as he watched his triumph slip away from him.

Sorento, Wyoming Territory

A train sat on the tracks at the depot, its relief valve venting steam. A small white sign nailed to the railroad depot identified the town as Sorento, Wyoming Territory. The town was small, with a posted population of two hundred fifteen, but it was busy beyond its size because it was a railhead to which surrounding ranchers brought their cattle.

The air of the town was perfumed with the strong odor of the several hundred cows that were now waiting in feeder lots awaiting shipment.

Trent Williams dismounted in front of a small building that had a sign out front identifying it as the Indian agency. A small bell was attached to the door, and it rang as he opened it to step inside. The inside of the building was bare of any type of decoration, and consisted only of a waist-high counter that separated the entrance from the rest of the building.

Shortly after Williams stepped inside, a large man with muttonchops and chin whiskers came into the room. He was wearing a three-piece suit with a vest that was stretched by his girth.

"Yes, can I help you?" he asked.

"I'm looking for Mr. Abernathey. Colin Abernathy."

"I'm afraid Mr. Abernathy isn't here. His office is in Laramie. My name is Cephus Malone. May I help you?"

"I don't understand. Isn't Abernathy the purchasing agent for cattle to be used to supply the Indians?"

"Yes, he is, but he is in Washington right now and won't be back until the fifth of next month," the man answered. "In the meantime, I am authorized to accept delivery of the cattle, and to give you a receipt which will be redeemed by Mr. Abernathy for the appropriate amount. I'm Cephus Malone. Do you have cattle?"

"Yes," Williams said.

Malone smiled. "Ahh, then you must be Mr. Kirby Jensen. Well, Mr. Jensen, I must confess that you got here much sooner than I thought you would. You have three thousand head for me, I believe?"

Williams didn't know anything about Kirby Jensen or his cattle, but for the time being it he thought it might be a good idea to go along with Malone's belief that he was Jensen.

"Yes, three thousand head."

"Good, good. As soon as I make an inventory of the cattle, I can issue a government draft for the funds. Where are the cattle? Just outside of town?"

"Uh, no, the herd isn't here yet."

"Well, I can understand," Malone said. "It's a long way up here from Big Rock, Colorado. But the sooner you can get them here, the better."

"Yes, well, I just wanted to check and see if you still wanted to purchase the cattle."

"Mind you, in order to secure the purchase you must be the first one to deliver the cattle," Malone said. "And I must warn you, you are not the only one in the picture. A man named Trent Williams has also contacted us for possible delivery."

"Yes, I understand," Williams replied. "I'll rejoin the herd and bring them up as fast as I can."

As Williams left Malone's office, his mind was racing with possibilities. If he could deliver over three thousand head, that would be over one hundred thousand dollars. All he had to do was get control of the three thousand head of cattle that a man named Kirby Jensen was bringing up from Colorado.

The way Williams saw it, there were two problems to contend with.

Problem number one was to find the herd.

Well, that shouldn't be too difficult. After all, given the mountains, passes, and rivers, how many ways up from Big Rock, Colorado, were there?

Problem number two would be to take the herd once he found it.

That shouldn't be too difficult either. With three thousand head, he could afford to hire a band of men to do the job for him and still have more money than he would have had had he been able to take Jason Adams's herd.

He could afford such a band of men, and he knew just where to find them.

Before going to bed that night, Trent Williams sent a telegram back to Salcedo. The recipient of the telegram was a man name Will Staley. Staley was the former sheriff, but had been defeated in the last election because of accusations that he had been in cahoots with a cattle rustler.

Staley denied the accusations, but was defeated anyway. Now he operated a private cattle protective agency going after rustlers. Although he was no longer a sheriff, and no longer had territorial authority to make arrests, he compensated for that by declaring himself a bounty hunter, and indeed, he did collect bounty on those who were wanted. But his primary income came from the cattlemen who hired him. There were those who said that Staley didn't always let the law get in the way of getting the job done, especially if there was enough money involved.

Williams was sure that he could offer Staley enough money to get the job done. But he could pay only if Staley succeeded in getting a herd for him. And the herd Malone had mentioned, the one belonging to a man named Kirby Jensen, would be that herd.

Chapter Seventeen

It had been five days since they came through the snow and were again on dry ground. In fact, as far as Andy was concerned, it was too dry. The reason for that was that he was riding drag and eating the dust kicked up by the herd.

It was because he was riding drag that he was the first to see the Indians. He wasn't sure he actually saw them because it was only a slight movement, a shadow within a shadow that caught his eye. He dismounted and pretended to be working on his saddle while actually looking behind him.

There! He saw it again, and this time there was no question. Three Indians, riding in line, moved through a cut in the ridge. They were bending low over their horses, obviously trying to remain unseen.

Andy remounted, then rode, not at a gallop but at a quick pace, until he caught up with Smoke.

"Smoke, there's some Indians on our tail," he said.

"How many?"

"I don't know," Andy said. "But they are trying their

damn'dest to stay out of sight, so I know that they are up to no good."

Smoke stroked his chin and looked out over the herd. "Andy, do you think you can get to the other side of the herd without letting the Indians know that you are on to them?"

"Yeah," Andy said. "I think so."

"All right, you get over there, tell Billy, Mike, and the Butrum boys that, at my signal, I want them to get the herd moving as fast as we can. The river's not more than a mile ahead and Sally is already set up there. If we can get the herd across, we'll make our stand there."

"Right," Andy said as he started around the herd.

"Pearlie!" Smoke called.

Pearlie turned his horse and rode back to see what Smoke wanted.

"Andy has spotted some Indians behind us. We're going to try and get the herd across the river, then turn to face them. Send Cal on up to be with Sally. Have them pick out some defensive positions for us, then help the others drive the herd."

"Smoke, isn't there a chance of spookin' the cows into a stampede if we try and hurry them now?"

"I don't think so. They're tired and they're headed toward water. I don't think they'll scatter. And I know this area. Once they get on the other side, there's no way they can go except the way we want them to go. Hell, I hope they do run, it'll keep 'em out of the line of fire. Now, get goin'.'"

"Right," Pearlie replied.

Smoke watched Pearlie ride back up to deliver his

message to Cal. He saw Cal ride off at a rapid clip, and not until Cal was at least half a mile away did he raise his pistol and fire.

"Let's go!" he shouted. "Move 'em out! Move 'em out!"

The cattle started forward at a gallop with the cowboys on both sides urging them on with whoops and shouts and waving their hats.

"Here, cows, run!" Smoke heard Billy calling. "Run, cows, run!"

Smoke rode to the rear of the herd, pulled his rifle, then looked back. The Indians, realizing then that they had been seen, gave up all pretense of trying to keep out of sight. They started after the cattle.

Smoke sighted on one of the Indians and squeezed the trigger. The Indian grabbed his chest, then fell from his galloping pony. That caused the other Indians to pull up for a moment. It was a moment only, but that gave Smoke the chance to turn and catch up with the herd.

By now the leading animals of the herd were crossing the river, their hooves churning up water ahead of the onrushing cattle behind them.

"Pearlie, you and Andy grab your rifles," Smoke said. He pointed to the neck of a small island that faced the western bank of the river, the direction from which they had just come.

"See if the two of you can squirm down through the tall grass. Take a position as near to the point as you can get, and do as much damage as you can when the Indians start across the water."

"Right!" Pearlie called back. "Andy, let's go!"

"The rest of you," Smoke ordered. "Find yourselves a good spot and get ready."

As the men got on their knees and began looking around for a rock or hill or tree log to provide them with cover and concealment, Smoke walked back to the chuck wagon, where he saw Sally making herself a firing position from behind one of the wheels.

"Sally, you're on your own," Smoke said. "When the shooting starts, I'm going to be moving around."

"You do what you have to do, Smoke," Sally replied. "I've got a good position here. I'll be all right and, I suspect, I might even get off a shot or two."

Despite the seriousness of the situation, Smoke laughed. "You might get off a shot or two, huh?" he said. He knew that, next to him, Sally was probably the best shot there. And he knew that nobody had more courage. "Just make sure you know who you are shooting."

"Any more snide remarks like that, Smoke Jensen, and you'll be my target," Sally quipped.

Smoke kissed her, and they held the kiss a moment longer than they normally would have.

"You be careful with all your moving around," Sally said as Smoke took his leave of her.

Smoke hurried back to see how the others were positioned, and where they were deployed.

"All right, now remember, Pearlie and Andy will shoot first!" Smoke said. "So don't be spooked into shooting when you hear them. I want you to hold your fire until the last possible moment. Then make your shots count!"

"Smoke, here they are! I can hear 'em coming!" Jules said nervously. His announcement wasn't necessary, however, for by then everyone could hear them. Above the drumming of the hoofbeats came the cries of the warriors themselves, yipping and barking and screaming at the top of their lungs.

The Indians crested the bluff just before the river; then, without a pause, they rushed down the hill toward the water, their horses sounding like thunder.

"Remember, hold your fire until the last possible moment," Smoke shouted to the others. "In fact, hold your fire until I give you the word!"

The Indians stopped just at the water's edge, then holding their rifles over their heads, began shouting guttural challenges to the men who were dug in on the island.

"Hu ihpeya wicayapo!"

"Huka!"

"Huka hey!"

"They're working up their courage," Smoke said. "Check your rifles, make sure you have a shell in the chamber."

The men opened the breaches and checked the chambers, then closed them and prepared for the attack.

The Indians rushed into the water, riding hard across the fifty-yard-wide shallows, whooping, hollering, and gesturing with rifles and lances. Then two of warriors pulled ahead of the others, and when they were halfway across the water, Smoke heard two distinct shots from the point of the island. The two warriors in front went down.

The remaining Indians crossed the river, then started up the sandy point.

"Fire!" Smoke shouted.

Smoke, Sally, Billy, Mike, Hank, LeRoy, and Jules fired as one. Four of the Indians went down, not because a couple of them had missed, but because a couple of them had fired at the same target. The devastating volley was effective, for the warriors who survived swerved to the right and left, riding by, rather than over, the cowboys' positions.

The Indians regrouped on the east bank of the river.

"Turn around!" Smoke yelled. "They'll be coming from behind us this time!"

The cowboys had just barely managed to switch positions when the Indians turned and rode back in a second charge. They were met with another volley, this one as crushing as the first had been. Again, a significant number of the Indians in the middle of the charge went down.

The Cheyenne pulled back to the west bank of the river to regroup, watched anxiously by the men on the island. By now the river was strewn with dead Indians. There were at least eight or ten of them, lying facedown in the shallow water as the current parted around them.

"Anyone hit?" Smoke called.

"Yeah, I been hit," LeRoy called back, his voice strained. "How bad is it?" Smoke asked.

"I—I reckon it's killed me," LeRoy said, his voice growing weaker.

"LeRoy!" Hank called, moving quickly to his brother's side.

"Hang on, LeRoy," Smoke said. "We're going to get

out of here. We'll be having drinks in a saloon in a few days, telling tall tales about this fight."

"You fellas have a drink to me," LeRoy said.

"LeRoy! LeRoy!" Hank called anxiously.

"How is he?" Smoke called.

"He's dead," Hank said in a tone that reflected both his shock and his sorrow. "I can't believe this. My brother is dead."

"I'm sorry, Hank. He was a good man." Smoke looked at all who had gathered around him. "You are all good men," he said.

"Smoke, what about Pearlie and Andy?" Cal asked. "You think they are all right?"

"Good question. I'd better go get them."

"Why don't you just call 'em in?" Billy asked.

"No, I can't do that. If the Indians hear us, that will make Pearlie and Andy easy targets. I'll go get them. Cal, you're in charge while I'm gone."

"Right," Cal replied.

Smoke worked his way down through the tall grass until he reached the point. Looking up, he saw both Pearlie and Andy behind tall clumps of grass, just on the other side of an open sandbar.

"Pearlie, you and Andy all right?" Smoke called to them, just loudly enough to be heard.

"Yeah, we're fine," Pearlie replied.

"Come on back with the rest of us now," Smoke said. "We've lost whatever advantage we had by having you out here."

"All right," Pearlie said. "Andy, you go first, I'll cover you."

Nodding, Andy bent over at the waist and darted

across the open bar of sand until he reached the tall grass.

"All right, Pearlie, it's your turn," Andy called back.

Duplicating Andy, Pearlie darted across the sandbar, then dived into the grass alongside Smoke and Andy.

"Anyone hit back there?" Pearlie asked.

"Yeah. LeRoy was killed," Smoke said grimly.

"Damn."

"Come on, let's get back."

The three men wriggled through the grass on their bellies until the reached a slight depression that allowed them to stand up. Once up, they were able to move quickly until they were back with the others.

"You think they're going to come back?" Mike asked.

Smoke shook his head. "I don't know," he said. "I wish I could see them well enough to know what is going on."

"I have a pair of army binoculars," Andy offered. "Would that help?"

"It might," Smoke said. "Let me see them."

Andy hurried back to where the horses were tied. He fished the binoculars from his saddlebag, then took them back and handed them to Smoke.

"These are good-looking glasses," Smoke said.

"Yeah," Andy replied. He smiled. "I took them from Sergeant Caviness."

"Good," Mike said. "I hope the son of a bitch had to pay the army for them."

The others laughed.

Smoke raised the binoculars to look across the water. He saw one Indian who was obviously in charge, riding back and forth in front of the others, holding a rifle over his head and shouting.

"Somebody seems to be stirring them up," Smoke said.

"May I take a look?" Andy asked.

"Sure, they're your glasses," Smoke said, handing the binoculars to the former soldier.

Andy lifted the binoculars to study the Indians. "I'll be damned," he said.

"What is it?"

"It's Walking Bear," Andy said.

"Who?"

"Walking Bear," Andy said, lowering his glasses.

"You know him, Andy?" Billy asked.

Andy shook his head. "Can't say as I know him exactly," he replied. "But he's been givin' the army some trouble for a long time now. He was part of Red Eagle's camp, but when Red Eagle went to reservation, Walking Bear took a lot of warriors with him and left. The army's been after him ever since then, but he's been like a ghost. No one's been able to find him."

"Looks like we just did," Smoke said.

"Yes, sir, it does at that," Andy said.

"How bad is this Walking Bear fella?" Mike asked.

"Pretty bad. Just before I got out of the army, Walking Bear attacked a platoon of soldiers that was escortin' a supply wagon. He kilt ever' soldier in that platoon."

"Are you sure this is Walking Bear?" Smoke asked.

Andy nodded. "Oh, yeah, I'm sure," he said.

"Sally," Smoke called. "Come here for a moment, would you?"

Sally walked over to where Smoke and Andy were

standing. Smoke took the binoculars from Andy and handed them to Sally.

"Take a look at the Indian in front," Smoke said. "The one riding back and forth, yelling at the others. Do you see him?"

Sally held the binoculars to her eyes for a moment.

"I see him," she said.

"Next time they come after us, shoot him. Take your time, get a good shot. But you need to kill him."

"All right," Sally answered. She handed the glasses back to Andy.

"Whoa, hold it," Hank said. "You're giving that job to her?"

"Yes."

"But she's a woman."

Pearlie and Cal laughed.

"What is it?" Hank asked.

"She may be a woman but when it comes to shootin'," said Pearlie, "'bout the only one here better'n she is with a rifle would be Smoke his ownself. And I'm not all that sure he's better."

"Smoke," Andy said, lowering the binoculars. "Looks like ole' Walkin' Bear's got 'em worked up into comin' again."

"All right, everyone, get ready! They're coming back!" Smoke warned.

Looking around, he saw that Sally had repositioned herself. No longer behind the wagon wheel, she was now behind a fallen tree, resting the barrel of her rifle on the log. She thumbed back the hammer, then sighted down the barrel.

With Walking Bear in the lead, the Cheyenne started another attack.

The Indians came again, their horses leaping over the bodies of the warriors and horses who had fallen before. Sally waited for a good shot, but Walking Bear was bending low over his horse in such a way as to keep behind his horse. It was difficult for Sally to get a good sight picture, and the first time she fired, she missed.

Quickly, she jacked another shell into the chamber and waited for another opportunity.

For some unknown reason, Walking Bear sat upright for just a second, and that gave Sally the opening she was looking for. She squeezed the trigger and her bullet hit Walking Bear right in the middle of his chest. She saw the look of surprise on his face; then she saw him drop his rifle and clasp his hand over his wound. He weaved back and forth for just a second before tumbling from the saddle.

When the others saw their leader go down, they stopped and milled about for a moment, uncertain as to what they should do. One or two started forward, but it wasn't a concerted charge and, like Walking Bear before them, they were shot down.

By now well over half their party lay dead on both banks of the river, in the water, and on the sandy beaches of the island. They had started the fight with the numerical advantage, but realized now that they were outnumbered.

One of the Indians turned and started riding away. Almost instantly, the others followed.

"Run! Run, you cowards!" Andy shouted, shooting at them as they fled.

The other cowboys began shooting as well, making certain to give the Indians a good send-off. Then, they began laughing and congratulating each other on the good fight.

"If you want to know who gets the most congratulatin', it should be Miz Sally," Andy said. "When she took ole Walkin' Bear down, she took the fight right out of 'em."

"Let's hear it for Miz Sally!" Billy shouted.

"Hurrah! Hurrah!" the others called.

With all the laughing and self-congratulations, the men forgot all about Hank, until Sally spoke up. She saw him over by his brother's body, hanging his head in sorrow.

"Hank," she said. "We want you to know how sorry we are about LeRoy. He was a good man."

"Thank you, ma'am," Hank said.

Chapter Eighteen

A range in Wyoming

A small herd of no more than one hundred cows moved through the darkness, watched over by three riders. A calf called for its mother and, in the distance, a coyote sent up its long, lonesome wail. The moon was a thin sliver of silver, but the night was alive with stars . . . from the very bright, shining lights all the way down to those stars that weren't visible as individual bodies at all, but whose glow added to the luminous powder that dusted the distant sky.

"Damn, Bobby, but it's cold," one of the riders said, the vapor of his breath glowing in the moonlight.

"Yeah, well, I tell you, if it wasn't this cold, we prob'ly wouldn't of been able to steal these critters. They'd of been someone watchin' 'em," Bobby said.

"Pat's right, though. Stealin' cows on a cold night like this is damn near as hard as punchin' 'em," a third rider said.

"Well, now, let me ask you this, Deekus. Would you rather be ridin' out here in the cold tonight, pushin' cows we'll be gettin' five, maybe ten dollars a head for? Or would you rather be punchin' cows for someone at twenty dollars a month and found?" Bobby asked.

"Hell, you put it like that, I can take bein' cold for a while," Deekus said.

"Hey, Deekus, what are you goin' to do with your money?" Pat asked.

"I'm goin' to a whorehouse and get me a woman," Deekus said. "What about you?"

"I don't know, get some new duds, I reckon."

"Duds? You goin' to waste your money on clothes when you could get you a woman?"

"Why, dress me up in some new duds and I can get me a woman without payin' for it," Pat said.

"Whoo, boy," Deekus said, laughing. "Did you hear that, Bobby? We got us a lover boy here."

Bobby laughed.

"Yeah, well, you just watch," Pat said. "You spend all your money on a woman and it's over with. You make yourself look good so's a woman wants you, why, you can get you a woman anytime you want, and you still got your new duds."

Bobby laughed again. "Seems like ole Pat has got it all figured out," he said.

The calf's call for his mother came again, this time with more insistence. The mother's answer had a degree of anxiousness to it.

"Damn," Bobby said. "I told you we should'a left the heifer and her calf alone. Now I got to go get 'em back together."

"Hell, why bother? It'll find its own way back."

"I don't think so. And if it starts settin' up too much of a racket, well, the three of us won't be able to handle the rest of the cows," Bobby said, slapping his legs against the side of his horse and riding off, disappearing in the darkness.

"Bobby's as bad as an ole mama cow himself," Deekus said, "watchin' out for 'em like that."

"Yeah, but he's prob'ly right. In this cold, we don't need the cows givin' us any trouble."

Suddenly, from the darkness came the sound of a gunshot.

"What was that?" Pat asked.

"Sounded like a gunshot," Deekus answered.

"Bobby must'a seen a snake or something."

"At night?" Deekus asked.

"A wolf maybe?"

The two boys waited for a moment longer, but heard nothing else.

"He ought to be back by now, shouldn't he?" Pat asked.

They were quiet for a moment longer. Then Deekus called out. "Bobby? Bobby, you out there?"

"Bobby?" Pat shouted, adding his own call.

"I don't like this," Deekus said.

"What do you think is going on?"

"I don't know, but I think we better check."

Pulling their guns, Deekus and Pat rode into the night in search of their friend.

A moment later, gunshots erupted in the night, the muzzle flashes lighting up the herd.

"Jesus! What's happening? Who is it? They're all

around us!" Pat shouted in terror, firing his gun wildly in the dark.

"Throw down your guns!" a voice called from the dark. "Do it now, or we'll kill your friend, then we'll kill you!"

"Pat, Deekus, do what they say!" Bobby called from the darkness. "They're all around you!"

Neither Deekus nor Pat reacted, and there was another shot from the dark.

"Oww!" Deekus called out as a bullet hit him in the shoulder. He dropped his gun.

Seeing Deekus hit, Pat threw down his gun as well. He put his hands in the air.

"We quit! We quit!" he called.

The two young men sat quietly as they watched over a dozen riders materialize from the dark.

"Who are you?" Pat asked.

One rider rode in front of the others. He was a powerfully built man with hat pulled low over a bald head and brow-less eyes.

"The name is Staley, boys. Will Staley," the rider said. "You should'a known better than to steal them cows in my country."

"Staley? What are you doin' here? You ain't the sheriff no more," Pat said.

"Nope, I ain't," Staley said.

"Then that means you got no jurisdiction over us."

Staley chuckled. "No, all that means is that the judge and jury got no jurisdiction over me."

"The judge and jury got no jurisdiction over you? What are you talkin' about?" Pat asked.

"I'm talkin' about hangin' you boys as cow thieves,"

Staley said. "When I was sheriff, I had to have a judge give me the word to do it. Now, I don't need nobody's word."

"What?" Deekus asked, suddenly understanding what Staley had in mind. "No, what are you doing?"

"Get 'em over there under that tree," Staley said.

"Wait, you can't do this! You got no right!" Pat said, but even as he was calling out in terror, Staley's men were coming toward him.

Within minutes, Deekus, Pat, and Bobby were sitting on their horses, their hands bound behind them. Three ropes were tossed over an outstretched tree limb; then the nooses were looped around the necks of the young cattle rustlers.

"You boys got 'ny last words?" Staley asked.

"You got no right to do this, Staley," Deekus said. "You ain't no lawman."

"You had no right to steal them cows," Staley replied.

"Stealin' a few cows ain't the same as murder and you know it. What you're doin' here is no more'n murder."

"That your say?"

"That's my say," Deekus said.

"What about you other two boys? You got 'nything to say before you go to meet your Maker?"

Bobby and Pat gritted their teeth to keep from crying out in terror. They looked at Staley and his riders through eyes that reflected their panic, but they said nothing.

"All right, you boys don't want to say nothin', I'll go along with that," Staley said.

Staley looked at the three men who were behind the horses of the rustlers. He nodded, and all three struck the rustlers' horses. The three horses leaped ahead, and the ropes that hung down from the tree pulled the rustlers from their saddles. The limb creaked and bent, but not before jerking the men up short. Pat and Bobby died quickly, but Deekus didn't. He hung there for several minutes, lifting his legs up as if by so doing he could ease the pressure on his neck. He made guttural, gurgling sounds and his eyes were opened wide in terror. One of the men pulled his pistol and pointed it Deekus.

"No!" Staley called out. "Let 'im die natural."

It took almost another full minute for Deekus to die. Finally, he quit twitching and hung there as quietly and as still as the other two.

"Put the signs on 'em," Staley said. "We'll leave 'em here as a warnin' to other cow thieves."

One of Staley's men rode up to the three dead rustlers, then pinned a sign onto each one of them.

COW RUSTLERS

CAUGHT AND HUNG BY THE

CATTLEMEN'S PROTECTIVE

ASSOCIATION

"That's, good," Staley said. "Now we'll take the fifty cows back to Dawkins and collect our pay."

"Fifty cows? You mean we ain't goin' to take 'em all back? They's about a hunnert cows here," one of Staley's deputies said.

"No, you are mistaken. I only see fifty cows here," Staley said pointedly.

The deputy realized then what Staley was saying. "Oh," he replied, nodding in agreement. "Yeah, now that I recount them, fifty is all I get as well."

Trent Williams was standing at the front window of the bank, looking out onto Salcedo's main street when he saw Staley and his men riding back into town. They made a rather imposing sight, ten men, all wearing long trench coats and wide-brimmed hats pulled low over their eyes. Stopping in front of a building that bore a sign reading CATTLEMEN'S PROTEC-TIVE ASSOCIATION, Staley dismounted, then gave the reins of his horse to one of the others. All the rest of the men rode on down to the livery, but Staley, after raking the bottoms of his boots in the edge of the board porch, went into his office.

Williams turned away from the window and saw Gilbert, his chief teller, dealing with a customer. The customer, a woman, received a deposit slip, then turned toward the door. She smiled and nodded her head at Williams.

"Mr. Williams," she said.

"Mrs. Rittenhouse," Williams replied.

Williams waited until Mrs. Rittenhouse left the bank. Then he called out to his teller.

"Mr. Gilbert?"

"Yes, Mr. Williams?" Gilbert replied.

"I'm going to be out of the bank for a short while. You handle anything that comes up."

"Yes, Mr. Williams."

Williams returned to his office, got his hat, then left the bank.

When Williams stepped into the building belonging to the Cattlemen's Protective Association a few minutes later, he saw that Staley had the door of the little stove open and was throwing wood into the flames. Though the fire was going, it had not yet built up enough heat to push back the cold, and Staley was still wearing his coat.

"Sheriff Staley?" Williams said.

"I'm no longer the sheriff," Staley said.

"I'm sorry. You were sheriff for so long that it seems natural to call you that."

"What do you want, Williams?"

"I, uh . . ." Williams cleared his throat. "Did you get my telegram, Sheri—uh, Mr. Staley?"

Staley turned toward him. "Yeah, I got your telegram," he said.

"Then you know that I have a proposition for you."

"I believe what you said was that you had a *profitable* proposition for me," Staley said, emphasizing the word "profitable."

"Yes. Indeed, it could be very profitable," Williams replied.

"How profitable?"

"Five thousand dollars profitable," Williams said.

"Seventy-five hundred," Staley replied.

"Seventy-five hundred?" Williams gasped. "What makes you think it should be seventy-five hundred dollars? You don't even know what the proposition is. Five thousand dollars is a lot of money, Mr. Staley."

"Yes, it is a lot of money," Staley agreed. "And it doesn't matter what the proposition is. If you are willing to pay me five thousand to do whatever it is you want done, that means you are making a lot more money than you are going to be paying me. I want seven thousand five hundred dollars from you or we don't do business."

Williams stroked his chin for a moment as he contemplated the demand. Finally, he nodded.

"All right, seventy-five hundred dollars," he said. He pointed to Staley. "But I can only pay the money after the job is done."

"What is the job?"

"There is a herd of cattle coming up from Colorado," Williams said. "I need that herd."

"I see," Staley said. "You say you want the herd but . . ."

"I didn't say I *want* the herd, I said I *need* the herd," Williams replied. "Everything depends on it. Especially your"—he paused as if saying the amount of money was distasteful to him—"seventy-five hundred dollars."

"Uh-huh," Staley replied. The stove was beginning to put out a little warmth now and he took his coat off to hang on a hook on the wall. He was wearing a pistol belt and the holster was hanging low on the right side. The pistol was kicked out so that as his hand hung naturally, it was no more than an inch or so from the butt. Staley turned toward Williams.

"You aren't talking about buying this herd, are you?"

Williams shook his head in the negative.

"So what you are asking me to do is steal the herd?"

Williams let out a nervous sigh before he answered. "Yes."

"You do know, don't you, that I own the Cattlemen's Protective Association?" Staley said. "Stealing cows is not my business. My business is running down the outlaws who *do* steal cows, and dealing with them. In fact, we just came back from running down the outlaws who stole cows from Eric Dawkins."

"You found them?" Williams asked.

Staley nodded. "Found 'em and hung 'em. They're danglin' from a tree near Cobb's Crossing right now as a warnin' to anyone else who thinks they can get away with stealin' cows."

"I see," Williams said nervously. He put his finger to his shirt collar and pulled it away from his neck.

"And now you are asking me to steal cows?"

"I, uh, I'm sorry," Williams said. "I was led to believe that I could do business with you if the price was right."

Suddenly, and inexplicably, the frown on Staley's face was replaced by a smile.

"We can do business if the price is right," he said.

"Seventy-five hundred dollars?"

"Ten thousand."

Williams was silent for a long moment. Then, finally, he nodded.

"Ten thousand," he agreed.

"Write out a letter, hiring me to recover your stolen herd," Staley said.

"What? No, you don't understand. The herd isn't stolen, it's . . ."

"No, *you* don't understand," Staley told him. "If

I'm goin' after those cows, I'm not going to be left hanging out to dry. You're going to write a letter hiring the Cattlemen's Protective Association to recover your stolen herd."

"Wait a minute," Williams said. "If anything goes wrong, that would automatically transfer all the guilt to me."

Williams smiled. "Yeah, it will, won't it?" he said.

"All right, all right. You're a difficult man to work with, Mr. Staley, but I don't see as I have any choice. I'll do as you say."

"Good. That means that if you do everything I tell you to do, we'll get along just real good. Now, where do I find these cows?"

Chapter Nineteen

Mike was riding nighthawk when he heard the sound of hooves, not a restless shuffling of cows repositioning themselves in the night, but a steady clack of hooves on rock. Since the herd was at a halt, he looked around to discover the source of the sound. Then, in the moonlight, he saw a long dark line, ragged with heads and horns, moving away from the main herd.

At first, he wasn't sure of exactly what was going on; then, all at once, he realized what was happening. These cattle weren't merely wandering away; they were being taken away.

"Billy!" he shouted to the man who was riding nighthawk with him. "Look out! We got rustlers! Call the others!"

Billy was closer to the main camp than Mike, and he shouted back toward the chuck wagon where the others were sleeping.

"Smoke! Pearlie! Cal! Turn out! We got rustlers!"

Billy's shout not only awakened Smoke and the others, it also alerted the thieves to the fact that they had been spotted. Instantly thereafter, one of them fired a shot at the sound of Billy's voice. Billy saw the muzzle flash, then heard the bullet whiz by, amazingly close for a wild shot in the dark.

Billy shot back, and the crack of the guns right over the head of the stolen cows started them running. By now, rapid and sustained gunfire was coming from the camp itself as Smoke and the others rolled out of their blankets and began shooting. Sally was standing in the wagon, firing a rifle, adding her own effort to the fight.

Billy put his pistol away and raised his rifle. He aimed toward the dust and the swirling melee of cattle, waiting for one of the robbers to present a target. One horse appeared, but its saddle was empty. Then another horse appeared, this time with a rider who was shooting wildly.

Billy fired and the robber's horse broke stride, then fell, carrying his rider down with him, right in front of the running cattle. Downed horse and rider disappeared under the hooves of the maddened beasts.

So far, only the cattle that had been stolen were running. The main herd, though made restless by the flashes and explosions in the night, milled around, but resisted running.

Cal appeared alongside Billy then, having mounted more quickly than any of the others.

"Are the others coming?" Billy asked.

"Yes, they're right behind me," Cal replied. He pointed toward the running cattle. "Come on, let's get our cows back!"

By now Smoke, Pearlie, and Andy had joined them, and they spurred their horses into a gallop toward the fleeing cows. Within minutes they were riding alongside the running, lumbering animals.

"We've got to get to the front!" Smoke called.

Billy nodded, but didn't answer.

The cows were running as fast as they could run, which was about three quarters of the speed of the horses. But what the cattle lacked in speed, they made up for with their momentum. With lowered heads, wild eyes, and flopping tongues, the cattle ran as if there were no tomorrow.

Finally, Smoke reached the head of the column, rode to the front, and was able to turn them. Once the cows were turned, they lost their forward momentum, slowed their running to a trot, and finally to a walk. When that happened, the riders were able to turn them and start them back.

"What happened to the rustlers?" Pearlie asked.

"One of 'em went down," Billy said. "The others must've run away."

Suddenly they heard shots from back at the camp.

"What's that?" Mike asked. "What's going on?"

"Damn!" Smoke said. "These cows were just a diversion! They're after the entire herd!"

Sally, Jules, and Hank were firing as fast as they could operate the levers of their rifles.

"Lord!" Hank said. "There's got to be at least twenty of them. Where did they all . . . uhnnn!"

Grabbing his chest, Hank went down.

"Hank!" Jules shouted. He knelt beside his friend and put his hand on Hank's face. "Hank!"

Hank made no response.

"Miz Sally, Hank's been hit!" Jules called.

"Get up here, Jules," Sally called back to him. "Get up here in the wagon!"

"But Hank! I can't leave him!" Jules shouted.

Looking down toward the young cowboy, Sally could tell by the way Hank was spread-eagled on the ground that he was dead.

"Never mind Hank, it's too late for him," Sally said. Even as she was calling out to him, she was sighting down the barrel of her rifle. She pulled the trigger, the rifle kicked back against her shoulder, and she saw the outlaw in her sights go down.

With one final look at Hank to confirm that he really was dead, Jules dashed across the open area toward the wagon.

Sally saw one of the rustlers taking aim at Jules, and quickly jacking a shell into the chamber, she snapped a shot toward him. She missed, but she did keep him from shooting at Jules.

Jules scrambled up over the side and down into the wagon.

"Are you all right?" Sally called.

"Yes, ma'am, I ain't been hit none," Jules responded.

A bullet slammed into one of the bow frames of the wagon, then whistled off into the night, a darkened missile of death.

"Get up here and start shooting," Sally ordered.

"Yes, ma'am!"

For the next thirty seconds, Sally and Jules exchanged shots with the rustlers.

"Where'd all these folks come from?" Jules asked. "I thought Smoke was chasin' 'em down."

"That's what they wanted to happen," Sally replied. "They wanted to pull away all the men so they could waltz right in and take the cattle."

Sally punctuated her remarks with another shot from her rifle.

"Really?" Jules said, laughing. "Well, they sure made a mistake thinkin' that if all the men was gone they could just waltz in here."

Sally laughed as well. "You may be young, Jules Sanders, but if you can laugh at a time like this, you are a man in my book."

"Why, thank you, Miz Sally," Jules said as he fired at the rustlers.

"Staley, we've lost three men already," one of Staley's riders said.

"All right, Cord, break off the fight," Staley said. "Start moving the cows out."

"With them shootin' at us?"

"They're in a wagon," Staley said. "You think they're goin' to be able to run us down in a wagon?"

Cord laughed. "No."

"Then do like I said and start movin' out them cows before the others come back."

"Where did they go?" Jules asked, lowering his rifle and staring through the gun smoke out into the darkness. "I don't see any of them."

"I don't either," Sally said.

"Hoo boy, we must'a run 'em off!" Jules said excitedly.

Sally shook her head. "I don't think so," she said. "I think they have something else . . . the cows!" she suddenly said.

"What?"

"They're going after the herd!"

"What'll we do?"

Before Sally could answer, they heard the report of several gunshots from the darkness.

Sally smiled. "We don't have to do anything," she said. "Smoke's back!"

From their position in the chuck wagon, they couldn't actually see what was going on, but they could see the muzzle flashes in the night, and they could hear the reports of the guns being fired.

"I wish I was out there," Jules said. "I feel like I ain't doin' my part."

"Don't be silly," Sally said. "If you hadn't been here to hold them down for a while, they would already have the herd and be gone."

Jules smiled. "Yeah, that's right, ain't it? We held them down here until Smoke could get back."

The sound of the hoofbeats of the galloping horses spread its thunder over the valley. As Smoke led his men back to the herd, he saw the cattle rustlers moving into position to steal the herd. Pearlie saw it too.

"They're takin' the cows!" Pearlie shouted.

"Like hell they are," Smoke replied, firing the first shot.

The rustlers, surprised by the fact that someone was in front of them, returned fire. Bullets whistled back and forth in the dark; then, one of Smoke's men cried out.

"I'm hit!"

Looking around, Smoke saw that it was Andy. Andy weaved back and forth in the saddle, then grabbed hold of the saddle horn to keep from falling.

"Mike, see to him!" Smoke called.

"Hold on, Andy, I'm comin'!" Mike called, riding toward the stricken cowboy.

Even as Mike was moving toward Andy, Smoke shot at another one of the rustlers, a stocky, powerfully built man. As the man tumbled from his saddle he lost his hat, and Smoke could see that he was bald.

"Damn, they got Staley!" Cord called.

"We're outnumbered now," one of the other outlaws said. "I'm gettin' out of here!"

"I'm leavin' too," another said.

Cord watched the two men leave, then saw that only he and one other man remained.

"Let's go!" Cord shouted.

"What about Staley?"

"To hell with him!"

"Should we go after 'em, Smoke?" Pearlie called.

"No," Smoke said. "We need to get the herd back together. And we need to see to Andy. Anyone else hit?"

A quick appraisal of their situation showed that only Andy had been shot. Smoke hurried over to the young cowboy, who was now lying on the ground beside his horse. Mike was squatting down beside him.

"How bad is it?" Smoke asked.

"He's hurt bad," Mike replied. "We need to get him in to a doctor."

"Hrmmph," Andy said in a disapproving growl. "We both know there ain't nothin' a doctor could do for me, even if you could get me there in time. Which you can't."

"We'll get you back to the wagon," Smoke said. "Sally is about as good on patching up gunshot wounds as any doctor. Lord knows, she's patched me up a few times."

"I ain't goin' to make it, Smoke," Andy said. "There's no sense in you tryin' to fool me none."

Smoke sighed, then nodded. "I won't lie to you, Andy. You're hit hard."

Andy chuckled.

"What the hell you findin' to laugh about, Andy?" Billy asked.

"I owed Dooley ten dollars," Andy said. "I figured when he died I wouldn't have to pay it. Don't you know now that the first thing ole' Dooley is goin' to do when he sees me is hold out his hand for that money."

Despite the seriousness of Andy's wound, both Billy and Mike laughed. Smoke laughed as well.

"Boys, I'll tell you somethin' maybe you didn't know," Andy said. "This here dyin' ain't hurtin' me none a'tall."

Andy gasped a few more breaths, then stopped breathing.

"All right, boys, get him up on his horse. Mike, you take him back to the wagon. Pearlie, Cal, Billy, let's take care of the cows."

It was nearly dawn by the time all the cows that had been run off were back with the herd.

"What are we goin' to do now, Smoke?" Pearlie asked. "Them cows is near dead they're so tired. We goin' to have to give 'em a little break."

"We'll stay here twenty-four hours," Smoke said. "We could use a rest too. And it'll give us time to get Andy buried."

"And Hank," Jules said, coming up to join them.

"Hank too?"

Jules nodded. "Yes, sir, me 'n Mike got 'em both lyin' under canvas back at the wagon. Oh, and Miz Sally say's she's near 'bout got breakfast ready."

"Good, I've done worked up an appetite," Pearlie said.

"Miz Sally was a regular hellion, shootin' the bad guys with one hand and cookin' breakfast with the other."

"What?" Billy asked, shocked by the revelation. "You mean to tell me Miz Sally was fixin' breakfast and shootin' the bad guys all at the same time?"

"Well, maybe not for real," Jules agreed. "But she almost was. You should see her when she's got her dander up, Smoke," Jules said.

Smoke chuckled. "I have seen her, Jules," he said. "Believe me, I have seen her."

Chapter Twenty

The corpses of Hank and Andy were dressed in their best shirts as they lay side by side on the canvas that had been spread out alongside the two graves that had been dug for them. The cowboys had put on their best shirts as well for the impromptu funeral that Smoke was about to conduct.

"Are the others taken care of?" Smoke asked Pearlie. He was referring to the outlaws who had lost their lives in the failed attempt at cattle rustling.

"They're took care of," Pearlie said. "We found a draw that was big enough to hold them. The sides of the draw was real soft and it was easy enough to just drop the bodies into the hole and push all the dirt in. They're buried, all six of 'em."

"Did you recognize any of them?"

"No," Pearlie answered. "We pretty near figured out which one is the leader, though. Was the leader, I mean, seein' as he's as dead as the others."

"Are you talking about the stocky bald-headed one?" Smoke asked.

"Yeah," Pearlie answered. "How'd you know that?"

"After he went down, the fight seemed to go out of all the others," Smoke said.

"Yeah, that's pretty much the way I noticed it too."

"Smoke, are you goin' to say a few words for Hank and Andy?" Sally asked.

Smoke nodded and the men took off their hats, then stood, holding their hats in front of them.

Smoke cleared his throat.

"Lord, I don't have to tell you that I'm not much for prayin'," he said. "But I figure that when I'm prayin' for someone else, you'll more than likely listen, even to someone like me.

"I don't know much about what kind of life these two boys lived before they joined us on this drive. But on this drive they were good men. They rode night-hawk without complaining, their partners could always count on them to be wherever they were supposed to be on time, and they died with courage and honor.

"Lord, all the preachers tell us that you have a special place for men like these two we're sendin' you today. I want you to welcome them there. Go easy on them, Lord. They've been through blizzards, drought, Indian raids, and rustlers. I know you've got some good men with you up there, Lord. Well, sir, here are two more.

"Amen."

"Amen," the others said.

The men put their hats back on. Then Cal cleared his throat and looked at Mike and Billy.

"Better get your old shirts back on," he said. "We need to get these boys in the ground."

"All right," Billy said.

"Jules, you come with me, we need to get us a good count of how many cows we got left," Pearlie said.

"Yes, sir," Jules replied, starting toward his horse.

Smoke watched Jules and Pearlie ride away. Then he turned his attention to the bodies of Hank and Andy. Sally sewed the canvas covers closed around the two bodies; then, gently, Billy, Mike, and Cal, using ropes, lowered Hank and Andy into their graves. Smoke watched until the graves were closed, leaving two fresh mounds of dirt.

Sally scattered a few pieces of brightly colored glass over the two mounds.

"I broke this glass a few days ago," Sally said. "I intended to throw it away, I don't know why I kept it, but now I'm glad I did. It's not as nice as putting flowers on their graves, but it does add a little color."

"It's nice," Smoke said without elaboration.

With the funeral over, the others began drifting away. Sally had something that needed her attention and, for some time, Smoke was alone. He walked over to stand over the two graves. Finally, he saw Pearlie and Jules returning to the camp. Swinging down from his horse, Pearlie gave the reins of his horse to Jules, then walked over to give the report to Smoke.

"We got a good count, Smoke," Pearlie said. "We've still got a little over twenty-nine hundred. That means that on this whole drive, we've lost less than a hundred cows."

"And four good men," Smoke added, looking at the side-by-side graves where Hank and Andy lay buried.

He was referring also to Dooley and LeRoy, who were buried on the trail behind them.

"Yeah," Pearlie agreed. "They were four good men, all right."

"I'd trade every cow in the herd for them," Smoke said.

"Things like this happen, Smoke," Pearlie said. "You know this better'n anyone."

"Yeah, I know," Smoke said as he stroked his jaw. "Things like this happen."

Smoke walked over to the fire and poured himself a cup of coffee. He had just taken a swallow when Sally came up to him with her own cup. Seeing her, Smoke reached for the pot and poured her a cup as well.

"Are you all right?" Sally asked.

"I wish you hadn't come," Smoke said, making no reference to Sally's comment.

"Why?"

Smoke sighed. "A lot has happened."

"Smoke, I'm not made of sugar and spice and everything nice," she said, quoting the old nursery rhyme.

Smoke chuckled. "Well, I'll second the 'you aren't very nice' part," he said.

"What? Why, Smoke Jensen!" Sally gasped. "Are you saying I'm not nice?"

"No, I'm just saying that, sometimes, you can be a little difficult."

Sally made as if to throw her coffee on him. "Why, if I weren't nice, I'd throw this scalding cup on you right now," she said, laughing.

"Nah, that's not what's stopping you," Smoke said,

laughing with her. "You just don't want to waste the coffee, that's all."

"You found me out," Sally teased, laughing some more. "You didn't answer me," she added.

"What was the question?"

"I asked if you were all right."

"Yeah," Smoke replied. "Yeah, I'm all right."

"It was good to see the two of you laughing a moment ago," Cal said, coming up to them then.

"Why do you say that?" Smoke asked.

"No reason in particular," Cal said. "It's just that some of the boys was beginnin' to think that you was so upset over losin' Hank and LeRoy, and Andy and Dooley, that you wouldn't be able to keep goin'."

"Do the others want to turn back?" Smoke asked.

Cal shook his head. "No, sir, not a one of us wants to turn back," he said. "We started out on this here journey, and we aim to see to it that you get your cows through."

"Four good men lost their lives to get the cows this far," Smoke said.

"Yes, but think about it, Smoke. If we don't' go on, then those boys died for nothin'. Besides, it's farther to go back now than it is to go on ahead. Looks to me like we got no choice."

Smoke nodded. "That's true," he said. He sighed. "We've got no choice. Tell the boys to get a good day's rest. We're going on ahead tomorrow."

Cal smiled broadly. "Yes, sir!" he said. "I'll tell 'em just that."

Sally looked up at Smoke after Cal left. "What was that all about?" she asked.

"What was what all about?"

"You weren't about to turn back."

"No, I wasn't," Smoke said. "But this way, the men think they have talked me into it. And sometimes it's good to let a man think he is controlling his own destiny, even if he isn't."

Trent Williams looked up from his desk when Gilbert stepped into his office.

"Mr. Williams there is a—gentleman—here to see you," the teller said. The way he set the word "gentleman" apart from the rest of the sentence indicated that he believed the man was anything but a gentleman.

"Who is it?" Williams asked.

"I don't know, sir," Gilbert replied. "He didn't give his name, but he said that it had to do with some— cow—business. He said you would understand."

"Cow business?" Williams thought for a moment, then realized what it must be. "Very well, show him in."

Williams leaned back in his chair waiting, expecting to see Will Staley come through the door.

It wasn't Staley.

"Who are you?" Williams asked.

"The name is Cord. Trace Cord," the man said.

"What can I do for you, Mr. Cord? My teller said it had something to do with the cow business."

"Yes," Cord said.

"What sort of cow business?"

"The kind of business you hired Will Staley for."

"Oh," Williams said. He drummed his fingers on

the desk for a moment or two. "I see. So tell me, Mr. Cord, why didn't Mr. Staley come to discuss this?"

"He didn't come 'cause he's dead."

"Dead?" Williams asked, sitting back in his chair, surprised by the statement.

"Yeah, him and five others."

"What happened?"

"We ran into a hornets' nest, that's what happened."

"Am I to understand that you did not get the herd?"

"You ain't been listenin' to nothin' I've said, have you?" Cord asked. "No, we didn't get the herd. We're damn lucky they didn't kill all of us."

"I see," Williams said. "What am I to do now?"

"I don't care what you do now. All I care about is gettin' the money."

"What money would that be?"

"The money Staley was supposed to pay us."

Williams's smile was without mirth. "Why, Mr. Cord, you don't really think I'm going to pay you for failure, do you?"

"There wasn't nothin' said about failure. Only thing Staley said was that he would pay us to go with him. Besides, you set us up, you son of a bitch. You didn't tell us we was goin' to run into an army."

"When I pay to have something done, how it is done is none of my business," Williams said.

"Yeah, well, that's just it. I went with him, and now I want my pay."

"And if I refuse?"

"I'll go to the sheriff and tell him what you had planned," Cord said.

Williams stroked his chin. "You wouldn't do that. You would be incriminating yourself."

"Hell, I don't care nothin' about that. I've been in prison before, wouldn't bother me none to go back in. But a highfalutin fella like yourself? You'd have a real hard time in prison."

"How much did Staley say he would pay you?"

"Two hun . . . uh, five hundred dollars," Cord said.

"Five hundred dollars is a lot of money."

"Yeah. But that's what he said he would pay us."

"Us?"

"I'll be splitting the money with the others."

"I see," Williams said. He nodded. "All right, I suppose what's right is right. I'll give you the money."

"I thought you might see it my way," Cord said with a self-satisfied smile.

Williams opened the middle drawer of his desk, reached his hand in, wrapped his fingers around the butt of a Colt .44, then pulled the gun out.

"What?" Cord asked, surprised by sudden appearance of the gun. "What are you doing?"

"I'll not be blackmailed," Williams said, pulling the trigger.

The sound of the gunshot was exceptionally loud. The bullet caught Cord in the heart, and though he lived long enough to slap his hand over the wound in his chest, he was dead by the time his body hit the floor.

"Mr. Gilbert! Mr. Gilbert, come in here quickly!" Williams shouted.

Gilbert, the teller who had come in earlier, now came running into the room carrying a poker over his head. Williams was standing over Cord's body, holding a smoking pistol in his hand.

"Mr. Williams, what happened, sir?" Gilbert asked.

"I don't know," Williams answered, his face registering shock. "This man came in here and threatened to hold up the bank. I tried to talk him out of it, but he was quite obdurate. Then, it all happened so quickly. One minute I was arguing with him and the next minute"—Williams held up the pistol—"I was holding a smoking pistol and he was lying on the floor."

"Yes, well, don't worry, Mr. Williams," Gilbert said. "You did the right thing. A bank robber like that should be shot."

Chapter Twenty-one

The sheriff's inquiry had been fast and nonthreatening. Gilbert testified that Cord had come into the bank and presented himself in a belligerent manner, demanding to see Trent Williams. Gilbert further testified that he was worried about Mr. Williams, and therefore kept a close eye on the door to the bank office. Then, he heard Williams call out, heard a shot, and when he entered the office he saw Cord lying on the floor and Williams standing over him, holding a smoking gun.

Trent Williams did not dissent from Gilbert's account. He explained that Cord had come into the office, demanding that Williams empty the safe and give him all the money.

"Did he have a gun?" Williams was asked.

"Yes."

"Was the gun in his holster, or was he holding it in his hand?"

"I don't know," Williams said.

"Come on, Sheriff, what are you askin' Mr. Williams

all these questions for?" Gilbert asked. "We've already told you what happened."

The sheriff nodded. "All right, Mr. Williams, you're free to go. There will be no charges."

"Thank you," Williams said.

Williams told himself that shooting Cord had been necessary, but he was unnerved. He wasn't unnerved because he had had to shoot Cord. He was unnerved because Staley had failed to get the herd for him. Now what was he going to do?

At this very moment the answer to Williams's dilemma was just down the street from the bank, playing a game of solitaire in the saloon. The man was dressed all in black, including his hat, though the starkness was offset by the glitter of the silver and turquoise hatband. This was Quince Pardeen, and though he would have preferred a game of poker, nobody would play with him because everyone was afraid of him. Pardeen's reputation preceeded him now, even in the smallest towns.

Pardeen counted out three cards, but couldn't find a play. The second card of the three was a black seven. There would have been a play had the black seven come up on top, but unfortunately, it was one card down and therefore useless to him. Pardeen glared at it for a moment, then, with a shrug, played it anyway.

The batwing doors swung open and a cowboy came in and walked over to the bar. He ordered a whiskey, then looked around and saw Pardeen sitting at the table, calmly playing cards.

"Ain't you the one they call Pardeen?" the cowboy asked.

Pardeen didn't answer.

"Yeah, that's who you are, all right," the cowboy said. "You're Quince Pardeen."

Though the cowboy wasn't telling the people in the saloon anything they didn't already know, everyone remained silent. The cowboy's tone of voice was challenging, and everyone knew that Pardeen was not a man to be challenged.

"My name is Carl Logan," the cowboy said. "My brother's name was John Logan. I reckon you've heard that name."

Pardeen made no response.

"John was a sheriff, an honest man whose only job was to protect the people of his town. But you shot him down in cold blood," the cowboy continued.

"Mister, do you know who you are talkin' to?" another man asked.

The cowboy looked at the questioner. "Yeah," he replied, "I know who I'm talkin' to. And I know who you are too, Corbett. You're the little piece of dung that hangs on Pardeen's ass all the time. They's some that says you're the one that helped Pardeen break out of jail where he was waitin' to be hung for killin' my brother."

Finally, Pardeen looked up from his cards. The expression on his face was one of boredom, as if he shouldn't have to deal with people like this belligerent cowboy.

"You talkin' to me, friend?"

"Mister, I'm not your friend."

Pardeen smiled coldly. "Oh, that's too bad," he said.

"You see, I generally give my friends some leeway when they make a mistake. But seein' as you aren't my friend, then I don't see much need in cuttin' you any slack a'tall."

"I ain't askin' for any slack from you, you low-assed son of a bitch," the cowboy said.

The others in the saloon gasped at the audacity of Logan's words.

"I'm tryin' to get you riled enough to fight," Logan said. He doubled his fists. "Because I aim to beat you to a pulp."

Pardeen looked up from the cards again. This time the nonchalance was gone. Instead, his eyes were narrowed menacingly.

"If you got somethin' stickin' in your craw, cowboy, I think maybe you'd better just spit it out," Pardeen said coldly.

"I done spit it out," Logan said. "I told you, I aim to beat you to a pulp; then I'm goin' to personally turn you over to the sheriff so you can get hung proper."

Pardeen looked surprised. "A fistfight?" he asked. "Did I hear you right? You are challenging me to a fistfight?"

"Yeah," Logan said. He looked over at Corbett. "I know there's two of you and one of me. But I'd say that makes the odds about even. Come on, I think I'm goin' to enjoy this." He made his hands into fists, then held them out in front of his face, moving his right hand in tiny circles. "Come on," he said. "I'm goin' to put the lights out for both of you."

Pardeen smiled, a low, evil smile. "Huh-uh," he said.

"If me'n you are goin' to fight, mister, it's goin' to be permanent."

"You mean a gunfight? No, I ain't goin' to get into no gunfight with the likes of you," Logan said. "Besides, like I said, there's two of you. I figure with the two of you, it might just about make a fistfight come out even."

"You can keep me out of this one, mister," Corbett said. "This just between the two of you." Corbett stood up and walked away, leaving the floor to the two players. Pardeen, in the meantime, stood up and stepped away from the table. He let his arm hang down alongside his pistol and he looked at the cowboy through cold, ruthless eyes.

"Well, what about it, Mr. Logan?" Pardeen said. "You're the one that asked me to dance."

Logan shook his head. "No, I told you, this ain't the kind of fight I'm talkin' about."

"I'll let you draw first," Pardeen offered.

"I told you, I ain't drawin' on you," Logan said. He doubled up his fists again. "But if you'd like to come over here and take your beatin' like a man, I'd be glad to oblige you."

"I said draw," Pardeen repeated in a cold, flat voice.

The others in the saloon began, quietly but deliberately, to get out of the way of any flying lead.

Logan shook his head slowly. "I told you, I ain't goin' to draw on you," he said. He smiled. "You might'a noticed that I'm not wearin' a gun."

"I'll give you time to get yourself heeled," Pardeen offered.

"I told you, I ain't goin' to get into no gunfight with you."

"Somebody give Mr. Logan a gun," Pardeen said coldly. He pulled his lips into a sinister smile. "He seems to have come to this fight unprepared."

"I don't want a gun," Peabody said.

When no one offered Logan their gun, Pardeen pointed to a cowboy who was standing at the far end of the bar. "I see that you are wearing a gun. Give it to him."

"He don't want a gun," the man said. "I ain't goin' to do that. If I give him a gun, you'll kill him."

"That's right."

"Well, I don't want no part of it."

"You got no choice, friend. You'll either give him your gun or you had better be ready to use it yourself," Pardeen said. He turned three quarters of the way toward the armed cowboy. "Which will it be?"

The cowboy paused for just a moment longer, then sighed in defeat. "All right, all right. If you put it that way, I reckon I'll do whatever you want." He took his gun out of the holster and laid it on the bar. "Sorry, Logan," he said. He gave the gun a shove and it slid halfway down the bar, knocking two glasses aside, then stopping just beside Logan's hand. It rocked back and forth for a moment, making a little sound that, in the now-silent bar, seemed amost deafening.

"Pick it up," Pardeen said to Logan.

Logan looked at the pistol, but made no effort to pick it up. A line of perspiration beads broke out on his upper lip.

"No, I ain't goin' to do it."

Pardeen drew his pistol and fired. There was a flash of light and a roar of exploding gunpowder. A billowing cloud of acrid, blue smoke rolled from the end of Pardeen's pistol, then began rising to the ceiling.

For a moment the entire saloon thought Pardeen had killed Logan, but that impression dissolved when they saw that Logan was still standing. He wasn't unscathed, though, for he was holding his hand to the side of his head with blood spilling through his fingers. Pardeen had shot off a piece of Logan's earlobe.

"Pick up the gun," Pardeen ordered.

"No."

There was a second shot and Peabody's right earlobe, like his left, turned into a ragged, bloody piece of flesh.

"Mister, you better do somethin'," Corbett said. "Else ole Quince here is goin' to carve you up like a Christmas turkey."

Logan stood there holding his hands over his ears as he stared at Pardeen. Both hands were red with blood.

"Pick it up!"

"No!"

"Are you left-handed or right-handed?" Pardeen asked.

"What?"

"Left or right."

"Why do you ask that?"

"I figure you are probably right-handed," Pardeen said. "Am I right?"

"Whether I'm right-handed or left-handed ain't none of your business," Logan said.

"You better hope I'm right," Pardeen said. He pulled his gun and shot a third time. This time his bullet took one of the fingers off Logan's left hand.

Logan cried out in pain, then grabbed his hand. "You're crazy!" he said.

"Pick up the gun," Pardeen said calmly.

Logan stared at Pardeen through eyes that were wide with fear. Then the fear was replaced by blind rage. Logan reached for the pistol.

"I'll send you to hell, you son of a bitch!" Logan yelled.

Pardeen played with Logan the way a cat will play with a mouse. He waited until Logan had the gun in hand before he drew again. This time his bullet caught Logan in the forehead. Logan fell back against the bar, then slid down, dead before he reached the floor.

The sound of the gunshot brought two or three outsiders into the saloon, including the sheriff. He saw Logan sitting down against the bar, his eyes open and sightless, his hand clenched tightly around the unfired pistol.

"Oh, hell," the sheriff said quietly. He looked over at Pardeen. "Did you do this?"

"Yeah, I done it," Pardeen said. "But it was self-defense. Look at the gun in his hand. He was goin' to shoot me."

"Pardeen forced him into it, Sheriff," the bartender said. "Logan didn't want to fight but Pardeen egged him on."

"Pardeen didn't have any choice, Sheriff," a voice from the back of the saloon said. "He had to force a showdown now."

The sheriff looked toward the sound of the voice and saw Trent Williams.

"Mr. Williams, you are taking up for Pardeen?" the sheriff asked, surprised by statement.

"Believe me, it's not something I want to do,"

Williams said. "But when Mr. Logan spoke to me earlier today, he let it be known that he intended to kill Quince Pardeen. I believe if Pardeen had not forced a show-down here, Logan would have shot him in the back."

"Yeah," Corbett said. "That's what I think too."

"What have you got to say about this, Pardeen?" the sheriff asked.

"You heard what the man said, Sheriff," Pardeen replied. "I didn't have no choice. If I hadn't killed him, he would'a killed me."

The sheriff shook his head. "I don't know if I believe you or not," he said.

Pardeen smiled. "Oh, yeah, you believe me all right," he said easily. "You believe me because you are afraid to go against me. Otherwise, you would have arrested me the moment I came into town."

"No, I—I couldn't arrest you," the sheriff said. "I've heard what you did back in Puxico, but I've received no paper on you and I've got no authority."

"Well, Sheriff, if you do get some paper on me and you want to come arrest me, you know where you can find me," Pardeen taunted.

"You just—you just watch your step around here," the sheriff said, trying hard to keep his voice from breaking in fear. Turning, he walked out of the saloon, leaving Logan's body dead on the floor behind him.

Pardeen chuckled as the sheriff left; then, turning, he saw Trent Williams staring at him. He walked over to talk to him.

"Logan didn't really tell you he was going to kill me, did he?" Pardeen asked.

"No."

"Then why did you say that?"

Williams looked around the saloon to see if anyone was close enough to overhear their conversation. As everyone seemed to want to give Pardeen a very wide berth, there was nobody close by.

"I spoke up for you because I want to hire your services," Williams said.

"I'm not interested," Pardeen replied.

Pardeen's dismissive comment surprised Williams. "You're not interested? Why not? You haven't even heard what I want you to do."

"I know what you want me to do. You want me to kill someone. The answer is no. Kill him yourself," Pardeen said.

"You haven't heard my offer."

"It would have to be a very good offer to get me to change my mind," Pardeen said.

"Is ten thousand dollars good enough?" Williams asked.

"What?" Pardeen replied with a gasp. "Did you say ten thousand dollars?"

"Yes."

A smile spread across Pardeen's face, and this time the smile was genuine.

"I'll do it."

"You haven't asked who it is I want you to kill."

"I don't care who it is. For ten thousand dollars I'd kill my own grandma."

Chapter Twenty-two

Sorento, Wyoming Territory

The town was cold and dark when Williams, Pardeen, and Corbett arrived at around one in the morning. Tying their horses off behind the saloon, the three men moved up the alley toward the office of the Indian agency.

They were startled by the screech of a cat that jumped down from a fence, then ran across the alley in front of them.

The yap of a dog caused them to stop, then move into the shadows. The dog continued to bark.

"Cody, hush up!" an irritated voice shouted.

The dog continued to bark.

"I said shut up!" the voice shouted again.

The dog barked one more time, but this time its bark was interrupted by a yelp of pain.

"Damnit, when I tell you to shut up, I mean shut up," the voice said angrily.

A baby began crying.

The three men waited a moment longer; then when

everything had calmed down, they resumed their cautious movement down the alley.

"He lives in a small shack behind the agency," Williams said.

"What about the other man?" Pardeen asked. "The one who is the actual agent?"

"Don't worry about him. He lives in Laramie."

"I still don't know how killin' this man is going to get us any money."

"It's simple," Williams said. "Kirby Jensen—"

"Smoke Jensen," Pardeen said, interrupting.

"All right, Smoke Jensen," Williams continued. "He's bringing in three thousand head of cattle. He will turn the cattle over to Malone in return for a receipt, which he can then redeem for cash from Abernathy. Only, he isn't going to turn the cattle over to Malone, he's going to turn them over to me."

"Because?" Pardeen asked.

"Because he is going to think that I am Cephus Malone."

Reaching the little building behind the Indian agency, Williams tried the front door.

"I'll be damned," he whispered. "It isn't locked."

"Yeah, a lot of people don't lock their doors in these little towns," Pardeen replied, also in a whisper. "They figure they know everyone in town, so they figure they're safe."

Williams started in, then stopped and stepped back out onto the porch.

"What is it? What's wrong?"

"Don't make any noise, and tell me when it's done," Williams said.

Pardeen chuckled, then disappeared into the darkened interior of the little house. Williams and Corbett waited outside.

"Who's there? What is it?" a voice said from inside. "What are you doing in here?"

That was as far as the voice got until it turned into a muffled squealing sound.

A moment later, Pardeen came back outside. "It's done," he said.

"Are you sure he's dead?" Williams asked.

"Oh, yeah, he's dead," Pardeen said. "I cut his throat from ear to ear."

"Lock the door," Williams said. "By the time anyone discovers him it will be too late."

Smoke's riders didn't see the town until they reached the top of a long, sloping ridgeline. Jules was riding point, so he was the first to see Sorento, which was no more than a small group of buildings clustered around a railroad depot.

"Yahoo!" Jules shouted, taking off his hat and waving it over his head. Turning his horse, he galloped back to the others.

"We're here!" he shouted happily. "It's just over the hill! We're here, we're here, we're here!"

It had been twenty-eight days since Smoke and his outfit had left Sugarloaf. Twenty-eight days of drought, stampede, blizzard, and attacks from Indians and cattle rustlers. They had come through, though not without its cost. Four good men lay dead on the trail behind them.

Because they would be spending this night in town,

Sally had not gone ahead of them this morning as she normally did. On this, the last day of the drive, she kept the wagon alongside the herd.

Smoke stopped them when they reached the crest of the hill. They sat there for a moment, looking down at the little town below them.

"It sure don't look like much," Pearlie said. "Comin' all this way only to see a town that ain't even as big as Big Rock seems sort of . . ." He struggled for a word. "Sort of . . ."

"Anticlimactic," Sally suggested.

"Yeah, that," Pearlie said, though he had no idea what the word meant.

"Well, we didn't come here to visit the town," Smoke said. "We came here to sell our cattle. And if we can do that, then it doesn't matter what size the town is."

"You got that right," Cal said. "But the question now is, did we make it in time? Are we the first ones here?"

"We're the first ones here," Sally said.

"How do you know?"

"Look at the feeder lots," Sally said. "There aren't more than a couple of dozen cattle down there."

"Could be they already been delivered to the Indians," Billy said.

"No," Sally said. "If there had been that many cattle in the pens, we would still be able to smell it. We're the first."

"So, what do we do now, Smoke?" Billy asked.

"We'll keep the herd here while I go into town and contact Mr. Malone," Smoke answered. "Then, soon as I make the arrangements, I'll pay you boys off, then make arrangements for you and the horses to go back by train."

"Whooee," Jules said. "Think about that, boys. We'll be goin' home on the train. I ain't never been on no train before. I wonder what that'll be like."

"Why, shoot, it won't be like nothin'," Cal said. "You just sit there on the train and ride along with it, that's all."

"Sally, you want to come into town with me?" Smoke asked.

"Not yet," Sally said. "Since we won't be taking the wagon back, I'll need to spend some time packing the things that we will be shipping back home. But I tell you what, find us a hotel room while you are in town, would you? I wouldn't mind spending this night in a real bed."

"Yeah, I could go along with that myself," Smoke said. He swung into his saddle and looked back at the others. "I can't tell you how proud I am of you," he said. "Not many men could do what you just did, driving three thousand head of cattle five hundred miles in the wintertime."

"The reason not many men could do it is because there ain't that many dumb enough to try," Billy replied, and the others laughed.

"I'll be back in a couple of hours," Smoke said as he turned toward the town.

A small bell was suspended from the door so that it jingled as Smoke stepped into the Indian agency office.

"I'll be with you in just a moment," someone called from the back.

"No hurry," Smoke answered. "It's taken me a month to get here. I can wait a few more minutes, I reckon."

The man laughed as he came out front. "May I help you?"

"My name is Smoke Jensen," Smoke said. "Are you are Cephus Malone?"

"I am indeed, sir. Cephus Malone at your service."

"Then you are the man I'm looking for. I'm here to sell my cattle. That is, assuming I am the first."

"You are the first."

"Then, I take it that you are still interested in buying." Smoke chuckled. "Otherwise, I've had a hell of a long drive for nothing."

"Oh, yes, I am quite willing to buy your herd. As soon as you put your cows in the holding pens, I will issue you a receipt for payment. Then, all you have to do is send the receipt to Washington and they'll send you a bank draft for the amount."

"I have to send the receipt to Washington for payment? I thought all I had to do was present the receipt to Mr. Abernathy."

"No, no, Abernathy need not get involved. I'm the only one you will have to deal with. That is, except for the Indian Bureau in Washington."

"Yes, in Washington," Smoke repeated. It was obvious by the tone of his voice that he was not too thrilled with the idea of having to wait for payment.

"I can see that it is making you a little nervous to have to wait for your money. But if you can't depend on the United States government, who can you depend on?"

"I guess you're right," Smoke said. "All right, I'll go bring in the herd. I have them just outside town."

"Good, good. Believe me, Mr. Jensen, there are going to be a lot of happy Indians when these cattle are delivered."

"I hope so," Smoke said. "A happy Indian is a peaceful Indian."

The man chuckled. "That's true, Mr. Jensen," he said. "Yes, sir, truer words were never spoken. I like that. I may use that the next time I talk to the bureaucrats in Washington. A happy Indian is a peaceful Indian."

"You will want the cattle delivered to the holding pens, I suppose?"

"Yes."

"All right," Smoke said as he started toward the door.

"Wait, Mr. Jensen, don't you want the receipt?"

Smoke stopped. "Don't you want to count them first?"

"Oh, yes. Yes, indeed. I guess I was getting a little ahead of myself, wasn't I? Please, by all means, bring the cattle in. I'll count them, then I'll issue the receipt."

Smoke nodded, then left.

Pardeen came out of the back room then. "So that was the great Smoke Jensen," he said.

"That is how he identified himself," Williams, who had been posing as Cephus Malone, said. "I have no way of knowing for sure, since I've never met the man. But I have no reason to doubt that he is who he says he is, especially as he has delivered the herd."

"Not yet he ain't delivered it," Pardeen said.

"Oh, he's delivered it all right," Williams insisted. "He just hasn't put them in the feeder pens for us."

"Yeah, well, you'd better keep an eye on that one," Pardeen said. "He's as slick as they come."

"No," Williams replied. "It isn't my job to keep an eye on him. That's your job."

"Oh, you don't worry about that," Pardeen said. "I have something special in mind for him just as soon as all this is over."

The town of Sorento existed for the sole purpose of providing a railhead to ship out cattle for the neighboring ranches. Because of that, the facilities at the depot were equal to those of cities much bigger.

Included in the facilities were two very large feeder lots, and Smoke used both of them. While Cal, Billy, Mike, and Jules pushed the cows into the two large pens, Pearlie and Smoke sat on the top rail of the pens, counting them. Smoke had one pen and Pearlie the other. They counted the cows by the simple method of making a knot in a string of rawhide for every fifty cows that passed through the gate. This controlled counting method allowed them to arrive at a much more accurate number than the hasty count that had been taken in the field after the attempted rustling.

"I make if thirteen hundred and forty-two, Pearlie said.

"I've got fourteen hundred and eleven," Smoke said.

"That's twenty-seven hundred and fifty three," Pearlie said. He shook his head. "I didn't think we had lost that many."

"Pearlie, when you consider everything that we went through, I'm very pleasantly surprise we didn't lose more," Smoke said.

"Yeah, I guess you are right," Pearlie said. He smiled. "But I reckon it's enough to make the drive worth it, don't you think?"

"Oh, yes, it's more than worth it," Smoke agreed. "Especially considering that we might have as bad a winter as we did before."

"Here comes our man," Smoke said when he saw Trent Williams, the man he thought was Cephus Malone, coming toward him. Williams was carrying two pieces of paper.

"Well, you got them all counted, I see," Williams said.

"Twenty-seven hundred and fifty-three," Smoke said.

"Two thousand, seven hundred, and fifty-three," Williams repeated. "All right, all I need you to do is sign this bill of sale over to me, and I'll give you your receipt."

Smoke nodded, then signed the bill of sale.

Williams handed him a receipt. "Send this in to Washington, friend, and you'll be a rich man," he said. "And may I say that it was a pleasure doing business with you?"

"Thank you," Smoke replied. "Now, I want to treat my cowboys to the best dinner in town. Where do you recommend I take them?"

"Oh, well, I wouldn't presume to recommend one place over another," Williams said. "But knowing cowboys, I imagine anyplace that would let them in would be a welcome change to men who are used to nothing but whorehouses and saloons."

Smoke glared at Williams. "I don't think of my cowboys in that way, mister," he said. "I consider them to be good men. In fact, I would go so far as to say that I consider them to be among the finest men I have ever met."

Williams cleared his throat. "Well—uh—certainly I meant no disrespect to either you or your men," he said.

Sally came up to Smoke as Williams was walking away.

"What's wrong?" she asked.

"Nothing's wrong," Smoke replied. He held up the receipt. "We have the receipt, but I'll tell you the truth, Sally, if it weren't for the money, that's a fella I'd just as soon avoid."

Sally smiled. "Well, after this, we can avoid him," she said.

As it turned out, the hotel had a banquet room and Smoke rented it for the evening. He ordered a dinner to be prepared for his men, and all showed up, freshly scrubbed and wearing their best clothes.

As the wine was poured, Smoke lifted his glass to propose a toast.

"Sally, men," he said. "I would like to drink a toast to ones who didn't make it here with us but who, by their effort and their sacrifice, enabled us to make it. Here's to Dooley, Andy, Hank, and LeRoy."

"Hear, hear," Pearlie said, and all of them drank.

"And I'd like to propose a toast to the man who led us," Billy said.

"And to the woman who led him," Cal added, eliciting laughter as he held his glass toward Sally.

Again they drank a toast. Then waiters began bringing in the food.

"Oh, that looks good," Billy said as a plate was put before him.

"I heard that you men just brought a herd of cattle up," the headwaiter said. "I suppose after eating bad food on the trail, anything would look good to you."

Jules started to say something, but Billy held up his hand to stop him.

"Mister, I said this food looks good. I didn't say nothin' about how we ate on the trail 'cause the truth is, there ain't nothin' this here café can serve that will come close to bein' as good."

"Trail food?" the headwaiter asked incredulously. "I hardly think so."

"Mister, Miz Sally cooked all our food on the trail," Mike said. "And if you make another remark about how it wasn't no good, why I reckon I'll just have to box your ears for you."

"Mike!" Sally said.

"Miz Sally, I'm just takin' up for you is all," Mike said.

Despite herself, Sally couldn't help but laugh at her young "protector."

"Well, I thank you very much. But boxing this gentleman's ears is no way to do it."

"Madam," the headwaiter said. "Believe me, I meant no disrespect."

"And no disrespect was taken," Sally replied graciously.

"Say, Smoke, what time does the train leave tomorrow?" Billy asked.

"Around nine o'clock, I think," Smoke said. "I'll find out for sure right after breakfast tomorrow when I get the tickets."

"There ain't no reason we can't go out and have us a good time tonight, is there?" Billy asked.

"No reason at all," Smoke said. "You are all on your own time now."

"Good," Billy said. "It's been a long time on the trail. I aim to wash some of that trail dust away."

Chapter Twenty-three

Billy was standing in the Cattleman's Saloon when he looked up at the clock and saw that it was nearly midnight.

"Whoa," he said to the soiled dove who was keeping him company. "I'd better get back to the hotel and go to bed. I'm catching a train out of here tomorrow."

"Honey, you don't have to go all the way to the hotel just to get in bed," the girl said.

Billy laughed. "I have to give you credit, Lucy, you are all business," he said. "But Mr. Jensen has gone to all the trouble to rent hotel rooms for us. It ain't that often I get to stay in a hotel, and I aim to take advantage of it."

"You will buy me one more drink, though, won't you?" Lucy asked.

"Damn right I will," Billy said. "In fact, I'll have one with you."

Billy tapped his finger on the empty glass and when the bartender came to refill it, indicated that Lucy's glass should be refilled as well.

"Not from that bottle, Jake," Lucy said.

"I know your special bottle," Jake replied, putting the whiskey bottle away and getting another bottle from under the bar.

"Ha. That's tea, ain't it?" Billy said.

"Well, I . . ."

"I don't care if it's tea," Billy said. "Hell, you couldn't stay here and drink ever' night without becomin' a drunk."

"I'm glad you understand," Lucy said. She took a swallow of her tea, then smiled at him. "Go on, you were tellin' me about the cattle drive you were on."

"Yes, ma'am, I was, wasn't I? Well, it was quite a trip up here, I tell you."

"Oh, I think it would have been very frightening to have to face so many Indians," the girl said.

"Well, I don't mind tellin' you that some of the boys was afraid," Billy said. He took a swallow of his whiskey, then ran the back of his hand across his mouth. "But I wasn't none afraid, no, sir. And I helped Smoke buck up some of the others."

"Smoke?"

"Smoke Jensen is his name. He was our trail boss," Billy said. "Well, he was more'n that 'cause he actually owned the cows."

"That's a funny name," the girl said.

"It may be a funny name," Billy said. "But he's about the best man I've ever known. Faster with a gun than greased lightnin', but you'd never know it just to know him 'cause he's a fella that don't get riled any too easy." Billy waved his finger back and forth. "But you have to pity the fella that ever does get him riled."

"I've heard of Smoke Jensen before," a man standing just down the bar said. The man was dressed all in black, including his hat, though the starkness was offset by the glitter of the silver and turquoise hat-band. He continued to stare into his glass as he spoke.

"You've heard of him, have you, mister?" Billy said. "Well, then you can verify what I'm saying about the type man he is."

"I'll tell you what I know about him," the man in black said. "I know him to be a lying, back-shooting coward."

Upon hearing that unexpected description of Smoke, Billy slammed the glass down hard on the bar, then turned to face the man who had spoken.

"What did you say, mister?"

The man at the bar turned to face Billy. "You heard what I said. I said that Smoke Jensen is a yellow-bellied, lying coward."

"Mister, maybe you don't know this, but Smoke Jensen is a friend of mine," Billy said. "And I'll be askin' you to take that back."

"And if I don't?"

"If you don't, you'll be answerin' to me," Billy said.

"Are you challengin' me to a gunfight, boy?"

Billy had not intended for the altercation to go this far. He had thought that a few harsh words, if necessary even few punches, would be called for. He had no idea that it was being pushed to a gunfight.

"Well, no, not that," Billy said, thinking quickly. "I was thinkin' more along the lines of wipin' up this here saloon floor with your hide. I mean, you spoke some harsh and even rude words, but I'm not ready to get into a gunfight over it."

"Mister, it's too late for you to back out now," the

man said. "You're the one who invited me to this ball. Now either dance with me, or admit that you are a yellow-bellied, lying coward just like your friend Smoke Jensen."

Those were killing words and everyone in the saloon, including Lucy, moved out of the way to give the two men room.

"Pardeen, the boy's been drinkin'," the bartender said. "Ease up on him."

"You stay out of this, barkeep," Pardeen said.

Billy's face went white. "Pardeen?" Billy said. "Did he call you Pardeen?"

"Yeah, he called me Pardeen 'cause that's my name," Pardeen said. "You got a problem with my name, boy?"

"No, it's not that—it's just that . . ." Billy took a deep breath. "Well, maybe we got off on the wrong foot." Billy tried to force a smile. "Why don't we just both forget about some of the things we've said and go back to drinkin' in peace?"

"Too late for that, boy. You should'a thought of that before you called me out."

"I didn't exactly call you out," Billy said. "I just said that you would have to—answer to me," he finished, barely saying the last three words.

"I'm going to count to three," Pardeen said. "When I get to three, I'm going to kill you. So I expect you had better draw your gun."

"No—I . . ."

"One."

"Look, I don't want to do this!"

"Two."

Suddenly, Billy made a desperate grab for his pistol. He had the gun out and was coming up with it before Pardeen even started his draw. For just a second, Billy actually thought that he might have a chance, and he felt a surge of hope.

That hope was dashed, even as it was forming in his mind, when he felt a sudden crushing blow to his chest. Pardeen had drawn and fired so quickly that by the time Billy realized Pardeen had the gun in his hand, he had already been shot.

The impact of the bullet knocked Billy back against the bar. He dropped his pistol and slapped his hand over the wound in his chest. Then, turning his hand out, he watched in horror as the palm of his hand filled to over-flowing with his blood.

Billy looked around the saloon, into the faces of those who had just witnessed this. He saw horror and sadness in Lucy's face. He held his hand out toward her, tried to take a step, then collapsed.

The knocking was loud and insistent and even as Smoke was waking up, he was drawing his pistol from the holster that hung over the bedstead. He motioned for Sally to get out of bed and get into the corner.

"Yeah, who is it?" he called. Immediately after he called out, he moved to one side so as not to be where his voice had been.

"Mr. Jensen, my name is Joe Titus. I'm the deputy sheriff. I need to talk to you."

"What about?" Smoke called. Once more he moved after he had called out.

"Do you have a man working for you by the name of Billy Cantrell?"

Smiling, Smoke sighed and lowered his gun. He opened the door. The deputy was an older man, tall and weathered, with gunmetal-gray hair.

"What kind of trouble has Billy got himself into?" he asked. "A barroom fight?"

"No, sir," the deputy answered. "I'm sorry to have to tell you this, Mr. Jensen, but Billy Cantrell is dead."

"What? Are you serious?"

"Yes, sir. He got into a gunfight with a man by the name of Quince Pardeen. Pardeen killed him."

Smoke lowered his head and pinched the bridge of his nose.

"Did you say Quince Pardeen?"

"Yes, sir. Do you know him?"

"I've never met him, but I know who he is," Smoke said.

"Well, sir, then you know he's what they call a gunfighter. Too bad your man, Cantrell, didn't know that. If he had known that, he might not have started the fight."

"Wait a minute? Are you telling me that Billy started the fight with Pardeen?"

"Yes, sir, that's what ever'body in the saloon said. They was near all of 'em witnesses, and they all said that Cantrell called Pardeen out."

"Billy might have challenged him to a fistfight," Smoke said. "He had a habit of doing that. But he would have never challenged anyone to a gunfight, let alone someone like Pardeen."

"Yes, sir, that don't seem to make no sense to me neither," the deputy said. "But like I said, ever'one who witnessed the fight says that's exactly what happened."

"Where is Billy now?"

"He's down to the Welch Mortuary," the deputy said. "You can see him first thing in the morning if you'd like."

Smoke nodded. "Yes," he said. "I'd like to, thank you."

"It's me Pardeen is after," Smoke said to Sally after the deputy left. "He killed Billy to get to me."

"You don't know that," Sally said.

Smoke nodded. "Yeah, Sally, the sad truth is, I do know it."

The next morning, Smoke, Sally, Pearlie, Cal, Mike, and Jules were waiting outside the mortuary when Welch turned the sign from CLOSED to OPEN.

"Yes, sir, what can I do for you?" Welch asked as he opened the door.

"You have our friend's body here," Smoke said. "We would like to see him."

"Well, sir, I haven't prepared the body for viewing yet," Welch said.

"I don't care whether he is prepared for viewing yet or not. I want to see him," Smoke said with more insistence."

"Very good, sir," Welch replied. "As long as you know that the remains are in a distressed state."

"Where is he?"

"He is right in here, sir."

Smoke and the others followed Welch into the back room of the building where they saw not one, but two bodies.

"Was someone else killed last night?" Smoke asked. "I thought Billy was the only one killed in the shoot-out."

"Oh, no, that is Mr. Malone," Welch said, pointing to the other body. "The poor fellow was found murdered in his bed yesterday morning."

"Malone?"

"Yes, Cephus Malone. Did you know him?"

Smoke walked over to look at the body. He turned toward Welch.

"Are you saying *this* is Cephus Malone?"

"Yes."

"The Indian agent Cephus Malone?"

"Yes, do you know him?"

"And he was killed yesterday morning?"

"Apparently night before last," Welch said. "As I said, he was discovered yesterday morning. Someone broke into his house and cut his throat. The sheriff thinks it was robbery." Welch shook his head. "It is frightening to think that we would have such a person in our small town."

"Smoke, that's not—" Sally began, but Smoke interrupted her.

"—the man we gave our cattle to," he said, concluding her sentence.

At that very moment, the man Smoke did give his cattle to was standing down at the feeder lot, addressing the ten men Pardeen had rounded up for him.

"One hundred dollars," Williams was saying. "One hundred dollars to every man who helps me drive these cattle to the Indian agency in Laramie."

"Mister, am I hearing you right?" one of the men said. "All we have to do is drive these here cows no more'n ten miles, and you're givin' us one hundred dollars?"

"That's right."

The men started talking excitedly among themselves; then one of them asked the question that was on all their minds.

"What's the catch?"

"No catch."

"You say there is no catch, but when Pardeen hired us, he asked if we were willing to use our guns. Now he wouldn't ask that if he didn't think there was a chance we'd have to use them."

"It's not a catch exactly. It's more like a complication," Williams said.

"All right, what is the complication?"

"There may be some who don't want us to do this," Williams said. "They may try and stop us. I don't intend to be stopped."

"If any of you have a problem with that, walk away now," Pardeen said. "Because when the shooting starts, I'll kill anyone who tries to run away."

"You say some people may try to stop us. How many people are you talking about?"

"One less than they started out with," Pardeen said. "I killed one of them last night."

"That was the fella in the saloon?" one of the men asked.

"Yeah."

"I seen that happen. I was wonderin' why you was bracing him so. Now I guess I know."

"So, you still ain't told us how many there are," one of the others said.

"There's only six of 'em," Pardeen said. "And that's countin' both Jensen and his wife."

"Jensen?" someone said. "That wouldn't be a fella they call Smoke Jensen, would it?"

Pardeen stared at the questioner for a moment before he answered.

"You don't be worryin' about that," he said. "I'll take care of Mr. Smoke Jensen. And his wife," he added.

"So what you are sayin' is, while you're takin' care of Jensen, we're to take care of the rest?"

"Yes. That would be nine of you, and four of them."

"For one hundred dollars?"

"Yes."

"Hell, sounds like easy money to me."

"Me too," one of the others said.

"Count me in."

"What if the sheriff and his deputy get involved?" one of the men asked.

"Are you talking about Dawson and Titus?" one of the others asked. "Ha! If they think there's likely to be shooting, they'll both be hidin' under a bed somewhere. You don't have to worry about them."

"McHenry," Pardeen said. "How about wandering back up into town to see what you can find out?"

"All right," McHenry said.

* * *

Leaving the undertaker's establishment, Smoke, Sally, Pearlie, Cal, Mike, and Jules walked down to the sheriff's office to find out what they could about the murder of Billy Cantrell, and to report the theft of their herd. Sheriff Dawson met them outside on the boardwalk.

"What can I do for you?" Dawson asked.

"Well, to start with, you can arrest the man who killed Billy Cantrell," Smoke said. "Then you can serve a warrant on the man who killed Cephus Malone and stole my cattle."

"Hold on there," Dawson said. "What do you mean the man who killed Cephus Malone? How do you know who killed Cephus Malone?"

"I know because yesterday I sold my cattle to a man who claimed to be Cephus Malone. Obviously, he wasn't Malone since Malone was already dead."

"His name is Trent Williams," Sheriff Dawson said.

"What? You already know about this?"

"You are talking about the man whose cattle are in the feeder lot right now?"

"Yes," Smoke said. "Only they aren't his cows, they are my cows."

"Well, seems to me like that is a civil dispute. I don't get involved in civil disputes."

"You call murder a civil dispute?" Smoke asked incredulously.

"Murder? Well, now, that's a serious accusation," Dawson said. "You have no proof of that, though I admit it does look suspicious."

"Suspicious?" Smoke replied. "Sheriff, how much evidence do you need? I have a receipt, signed by a man who claims to be Cephus Malone. Only it turns out that he isn't Cephus Malone. That can only mean that he murdered Cephus Malone in order to get control of my cattle. I also think it is suspicious that Quince Pardeen, the man who murdered Billy Cantrell, has been seen down at the feeder lot this morning."

Sheriff Dawson shook his head. "Titus and I both talked to the eyewitnesses; they all said that your man drew first."

"Are you serious? Billy was forced into it," Smoke said. "I talked to those same witnesses, Sheriff, and they said that Pardeen told Billy he was going to kill him at the count of three—then he began counting."

"That was just a bluff. If your man had not drawn his pistol and then Pardeen killed him, it would have been murder."

"And Billy would have still been dead," Smoke said.

"Yes, well, the fact is, your man did draw first," the sheriff said. "And as long as all the witnesses swear to what they saw, no charges can be made."

"What about the fact that Pardeen and whoever he is with are about to steal my cattle?"

Dawson ran his hand through his hair, clearly agitated by the way the discussion was going.

The sheriff pointed toward the cow pens. "Maybe you don't know it, mister, but there are ten men down there, in addition to Pardeen. I've only got one deputy."

"So you have looked into it," Smoke said. "You do know that Williams is down there with my cattle."

"Yeah, I've looked into it," Dawson replied. "Like I said, it is suspicious. But I have no proof that anything illegal has happened."

"And you aren't going to get proof unless you go down there and ask a few questions," Smoke said.

Dawson shook his head. "Maybe you don't know this, but the men down there aren't just cowboys. They are a bad lot, all of them. More than half of them have been in jail at one time or another for robbery, assault, you name it."

"They aren't regular cowboys?"

"No."

"Then that is more evidence, isn't it? Sheriff, they are stealing my herd right before your eyes."

"Well, what do you want me to do about it? I told you, there's just me and Titus."

"Deputize us," Smoke said, taking in the others with a sweep of his hand. "We'll take care of the situation ourselves."

"I don't know that I can do that."

"Of course you can do it," Smoke said. "In fact, I am already a deputy back in Big Rock. All you have to do is grant me a professional courtesy as a visiting lawman. It's done all the time."

"All right, all right," Sheriff Dawson said. "You're deputized. Do what you feel must be done. But don't count on any help from either me or my deputy."

"At this point, Sheriff, you and your deputy would just get in our way," Smoke said.

Chapter Twenty-four

Jarred McHenry came back to the feeder lot to report to Williams and Pardeen on what he had just learned.

"The sheriff has deputized Smoke Jensen and the others," he said.

"Well, now, this is getting interesting," Pardeen said. They were holding the conversation just outside the fence of the feeder lot, and the air was redolent with the pungent smell of manure. Nearby was a stable where a half-dozen buckboards and wagons were parked and waiting to be rented. Someone from the stable was working on the wheel of one of the wagons, totally unaware of the impending showdown.

"We about to have us a shoot-out, ain't we?" one of the men asked, his voice betraying his nervousness over the prospect.

"I sure as hell hope so," Pardeen said.

"What do you mean, you hope so?"

"The stage has been set for me'n Smoke Jensen to

have us a meeting for a long time now," Pardeen said. "And this is as good a time and place as any."

"Well, I don't mind telling you boys, this isn't what I wanted," Williams said. He sighed. "But I'm afraid the fat is in the fire now."

Suddenly, and inexplicably, Jarred laughed.

"What it is? What are you laughin' at?" one of the others asked.

"Devil's food cake," Jarred said.

"What?"

"Devil's food cake," Jarred repeated. "You think it really is devil's food? What I'm askin' is, come supper time in hell tonight, you think they'll serve devil's food cake?"

One of the others shook his head. "Jarred, you are dumber than a cow turd."

They were quiet for a moment. Then Jarred growled, "We goin' to stand around 'n talk all day? Or are we goin' to get this thing done?"

"You're anxious, are you?" Pardeen asked.

"Some," Jarred admitted. "If we're goin' to do this, let's get it done." He started toward town and some of the others began to follow.

"Wait," Williams called. The others turned to look at him.

"Didn't you say they were coming to us?"

"Yeah, that's what it sounded like," Jarred said.

"Then let's make them come to us. That way, we'll have the advantage. And when it's over, there won't be no question about it bein' murder or anything."

"Yeah, good idea," Pardeen said. "Hey, you," he called to the man who was working on the wagon wheel.

The man looked over toward Pardeen. "You talkin' to me?"

"Yeah, you," Pardeen repeated. "Come here."

Responding to the call, the man got up and walked over toward them, wiping his hands with a rag he carried in his back pocket.

"What's your name?" Pardeen asked.

"The name is Cooksie. I own this place." He pointed to the livery. "You need to board your horse, or rent a horse or a wagon?"

"Nah," Pardeen said. As he was talking, he took out his pistol and began checking the loads in the cylinder. Seeing this, the others did the same thing. "We need you to do something for us."

The expression on Cooksie's face reflected some anxiousness over seeing everyone suddenly check their pistols.

"What's going on here? What are you men about to do?"

"We're about to conduct a prayer meetin'," Pardeen said, and the others laughed.

"Yeah, a prayer meetin'," Jarred repeated with a low laugh.

"What?" Cooksie asked.

"Never you mind what we're about to do," Pardeen said. "You just go on down to the sheriff's office and tell them new deputies he just swore in that we're down here waitin' for 'em."

"You're about to get into a gunfight here, aren't you?" Cooksie asked.

"That's right."

Cooksie shook his head. "You boys don't really want to do this," he said, his voice high-pitched and nervous.

"Yeah," Pardeen said, looking pointedly at him. "We do. Now, you go down there and get them like we said. Then you stay the hell out of the way."

Smoke and the others were still standing in front of the sheriff's office, discussing the best way to deal with the situation at hand, when Cooksie came up to them.

"Is the sheriff and his new deputies in the office?" the stable owner asked.

"We're his new deputies," Smoke replied.

"You ain't wearin' no stars."

"We don't need any stars," Smoke said. "But if you doubt we are deputies, you can check with the sheriff. He is just inside."

"No, that's all right. Now that I think about it, I reckon you're the ones they was talkin' about anyway. They said new deputies."

"Who said it?"

"Well, the only ones I know are Jarred McHenry, Abner Coleman, Whizzer Magee, Lou Smith, the Parker brothers, and maybe three or four more with 'em."

"What about them?" Smoke asked.

"Well, sir, I don't rightly know what this is all about, but they said to tell you that they are down at the feeder lot waitin' for you."

"Are they now?" Smoke asked.

"Yes, sir. And that fella Pardeen? He's with them too."

Pearlie grinned broadly. "Pardeen too? Well, what

do you know, Smoke?" he said. "We must've been livin' right. Christmas is comin' early this year."

"Pardeen belongs to me," Smoke said.

"Dead is dead," Mike said. "The son of a bitch killed Billy, so I don't care who kills him, as long as he's dead." Then, realizing that Sally had overheard him swear, Mike apologized.

"Sorry 'bout usin' them words like that, Miz Sally."

"No need to apologize, Mike," Sally replied. "Pardeen is a son of a bitch."

Jules laughed. Then he and the others checked their guns and the loads, then replaced the weapons loosely in their holsters.

"A shoot-out!" Cooksie shouted then, running down the street. "Stay off the streets, ever'body, there's going to be a shoot-out!"

Cooksie's shouts were picked up by others, but what he intended to be a warning had just the opposite effect. People began pouring out into the street from all the stores and houses. What they saw was five men and a woman walking resolutely toward this rendevous with destiny. What they didn't see was one ounce of emotion in any of the faces of the six.

When they looked back toward the eleven the six would be facing, though, they saw faces that reflected the gamut of emotion, from resignation to fear to excitement. On Quince Pardeen's face was an expression of detachment.

Sheriff Dawson suddenly appeared, stepping out into the street. He held his hand up to stop Smoke and the others.

"Stop right there," he called. "I don't intend to have a bloodbath in my town."

"You want to go down there and arrest them, Sheriff?" Smoke asked.

Dawson looked at Smoke and the others for a moment. Then, shaking his head, he stepped back out of the street. "No," he said. "You folks are on your own now. I wash my hands of it."

Sally chuckled. "Why not?" she asked. "It worked for Pontius Pilate."

As Smoke, Sally, Pearlie, Cal, Mike, and Jules approached, Williams, Pardeen, and the others stepped out of the livery barn and stood facing them. The two groups stood no more than ten feet apart. Williams, Pardeen, McHenry, and the others were now boxed in, for the feeder lot was behind them, the livery barn on one side, and a house on the other. Smoke, Sally, Pearlie, Cal, Mike, and Jules were standing out in the open close to the street.

There was a moment of silence as the two parties confronted each other.

"Williams, this doesn't have to happen. You and your men lay your guns on the ground, then walk away and leave my cattle here, and this will all be over," Smoke said.

"Oh, it has to happen," Pardeen said. "Yes, sir, it has to happen." Pardeen allowed a snide smile to spread across his face.

"Pardeen, you aren't a part of this offer. I was talking to Williams," Smoke said. "You killed Billy, so I'm going to kill you, no matter what Williams does."

The smile left Pardeen's face. Then he made the

first move, reaching for and pulling his .45 so fast that to some of the bystanders, it appeared as if he had been holding the gun all along.

"No!" Williams suddenly shouted. He took a couple of hesitant steps backward. "No, wait! We'll be killed!" Williams turned and ran through the open door of the barn behind them. "No, don't shoot us, don't shoot us!" he begged.

"Williams, you lily-livered coward!" Jarred McHenry shouted.

Although Pardeen had drawn first, the first shot came from Smoke's gun. He fired and the recoil kicked his hand up. Pardeen called out in pain, then grabbed his stomach as blood spilled between his fingers. But even as Pardeen went down, Magee shot at Smoke but missed. Sally shot Magee, hitting him in the chest. Smith fired at Mike as Pearlie fired at Coleman, hitting him between the eyes.

After that, guns began to roar in rapid succession. Both Parkers went down, then three other gunmen, leaving only Smith and McHenry. Smoke killed Smith, while a bullet from Cal's pistol tore through McHenry's right hand. Another hit him in the chest.

McHenry staggered back against a window of the vacant house, then slid slowly to the ground. He switched his pistol to his left hand. Sitting there on the ground with his legs crossed, and resting his pistol on his shattered arm, he shot with his left hand. His bullet hit Sally in the arm, spinning her around. Smoke shot McHenry again, this time in the forehead, knocking him back against the house.

"Sally, are you all right?" Smoke shouted.

"Yes," Sally answered. "It's not much more than a nick."

Suddenly, out of the corner of her eye, Sally saw Williams reappear in the door of the barn, holding a rifle. Williams fired, and Mike went down. Smoke, Pearlie, and Cal all fired at the same time and their bullets slammed into Williams's chest. He stumbled out into the street and lurched over toward the people who had crowded around to watch. Unable to shoot for fear of hitting someone in the crowd, Smoke held his fire.

Williams grabbed onto the post that supported the roof over the boot repair shop. He coughed once and blood bubbled from his lips; then he fell back, dead in the dirt.

Of all those involved in the fight, not one of the gunmen with Williams was left alive. Smoke, Pearlie, Cal, and Jules were unscathed. Sally had a bullet in her arm, and Mike was dead.

"Mike!" Sally shouted. "Oh, Smoke, they got Mike."

Smoke went over to look down at the young man, then shook his head sadly.

The fight had been witnessed by scores of people, and now Smoke could see them moving closer to look at the bodies of the slain. None of the townspeople said anything. Their looks weren't of pity, or compassion, or even hate. Most were of morbid curiosity, as if they were experiencing a sensual pleasure from being so close to death while themselves avoiding it.

"Did you ever seen anythin' like this?" someone asked.

"Never," another answered.

"It was over in a hurry, wasn't it?" someone asked.

"Thirty-seven seconds," another said, holding a watch in his hand. "I timed it."

One of them came over to look down at Mike.

"Get away from him," Smoke said.

"I don't mean nothin' by it, mister. I'm just goin' to look."

"I said get away!" Smoke shouted, pulling his pistol and pointing it at the curious townsman. The citizen backed away quickly, holding his hands up.

Two days later, Smoke, Sally, Pearlie, Cal, and Jules were standing on the platform at the depot, waiting for the train that would take them back home. Sally had been treated by a doctor and her arm was in a sling. The bodies of Mike and Billy were in coffins, and would be put on the baggage car of the same train. The cattle were gone, and Smoke had a certified bank draft for $97,250.00, the amount he and Colin Abernathy agreed upon after Abernathy came personally to take delivery of the cattle. They heard the sound of the train in the distance.

"Here it comes," Jules said excitedly.

"Are you anxious to get home?" Sally asked.

"Yes, ma'am," Jules said. "I'll be glad to give this money to Ma and Pa. Plus," he added with a broad grin, "this here will be the first time I ever rode on a train."

The smile left his lips. "It's the first time either Billy or Mike ever rode on a train too. They was really lookin' forward to it."

Sheriff Dawson came up to them then. "I thought

you might like to know that an inquest was held, and it was found that the shootin' and killin' was all justified," he said.

Smoke just nodded, but said nothing.

Dawson smiled. "And you'll be goin' home with almost one hundred thousand dollars. I reckon this is one trip you'll be real glad you made."

"Oh, yeah, I'm just all broke out with joy," Smoke replied.

"You don't sound all that happy."

"Mike, Billy, Hank, Andy, LeRoy, and Dooley," Smoke said.

"I don't understand."

"No," Smoke said. "You wouldn't."

The train pulled into the station then, chugging, clanging, spewing steam and dripping glowing embers onto the track bed.

"Come on, Sally," Smoke said. "Let's go home."

J. A. Johnstone on William W. Johnstone
"When the Truth Becomes Legend"

William W. Johnstone was born in southern Missouri, the youngest of four children. He was raised with strong moral and family values by his minister father, and tutored by his schoolteacher mother. Despite this, he quit school at age fifteen.

"I have the highest respect for education," he says, "but such is the folly of youth, and wanting to see the world beyond the four walls and the blackboard." True to this vow, Bill attempted to enlist in the French Foreign Legion ("I saw Gary Cooper in *Beau Geste* when I was a kid and I thought the French Foreign Legion would be fun") but was rejected, thankfully, for being underage. Instead, he joined a traveling carnival and did all kinds of odd jobs. It was listening to the veteran carny folk, some of whom had been on the circuit since the late 1800s, telling amazing tales about their experiences which planted the storytelling seed in Bill's imagination.

"They were honest people, despite the bad reputation traveling carny shows had back then," Bill remembers. "Of course, there were exceptions. There was one guy named Picky, who got that name because he was a master pickpocket. He could steal a man's socks right off his feet without him knowing. Believe me, Picky got us chased out of more than a few towns."

After a few months of this grueling existence, Bill returned home and finished high school. Next came stints as a deputy sheriff in the Tallulah, LA. Sheriff's Department, followed by a hitch in the U.S. Army. Then he began a career in radio broadcasting at KTLD in Tallulah, Louisiana, that would last sixteen years. It was here that he fine-tuned his storytelling skills. He turned to writing in 1970, but it wouldn't be until 1979 until his first novel, *The Devil's Kiss*, was published. Thus began the full-time writing career of William W. Johnstone. He wrote horror (*The Uninvited*), thrillers (*The Last of the Dog Team*), even a romance novel or two. Then, in February 1983, *Out of the Ashes* was published. Searching for his missing family in the aftermath of a post-apocalyptic America, rebel mercenary and patriot Ben Raines is united with the civilians of the Resistance forces and moves to the forefront of a revolution for the nation's future.

Out of the Ashes was a smash. The series would continue for the next twenty years, winning Bill three generations of fans all over the world. The series was often imitated but never duplicated. "We all tried to copy *The Ashes* series," said one publishing executive, "but Bill's uncanny ability, both then and now, to predict in which direction the political winds were blowing, brought a dead-on timeliness to the table no one else could capture." *The Ashes* series would end its run with more than thirty-four books and twenty million copies in print, making it one of the most successful men's action series in American book publishing. (*The Ashes* series also, Bill notes with a touch of pride, got him on the FBI's Watch List for its less than flattering portrayal of spineless politicians and the growing power of big government over our lives, among other things. "In that respect," says collaborator J. A. Johnstone, "Bill was years ahead of his time.")

Always steps ahead of the political curve, Bill's recent thrillers, written with J. A. Johnstone, include *Vengeance Is Mine, Invasion USA, Border War, Jackknife, Remember the Alamo, Home Invasion, Phoenix Rising, The Blood of Patriots, The Bleeding Edge,* and the upcoming *Suicide Mission.*

It is with the Western, though, that Bill found his greatest success and propelled him onto both the *USA Today* and *New York Times* bestseller lists.

Bill's western series, co-authored by J. A. Johnstone, include *The Mountain Man, Matt Jensen the Last Mountain Man, Preacher, The Family Jensen, Luke Jensen Bounty Hunter, Eagles, MacCallister* (an *Eagles* spinoff), *Sidewinders, The Brothers O'Brien, Sixkiller, Blood Bond, The Last Gunfighter,* and the upcoming new series *Flintlock* and *The Trail West.* Coming in May 2013 is the hardcover western *Butch Cassidy, The Lost Years.*

"The Western," Bill says, "is one of the few true art forms that is one hundred percent American. I liken the Western as America's version of England's Arthurian legends, like the Knights of the Round Table or Robin Hood and his Merry Men. Starting with the 1902 publication of *The Virginian* by Owen Wister, and followed by the greats like Zane Grey, Max Brand, Ernest Haycox, and of course Louis L'Amour, the Western has helped to shape define the cultural landscape of America.

"I'm no goggle-eyed college academic, so when my fans ask me why the Western is as popular now as it was a century ago, I don't offer a 200-page thesis. Instead, I can only offer this: The Western is honest. In this great country, which is suffering under the yoke of political correctness, the Western harks back to an era when justice was sure and swift. Steal a man's horse, rustle his cattle, rob a bank, a stagecoach, or a train, you were hunted down and fitted with a hangman's noose. One size fit all.

"Sure, we westerners are prone to a little embellishment and exaggeration and, I admit it, occasionally play a little fast and loose with the facts. But we do so for a very good reason—to enhance the enjoyment of readers.

"It was Owen Wister, in *The Virginian* who first coined the phrase '*When you call me that, smile.*' Legend has it that Wister actually heard those words spoken by a deputy sheriff in Medicine Bow, Wyoming, when another poker player called him a son-of-a-bitch.

"Did it really happen, or is it one of those myths that have passed down from one generation to the next? I honestly don't know. But there's a line in one of my favorite Westerns of all time, The Man who Shot Liberty Valance, where the newspaper editor tells the young reporter, 'When the truth becomes legend, print the legend.'

"These are the words I live by."

TURN THE PAGE FOR AN EXCITING PREVIEW

**Duff MacCallister is heir to a fierce family
of fighting Scotsmen. In a new land, in the
extraordinary new saga by bestselling authors
William W. Johnstone and J. A. Johnstone,
Duff gives new meaning to the words** *without mercy*

CUT OFF THE HEAD—THE BEAST WILL DIE.

The Indians around Fort Laramie, Wyoming, are
peaceful. Or so it has seemed—until killers ambush
a detail of U.S. soldiers and an officer's wife.
One man, an ambitious cavalry officer, flees the
carnage and lives to tell the story—his own story,
an outright lie. When Duff MacCallister and a few
brave men go after the attackers, they discover the
officer's wife is very much alive and at the cold,
merciless hands of the sadistic warrior Yellow Hawk.
To free the woman, Duff touches off a fierce battle.
And when he finds himself surrounded by
the blood-crazed renegades, MacCallister knows
there is only one way out—by going after
Yellow Hawk himself . . .

MacCallister: The Eagles Legacy
DRY GULCH AMBUSH

by
USA TODAY BESTSELLING AUTHOR
WILLIAM W. JOHNSTONE
with J. A. Johnstone

On sale now, wherever Pinnacle Books are sold!

Prologue

Argonne Forest, October 3, 1918

The American attack had begun at 5:30 a.m. on September 26, but the results were less than hoped. The Fifth and Third Corps were successful, but the 79th Division failed to capture the town of Montfaucon, and the 28th Division was stopped cold by formidable German resistance. The 91st Division was forced out of the village of Épinonville, and the 37th Division failed in its attempt to advance at d'Argonne. The result was an attack that ground to a halt, and for the next two days the American troops dug in, and waited for orders for the next move.

The entrenched infantrymen became passive participants as the Allied and German artillery continued to exchange fire. As they passed overhead, the shells from the French 75's, and the American 155 heavy guns would make a sound similar to that of an unattached railroad car rolling down a track. That made it easy to tell the outgoing fire from the incoming fire, because the arming bands on the

German 105 howitzer shells would emit a high-pitched, bansheelike whistle.

"Incoming!" someone yelled, though the warning wasn't necessary as everyone could hear the shell come screaming in. The intensity of the whistle would also give some indication as to how far away the shell would be, and Duff Tavish MacCallister, Jr., who had his Springfield '03 rifle disassembled and spread on a sheet of canvas before him, didn't even bother to duck.

The impact was some two hundred yards away, and Tavish, as he was called, heard the heavy thump of the explosion, then a whirring sound of the shrapnel that spread out within the hundred-foot bursting radius of the shell. He was cleaning his rifle, and he picked up the barrel and looked down inside. That was when his platoon leader, Lieutenant Fillion, arrived in an olive drab, open body Dodge touring car.

Tavish stood up and smiled, saluting the lieutenant when he stepped out of the car.

"Well now, Lieutenant, when did you get so high-falutin' that you rated a car like that?"

"It's not me, Sergeant. It's you. General Pershing wants to speak with you, and he sent his car."

"Wait a minute. The general wants to talk to me?"

"He wants to speak with Sergeant Duff Tavish MacCallister, Jr., personally, and he emphasized junior. I'm to take you to him."

"All right, sir," Tavish said. "Give me a moment to put my rifle together."

It took but a moment to reassemble the rifle, and then Tavish followed the lieutenant back to the car.

"Sergeant MacCallister, do you know the general?" Lieutenant Fillion asked.

"No, sir. Oh, I mean I recognize him when I see him, but you sure couldn't say that I know him. Do you know why he wants to see me?"

"I don't have the slightest idea," Fillion said. "I thought perhaps you would know."

"I'm afraid not, Lieutenant."

When the car arrived at the Château de Chaumont, Tavish was taken up to the castle. A guard saluted Lieutenant Fillion, who returned the salute.

"Sergeant, would you clear your weapon please?" the guard asked.

Tavish operated the bolt several times until the five .30-caliber rounds had been ejected. He left the bolt open, and the guard nodded, indicating that he could go in.

Inside the castle was a great room that was filled with tables manned by soldiers. In one corner of the room was a field telephone switchboard, and the operator was busily pulling and connecting cords. Attached to the back wall was a large map, marked with pins, and pieces of paper. There were at least four staff officers studying the map, one of whom was General John J. Pershing.

"Wait here, Sergeant," Lieutenant Fillion ordered.

"Yes, sir," Tavish said.

Fillion spoke to a major, who approached a colonel, who was one of the staff officers. The colonel looked back at Tavish, nodded, and then spoke to General Pershing. Pershing nodded, and then approached

Sergeant MacCallister and Lieutenant Fillion, with a broad smile spread across his face.

Both Tavish and Lieutenant Fillion came to attention and saluted him.

"At ease, at ease," Pershing said easily, returning the salute, and then offering his hand to Tavish.

"Sergeant, would your father be a big, ugly Scotsman who owns a ranch just outside Chugwater, Wyoming, called Sky Meadow?"

Tavish smiled. "I wouldn't call him ugly, General. But he is a big Scotsman who owns Sky Meadow."

"I thought so. The name, Duff Tavish MacCallister, Jr. gave me a hint. Then, when I checked your service file and saw that you had fired the maximum score on the KD range for rifle, I knew it had to be you. I'm a pretty good shot myself. Did you know that?"

"No, sir, though, as a general, I would expect you to be good at just about anything you attempted."

Pershing laughed out loud. "Spoken like a true diplomat. But I'm talking about when I was a lieutenant. I was rated second in pistol, and fifth in rifle, out of all soldiers in the entire U.S. Army. That's pretty good, wouldn't you say?"

"Yes, sir, I would say that's damn g . . . that is, I mean, very good, sir."

Pershing laughed again. "Damn good describes it, I would say."

"Yes, sir."

"I see you brought your rifle with you."

"Yes, sir, but it's cleared, sir," MacCallister said.

"Yes, your bolt is open and I can see that. Come out back with me. Major Purcell, the little demonstration

I asked you to arrange a bit earlier. Did you take care of setting things up?"

"Yes, General, I did."

"Good. Gentlemen, I invite you all out back. Sergeant MacCallister is going to put on a display of marksmanship, the likes of which none of you have ever seen. Sergeant MacCallister, are you ready?"

"I beg your pardon, sir, but I'm not sure what this is all about," Tavish said with a puzzled expression on his face.

"I'll tell you what I'm talking about, Sergeant. I'm setting you up," General Pershing said. "I'm going to have you attempt a very difficult shot. And I'm putting pressure on you, by having as big an audience as I can arrange. You see, it is important that you have pressure, even if it is simulated pressure. Because if you miss this shot now, you will have embarrassed yourself, me, your company, and your father."

"My dad?"

"I'll get to that later. In the meantime, if you can make this shot, and Sergeant MacCallister, I sincerely hope that you can make it, then I'm going to have a very special assignment for you—an assignment that could well be the means of ending this war. Are you game to try?"

"Yes, sir," Tavish said.

"I never doubted for a minute. Gentlemen," he said to the officers who were still gathered around. "Let's go out back."

Tavish followed General Pershing and half a dozen of his staff officers outside to the walled-in grounds behind the castle. He looked around once they were there, and saw a table some distance away. Sitting on the table was a wine bottle, and sticking out the top of the wine bottle was a candle. A tiny flame was perched, motionless, on top of the candle.

"I imagine you are wondering about the candle," General Pershing said.

"Yes, sir, I am," Tavish admitted.

"How far away is that candle, Major Purcell?"

"It is exactly two hundred and eighty-seven yards, General," the major replied.

"There's your range, Sergeant. Two hundred and eighty-seven yards. And, because we are inside the walled grounds of the castle, you have no wind to worry about. It should be an easy shot."

"You want me to shoot the bottle from here, General?"

"Heavens no, Sergeant. I want you to extinguish the flame, without harm to the candle or the bottle."

"What the hell?" someone in the group said. "Nobody can do that."

"I don't know, I bet a really good shot could," another said.

"Gentlemen, I am betting that the sergeant can do it," General Pershing said. "And I will personally cover up to twenty-five bets, as long as none of them are over a dollar."

"You've got yourself a bet, General," a colonel said.

"I want some of that, too," another officer said.

"Major Purcell, will you hold the bets, please?" General Pershing asked.

"Yes, sir, General," Purcell answered.

Pershing looked up at Tavish and smiled.

"There you go, Sergeant. There's a little more pressure on you now. If you don't make the shot, you are going to cost me twenty-five dollars. And I don't like losing money."

A few of the officers laughed.

"Are you getting nervous, Sergeant?" General Pershing asked.

"No, sir," Tavish said.

"No? Why not?"

"Because I'll make the shot, General," Tavish said easily, confidently.

"Well, Sergeant, that's a little arrogant, don't you think?" a captain asked, with a derisive tone in his voice.

General Pershing held out his hand. "It isn't arrogance at all, Captain, it's confidence," he said. Then, stepping back, he held his hand out in a sweeping motion. "Sergeant MacCallister, the stage is yours."

"Thank you, General," Tavish said. He took a single round from the ammunition pouch on his web belt, rubbed the point of it against the side of his nose, then put it into the chamber of the rifle, and closed the bolt.

"Don't get nervous now, Sergeant," one of the officers said.

Tavish paid no attention to the kibitzer. Instead, he raised the rifle to his shoulder, leaned his head down against the stock, and set up his sight-picture between the rear and front sights. He rested the nonflickering flame just on top of the front sight, took in a breath, let half of it out, then held it, and slowly began squeezing the trigger.

The rifle boomed, and the recoil rocked the end of the barrel up, but nobody was looking at the rifle. They were looking at the candle flame, which was instantly snuffed.

The crowd cheered and applauded, even those who had bet and lost a dollar.

General Pershing collected the money, and then gave all of it to Lieutenant Fillion. "Lieutenant, you and Sergeant MacCallister are in the same company, are you not?"

"Yes, sir, A company, 1st Battalion, 38th Regiment of the Third Infantry Division."

"I believe the commanding officer of that company is Captain Royal?" Pershing asked.

"Yes, sir."

"Give him this money and tell him to use it to throw a party for his company the next time they are off the line."

"Yes, sir!" Fillion said with a broad smile.

"Sergeant, come with me."

Not only Tavish, but Lieutenant Fillion and Major Purcell, who was General Pershing's adjutant, started with him as well.

"No, gentlemen," Pershing said, holding out his hand to stop them. "I want to speak to the sergeant alone."

Tavish went back into the castle with Pershing, through the great room, and to a smaller room off the great room. There, Pershing poured two glasses of wine and handed one glass to Tavish. "To fallen comrades," he said, holding his glass out, inviting a toast.

"To fallen comrades," Tavish repeated.

"Before I tell you what task I have in mind, I want to talk to you a bit about your father . . . about my personal encounter with him, and also what I learned about him from Colonel Gibbon, who was once my commanding officer. It might be a rather long story, if you have the patience to hear me out."

"General, I'll stay here as long as it takes, and feel honored to do so," Tavish replied.

Pershing opened a silver cigarette case, offered one to Tavish, and when he declined, lit one for himself before he continued.

"It all began in Chugwater, Wyoming, in 1888."

Chapter One

Chugwater, Wyoming, July 4, 1888

Chugwater, Wyoming, July 4, 1888

There was a banner that stretched all the way across First Street from Bob Guthrie's Lumber Supply to Fred Matthews' Warehouse. The banner read:

HAPPY 112TH BIRTHDAY
TO THE UNITED STATES OF AMERICA
FROM THE PEOPLE OF CHUGWATER, WYOMING

The entire town was turned out for the Independence Day celebration, with First Street turned into a midway of sorts. On each side of the street, the ladies from town and from the surrounding farms and ranches were manning booths where they sold everything from home-canned tomatoes, to baked goods, to quilts. A traveling medicine man had set up his operation at the far end of the street and the barker was doing a brisk business.

The most important event of the day, however, was the big shooting contest, and after two hours of participation, the field had been narrowed down to four people: Elmer Gleason, Biff Johnson, a visiting U.S. Army lieutenant named John Pershing, and Duff MacCallister.

Elmer Gleason was Duff's ranch foreman. Biff Johnson, who was one of Duff's closest friends, owned Fiddler's Green Saloon. Biff, who had served with Lieutenant Pershing during the Apache campaigns in New Mexico and Arizona, was well aware of the young officer's marksmanship, and had invited him to participate in the shooting match. The competition among the four men, though spirited, was friendly.

For several minutes, as bets were made and covered, the four shooters matched each other shot for shot, with no apparent separation between them.

Rarely had such shooting been seen anywhere, and as word spread through the town of the amazing accuracy shown by the four shooters, the ladies who were manning the booths, and then even the medicine show barker, closed down their own operations so they could witness the magnificent marksmanship that was on display here today.

Each of the shooters had their own supporters, and Duff's biggest supporter was Meagan Parker, owner of the Ladies' Emporium, a dress shop which was next door to Fiddler's Green.

Finally the judges conferred, and then decided to move the target farther away. They did that, and the four men stayed neck and neck until they were shooting from two hundred yards. At the two hundred yard mark, Biff Johnson fell out of the contest, one of his bullets striking three-fourths of the way in, and one-fourth of the way out of the bull's-eye.

There were no other dropouts until the three hundred yard range, when Elmer dropped out. Now, only Duff and Lieutenant Pershing remained.

"We're out of targets. What are we going to do now?"

"Light a candle," Duff suggested. "We'll use that as the target." A candle was lit, and Lieutenant Pershing fired first. The flame flickered at the pass of the bullet, but didn't go out.

"Hit," one of the judges said, observing the candle through a pair of field glasses.

"T'was nae a hit," Duff said.

"Sure it was," the judge said. "I saw the flame flicker."

"T'was but the wind of the passing bullet, t'was nae a hit. If it had been a hit, the candle would have gone out."

Pershing laughed. "There is no way you are going to snuff a candle from three hundred yards. Not unless you hit the candle. And we aren't shooting at the candle, we're shooting at the flame."

"I can do it," Duff said, matter-of-factly.

"If you can put the flame out from here, Mr. MacCallister, I'll hold that you're a better man than I am," Pershing said.

"I tell you what," Duff said. "If I can nae snuff the candle with this shot, I'll be declarin' you the winner. If I snuff it, I'm the winner."

"You don't have to that, Mr. MacCallister," Pershing said. "You're putting it all on the line with one shot."

"Aye, but there's other things to do today than stand here shooting until nightfall. And as good as you are, 'tis likely to come down to that."

"I'll say there's other things to do, today," Meagan said. "You'll not be forgetting there's a dance tonight, Duff MacCallister."

"Sure 'n how would I be forgettin' the dance, now, when I'll be takin' the prettiest lady in Laramie County, aye, and in the whole territory of Wyoming."

Shortly after Duff MacCallister had arrived in Chugwater, eight men had come to kill him, and before it was over, all eight were lying dead in the street. Duff hadn't done it without help.

A man, who was on the roof of the Ladies' Emporium with a bead on Duff, was shot by Biff Johnson. Fred Matthews had tossed Duff a loaded revolver just in time, and Meagan Parker risked her own life to hold up a mirror that showed Duff where two men were lying in wait for him.

Meagan and Duff had maintained a "special" relationship ever since.

"Now, you're saying you are going to snuff the flame, without hitting the candle, is that right?" Pershing asked.

"Aye."

"All right, Mr. MacCallister," Pershing agreed. "If you can do that, you sure as hell deserve to win."

A buzz of excitement passed through the crowd as news of the arrangement moved quickly from mouth to mouth. The contest was to end, right here and right now, on one all-or-nothing shot.

All the contestants had been using the same rifle to

ensure fairness. That rifle, a 45- caliber Whitworth, was furnished by the marksmanship committee. The Whitworth had a long, heavy, octagon-shaped barrel of the type favored by Berdan's Sharpshooters during the Civil War. It was especially designed for accuracy.

Preparing for the shot, Duff poured in the powder, and then tapped a paper wad down to seal in the powder. Next, he used a bullet starter, which was a pistonlike arrangement that helped to seat the bullet, which was slightly larger than the diameter of the lands, but not quite as large as the diameter of the grooves. The end of the piston was shaped to fit the nose of the bullet. With a smart blow from the palm of his hand, Duff drove the bullet down into the barrel, engaging it in the rifling. He then used a ramrod to push the bullet down until it was properly seated.

With the loading ritual completed, Duff picked up a little dirt from the street and dropped it, watching the drift of the dust. Next, he rubbed a little dust on the site bead at the end of the rifle barrel. Then, using the sling to help him hold the rifle steady, he aimed at the tiny, flickering flame three hundred yards away.

"Now, don't be getting all nervous," Pershing teased, just as Duff started to aim. A few laughed.

"'Tis thankin' you I am for that kind word of encouragement," Duff replied with a smile.

Duff aimed again. He took a deep breath, let half of it out, and slowly began to squeeze the trigger.

The rifle boomed and rocked back against his shoulder. A great billow of gun smoke obscured his vision of the target for a moment, but he didn't have to see it. The reaction of the crowd told him what had happened, as they cheered and applauded his shot. When the smoke drifted away he saw that the candle was still standing, but the flame had been extinguished.

The crowd rushed toward Duff to congratulate him, Lieutenant Pershing being the first one to do so.

"Folks," Biff said. "I can't afford a beer for ever' one, but I will stand a free beer to all the lads who took part in this shootin' contest. Come on over to Fiddler's Green."

"Good man, Biff," one of the shooters who had dropped out much earlier said.

"Tell me, why do you call this place Fiddler's Green?" someone asked Biff, as all the shooters stood at the bar drinking their free beer.

"I call it Fiddler's Green because I'm a retired first sergeant. I served with the lieutenant here down in Arizona, when we were chasing Apache."

"He did more than serve with me," Lieutenant Pershing said. "Every young officer needs a noncommissioned officer who'll take him under the wing and teach him things he didn't learn at the Point. Sergeant Johnson did that for me."

"It was my pleasure, Lieutenant. Before I was with General Cook, I was with General Custer and the Seventh Cavalry," Biff replied.

"How lucky you are to have left before his fateful battle," one of the shooters who had dropped out earlier said.

"Oh, but I didn't leave. I went on that last scout with him."

"I don't understand. How is it, then, that you weren't killed?"

"I wasn't killed because I was in D troop with Benteen. We came up to save Reno, but we were too late to help Custer."

"Now you can see why he calls this place Fiddler's Green," Lieutenant Pershing said.

"No, I don't see at all."

"You want to tell this young man who wouldn't know 'Stable Call' from 'Mess Call,' Lieutenant?" Biff invited.

"I would be glad to," Pershing said. "It's something all cavalrymen believe. We believe that anyone who has ever heard the bugle call "Boots and Saddles" will, when they die, go to a cool, shady place by a stream of sweet water. There, they will see all the other cavalrymen who have gone before them, and they will greet those who come after them as they await the final judgment. That place is called Fiddler's Green."

"Do you really believe that?"

"Why not?" Pershing replied. "If heaven is whatever you want it to be, who is to say that cavalrymen wouldn't want to be with their own kind?"

"Biff," Duff said. "Would ye be for settin' up all these gentleman shooters with another round on me?"

"With pleasure," Biff replied as the shooters responded in gratitude.

* * *

Next door to the saloon, in her apartment over the Ladies' Emporium, Meagan Parker was getting ready for the dance that evening. Meagan not only owned the Ladies' Emporium, she actually designed and made many of the dresses that she sold there, and she had designed and made the dress she would be wearing tonight. It had a very low neckline, no sleeves, and a tight, uplifting bodice. It was a dress that would show off her figure to perfection. She picked it up, and then held it in front of her as she looked in the mirror. She smiled at the image.

"Mr. Duff Tavish MacCallister, are you ready for Meagan?—because she's ready for you," she said. Laying the dress down, she went back to fill the tub for her bath.

The dance was being held in the ballroom of the Dunn Hotel. The hotel was on the corner of Bowie Avenue and First Street. The Ladies Garden Club had turned the ballroom into a showplace of patriotism, stringing red, white, and blue bunting all about, and displaying lithographs of Washington, Adams, Jefferson, and Lincoln on the walls.

All was in readiness for the dance.

Chapter Two

Meagan arrived before Duff and, after receiving compliments from the other women about her dress, as well as admiring glances from the men, she walked over to one side to keep an eye open for Duff. She didn't have to wait long.

Duff arrived within a few minutes after Meagan and he was in his kilt. For most men, in fact, for just about any other man Meagan knew, wearing such a get-up would have elicited a great deal of derisive laughter. But Duff towered over every other man there, not only in his height, but in his raw power, broad shoulders, powerful arms, and muscular legs, shown off by what he was wearing.

While in Scotland, Duff had been a captain of the Black Watch Regiment. Because of that he had a complete Black Watch uniform, which consisted of a Glengarry hat, with the cap-badge of the Black Watch, Saltire, the Lion Rampant and the Crown with the motto *Nemo Me Impune Lacessit* (No one provokes me with impunity), a kilt of blue-and-green tartan, black waistcoat, an embossed leather sporran which he wore around his waist, knee-high stockings, and the *sgian dubh,* or ceremonial knife, which he wore tucked into the right kilt stocking, with only the pommel visible. During his time with the Black Watch Regiment, he had been awarded the Victoria Cross, Great Britain's highest award for bravery, which was awarded him for his intrepidity, above and beyond the call of duty during the battle of Tel-el-Kebir in Egypt.

Duff was also carrying his bagpipes, having been asked by Biff Johnson to bring them. Biff's wife was Scottish, and she had a fondness for the pipes.

Duff and Meagan saw each other at about the same time and, with a big smile, Duff came toward her.

"Sure m'girl, an 'tis a vision of loveliness ye be, like the beauty of a field that is arrayed in the rainbow colors of sparkling dew."

Meagan laughed. "I swear, Duff, if ever the needle breaks on my sewing machine, I'll call upon your tongue, for it can weave magic with your words."

Lieutenant Pershing, who was in his full dress uniform, came up to Duff and Meagan.

"I'm glad to see that I'm not the only one in uniform, though I must say, Duff, yours is a bit more grand than my own." Pershing pointed toward the Victoria Cross. "And with a most impressive decoration," he added.

"Thank you."

Pershing smiled at Meagan. "And I do hope, Miss, that you will take pity on a lonely soldier, far from home, and save at least one place on your hop card for me tonight."

"Hop card?" Meagan asked with a puzzled expression on her face.

"Forgive me, that is how we referred to them at the Academy. I mean, of course, your dance card."

Meagan looked at Duff and smiled. "Of course, I will save a dance for you," she said.

Pershing made a slight bow with his head, then walked away.

"I must say, lass, it seemed to me as if you were quick to oblige the leftenant's request."

"Why not?" Meagan replied. "It can't do harm to let you know that you aren't the only rooster in the chicken house."

Duff laughed out loud.

"Ladies and gents!" someone shouted, and looking toward the sound, they saw R.W. Guthrie. Guthrie was mayor of Chugwater, and the master of ceremonies for the ball.

Conversations ended as everyone looked toward the mayor.

"I want to say a few words," Guthrie began.

"Oh, for heaven's sake, Mayor, you was just elected last year. You got three more years yet, don't go politickin' on us now," someone shouted, and the others laughed.

"No politicking," Guthrie replied with a good natured smile. "All I want to say is welcome to our Fourth of July dance. Now, grab your partners, and let the dancin' commence!"

The music began then and the caller started to shout. The floor became a swirl of color as the dancers responded to the caller's commands, the brightly colored dresses with the skirts whirling out, the jewels in the women's hair, at their necks, or on their bodices, sparkling in the light.

In between the calls, the fiddler worked the bow up and down the fiddle, bending over, kicking out one leg, then the other as he played, his movements as entertaining as the music itself. Then, when his riff was over, the caller would step up again.

After a few more dances, Guthrie came over to ask Duff if he would play the pipes.

"You're sure 'tis not against the wishes of the band?"

Guthrie smiled. "There ain't none of 'em ever heard the pipes and they're curious about it."

Duff chuckled. "I've found that love of the pipes is an acquired taste. There are some, even my friend Elmer, that find no joy in the pipes."

"But there's them that do," Elmer said, having overheard the conversation. "So don't you go deprivin' them none because of me."

"You did bring your pipes," Guthrie said. "I assume that means you are willing to play them."

"Ha!" Meagan said. "I'd like to see someone try to stop him."

Duff smiled. "Ye've talked me into it. I'll play."

"What are you going to play? I'll let the folks know."

"Duff, please," Meagan said. She put her hand on his arm. "'The Skye Boat Song.'"

Meagan knew what nobody else at the dance knew. The woman Duff was to have married back in Scotland was named after this song. Her name was Skye McGregor. It was because Duff had killed the men who killed Skye that he was forced to leave Scotland.

Duff nodded, and then picking up his pipes got ready as Guthrie made the announcement to all who were present.

"Ladies and gents, Mr. Duff MacCallister has agreed to play a tune for us on his bagpipes."

"The song Mr. MacCallister has chosen is a song of Scotland, called 'The Skye Boat Song.' Duff, the platform is yours," Fred said.

There was a scattering of applause as Duff moved up onto the platform. He inflated his bag, and there was a tone from the drone and chanter as Duff began to play.

After he finished, several came up to thank him for playing. Meagan, especially, was moved.

"Thank you for playing that song, Duff," Meagan said. "I know it is difficult for you, but you play so beautifully, and with such feeling. I know that you think about her when you play it."

"Meagan, I'm sorry if . . ." Duff started.

"Don't apologize for still being in love with Skye," Meagan said. "It is one of the things that make you so wonderful in my eyes."

"Ladies and gents, form your squares!" the caller shouted, and once again the ballroom was filled with happy dancers.

When the dance broke up just after midnight, Duff, leading his horse, walked Meagan back up First Street to her home, which was located on the second floor above her business.

"I have a bottle of Scotch in my apartment, if you would like a drink before your long ride out to your ranch," Meagan invited.

Meagan led the way up the outside stairs, and then unlocked the door to her apartment. Just inside the door was a lantern and she lit it, filling the room with a golden bubble of light. She poured a glass of Scotch for Duff, and a glass of wine for herself.

Duff held out the glass. "Here's tae the heath, the hill and the heather, the bonnet, the plaid, the kilt and the feather."

Meagan touched the wineglass to his whiskey. "To the copper penny: May it soon grow into a dime and then swell into many."

"Ah, I'll make a Scotsman out of you yet," Duff said as they drank to their toasts.

"How are my cattle doing?" Meagan asked. She had recently invested some money in the ranch, so was now half owner of the outstanding herd of Black Angus cattle that populated the fields of Sky Meadow.

"My cattle are growing fat, while yours are growing thin," Duff replied.

"How do you know which cattle are mine and which are yours?"

"Because mine are fat and yours are thin," Duff said, laughing.

"You may be Scottish instead of Irish, but you do have a bit of the blarney in you," Meagan said.

"I've recently made a deal with the United States Army to furnish them with two thousand head of cattle for beef. We'll be getting forty dollars a head, so you're about to make forty thousand dollars," Duff said.

"Oh, my!" Meagan said. "Why am I wasting time making dresses? I should be a full-time rancher."

"And where, I ask you, would you be for getting a

frock as lovely as the one you are wearing tonight? And 'tis nae just you; think of the foine ladies of this town who would have no place to go to buy dresses for to please their husbands."

"Ha! Do you think ladies dress only to please their husbands?" Meagan asked.

"And others," Duff added, the expression on his face giving indication of how pleased he was with what Meagan was wearing.

They talked awhile longer, speaking of cattle and business, sharing stories from their past. Then Duff put down his glass.

"I suppose I'd best get back to the ranch," he said, starting toward the door. She went with him, and just before he left, he put his finger to her chin then turned her face toward his so that they were but a breath apart. "Take care, Meagan, that ye dinnae put yourself in danger. I dinnae ken what I would do if something should happen to ye."

"I am always careful," she said.

Still holding his finger under her chin, Duff leaned forward, closing the distance between them. He kissed her, not hard and demanding, but as soft as the brush of a butterfly's wing.

When the kiss ended, Meagan reached up to touch her own lips, and she held her fingers there for a long moment. She knew that the kiss had sealed no bargain, nor by it, had he made any promise to her. It was what it was—a light, meaningless kiss.

No, it wasn't meaningless. She had very strong feelings for Duff, and she knew that he had strong feelings for her. She knew, too, that it wasn't because his heart was too full of Skye. He told her that he had accepted her death, was ready to get on with his life, and she believed him. But what he wasn't ready to do was love another woman, then lose her as he had lost Skye. Meagan knew that was what he meant when he said, *"Take care, Meagan, that ye dinnae put yourself in danger. I dinnae ken what I would do if something should happen to ye."*

With a smile and a nod, Duff walked down the steps, mounted his horse, and rode away. Meagan stayed on her balcony watching him until he disappeared in the dark. Overhead a meteor streaked through the night sky.

SPECIAL BONUS!

**Turn the page
for Chapters Seven, Eight, Nine, and Ten of**

TRAIL OF THE MOUNTAIN MAN,

one of Smoke's earliest western adventures.

Trail of the Mountain Man

by William W. Johnstone,
today's most popular western storyteller

Chapter Seven

Leaving Bob Colby with Sally, Smoke saddled Drifter, the midnight-black, wolf-eyed stallion. Sally fixed him a poke of food and he stashed that in the saddlebags. He stuffed extra cartridges into a pocket of his saddlebags, and made sure his belt loops were filled. He checked his Henry repeating rifle and returned it to the saddle boot.

He kissed Sally and swung up into the saddle, thinking that it had certainly been a short homecoming. He looked at Bob, standing tall and very young beside Sally.

"You stay with Sally, Bob. Don't leave her. I'll square that with your Pa."

"Yes, sir, Mister Smoke," the boy replied.

"Can you shoot a short gun, Bob?"

"Yes, sir. But I'm better with a rifle."

"Sally will loan you a spare pistol. Wear it at all times."

"Yes, sir. What are you gonna do, Mister Smoke?"

"Try to organize the small farmers and ranchers,

Bob. If we don't band together, none of us will have a chance of coming out of this alive."

Smoke wheeled Drifter and rode into the timber without looking back.

He headed across the country, taking the shortest route to Colby's spread. During his ride, Smoke spotted men staking out claims on land that had been filed on by small farmers and ranchers.

Finally he had enough of that and reined up. He stared hard at a group of men. "You have permission to dig on this land?"

"This is open land," a man challenged him.

"Wrong, mister. You're on Colby land. Filed on legally and worked. Don't be here when I get back."

But the miners and would-be miners were not going to be that easy to run off. "They told us in Fontana that this here land was open and ready for the takin'."

"Who told you that?"

"The man at Beeker's store. Some others at a saloon. They said all you folks up here were squattin' illegal-like, that if we wanted to dig, we could; and that's what we're all aimin' to do."

So that was Tilden's plan. Or at least part of it, Smoke thought. He could not fault the men seeking gold. They were greedy, but not land-greedy. Dig the gold, and get out. And if a miner, usually unarmed, was hurt, shot in any attempt to run them off, marshals would probably be called in.

Or . . . Smoke pondered, gazing from Drifter at the miners, Tilden might try to name a marshal for

Fontana, hold a mock election for a sheriff. Colorado had only been a state for a little over two years, and things were still a bit confused. This county had had a sheriff, Smoke recalled, but somebody had shot him and elections had not yet been held to replace the man. And even an illegally elected sheriff would still be the law until commissioners could be sent in and matters were straightened out.

Smoke felt that was the way Tilden was probably leaning. That's the way *he* would play it if Smoke was as amoral as Tilden Franklin.

"You men have been warned," he told the miners. "This is private property. And I don't give a damn what you were told in town. And don't think the men who own the land won't fight to keep it, for you'll be wrong if you do. You've been warned."

"We got the law on our side!" a miner said, considerable heat in his voice.

"What law?"

"Hell, man!" another miner said. "They's an election in town comin' up tomorrow. Gonna be a sheriff for a brand-new town. You won't talk so goddamned tough with the law lookin' over your shoulder, I betcha."

Smoke gazed at the men. "You're all greedy fools," he said softly. "And a lot of you are going to get hurt if you continue with this trespassing. Like I said, you've been warned."

Smoke rode on, putting his back to the men, showing them his contempt.

An hour later, he was in Colby's front yard. Wilbur

Mason had joined Colby by the corral at the sound of Drifter's hooves. A bloody bandage was tied around Wilbur's left arm, high up, close to the shoulder. But Smoke could tell by looking at the man that Wilbur was far from giving up. The man was angry and it showed.

"Boys," Smoke said. "You save anything, Wilbur?"

"Nothing, Matt . . . Smoke. You really the gunfighter?"

"Yes." He swung down and dropped Drifter's reins on the ground. "Do any of you know anything about an election coming up tomorrow in town?"

"No," they said together. Colby added, "What kind of election, Smoke?"

"Sheriff's election. Tilden may be a greedy bastard, but he's no fool. At the most, there is maybe twenty-five of us out here in the high country. There is probably two or three thousand men in Fontana by now. Our votes would be meaningless. And for sure, there will be Tilden men everywhere, ready to prod some of you into a fight if you show up by yourselves in town. So stay out until we can ride in in groups."

"Who's runnin' for sheriff?" Wilbur asked.

"I don't know. A TF man for sure, though. I'll check it out. Bob is staying with Sally, Colby. That all right with you?"

"Sure. He's a good boy, Smoke. And he'll stand fast facin' trouble. He's young, but he's solid."

"I know that. He said Adam was riding out to check the others . . . what's the word so far?"

"They're stayin', Smoke. Boy's asleep in the house now. He's wore out."

"I can imagine." His eyes caught movement near the house. Velvet. "Keep the women close by, Colby. This situation is shaping up to be a bad one."

"Velvet's just a kid, Smoke!" her father protested. "You don't think . . ." He refused to even speak the terrible words.

"She looks older than her years, Colby. And a lot of very rough people are moving into this area. Tilden Franklin will, I'm thinking, do anything to prod us all into something rash. He's made his intentions toward my wife public. So he's pulling out all the stops now."

Both Colby and Wilbur cursed Tilden Franklin.

Smoke waited until the men wound down. "How's your ammo situation?"

"Enough for a war," Colby said.

"Watch your backs." Smoke swung into the saddle and looked at the men. "A war? Well, that's what we've got, boys. And it's going to be a bad one. Some of us are not going to make it. I don't know about you boys, but I'm not running."

"We'll all stand," Wilbur said.

Smoke nodded. "The Indians have a saying." His eyes swept the land. "It's a good place to die."

Chapter Eight

Smoke touched base with as many small ranchers and farmers as he could that day, then slowly turned Drifter's head toward the town of Fontana. There was no bravado in what he was about to do, no sense of being a martyr. The area had to be checked out, and Smoke was the most likely candidate to do that.

But even he was not prepared for the sight that greeted him.

Long before he topped the crest overlooking the town of Fontana, he could see the lights. Long before the rip-roaring town came into view, he could hear the noise. Smoke topped the crest and sat, looking with amazement at the sight that lay beneath and before him.

Fontana had burst at the seams, growing in all directions within three days. From where he sat, Smoke could count fifty new saloons, most no more than hurriedly erected wooden frames covered with canvas. The town had spread a half mile out in any direction, and the streets were packed with shoulder-to-shoulder humanity.

Smoke spoke to Drifter softly and the big, mean-eyed stallion moved out. Smoke stabled Drifter in the oldest of the corrals—a dozen had suddenly burst forth around the area—and filled the trough with corn.

"Stay away from him," he warned the stable boy. "If anyone but me goes into that stall, he'll kill them."

"Yes, sir," the boy said. He gazed at Smoke with adoration-filled eyes. "You really the gunfighter Smoke Jensen?"

"Yes,"

"I'm on your side, Mister Smoke. Name's Billy."

Smoke extended his hand and the boy gravely shook it. Smoke studied the boy in the dim lantern light of the stable. Ragged clothes, shoes with the soles tied so that would not flop.

"How old are you, Billy?"

"Eleven, sir."

"Where are your folks?"

"Dead for more years than I can remember."

"I don't recall seeing you before. You been here long?"

"No, sir. I come in a couple weeks ago. I been stayin' down south of here, workin' in a stable. But the man who owned it married him a grass widow and her kids took over my job. I drifted. Ol' grump that owns this place gimme a job. I sleep here."

Smoke grinned at the "ol' grump" bit. He handed

the boy a double eagle. "Come light, you get yourself some clothes and shoes."

Billy looked at the twenty-dollar gold piece. "Wow!" he said.

Smoke led the boy to Drifter's stall and opened the gate, stepping inside. He motioned the boy in after him. "Pet him, Billy."

Billy cautiously petted the midnight-black stallion. Drifter stopped eating for a moment and swung his big head, looking at him through those yellow, killer-cold, wolf-like eyes. Then he resumed munching at the corn.

"He likes you," Smoke told the boy. "You'll be all right with him. Anyone comes in here and tries to hurt you, just get in the stall with Drifter. You won't be harmed."

The boy nodded and stepped back out with Smoke. "You be careful, Mister Smoke," he warned. "I don't say much to people, but I listen real good. I hear things."

They walked to the wide doors at the front of the stable. "What do you hear, Billy?"

Several gunshots split the torch- and lantern-lit night air of Fontana. A woman's shrill and artificial-sounding laughter drifted to man and boy. A dozen pianos, all playing different tunes, created a confusing, discordant cacophony in the soft air of summer in the high-up country.

"Some guy named of Monte Carson is gonna be elected the sheriff. Ain't no one runnin' agin him."

"I've heard of him. He's a good hand with a gun."

"Better than you?" There was doubt in Billy's voice at that.

"No," Smoke said.

"The boss of this area, that Mister Tilden Franklin, is supposed to have a bunch of gunhands comin' to be deputies."

"Who are they?"

"I ain't heard."

"What have you heard about me?"

"I heard two punchers talkin' yesterday afternoon, over by a tent saloon. Circle TF punchers. But I think they're more than just cowboys. They wore their guns low and tied down."

Very observant boy, Smoke thought.

"If they can angle you in for a backshoot, they'd do it. Talk is, though, this Mister Franklin is gonna let the law handle you. Legal-like, you know?"

"Yeah." Smoke patted the boy's shoulder. "You take good care of Drifter, Billy. And keep your ears clean and open. I'll check you later."

"Yes, sir, Mister Smoke."

Smoke stepped out of the stable and turned to his left. His right hand slipped the thong off the Colt's hammer. Smoke was dressed in black whipcord trousers, black shirt, and dark hat. His spurs jingled as he walked, his boots kicking up little pockets of dust as he headed for the short boardwalk that ran in front of Beeker's General Store, a saloon, and the gunsmith's shop. Smoke's eyes were in constant motion, noting and retaining everything he spotted.

Night seemed to color into day as he approached the boomtown area.

A drunk lurched out from between two tents, almost colliding with Smoke.

"Watch where you're goin' boy," the miner mush-mouthed at him.

Smoke ignored him and walked on.

"A good time comes reasonable," a heavily rouged and slightly overweight woman said, offering her charms to Smoke.

"I'm sure," Smoke told her. "But I'm married."

"Ain't you the lucky one," she said, and stepped back into the shadows of her darkened tent.

He grinned and walked on.

Smoke walked past Beeker's store and glanced in. The man had hired more help and was doing a land office business, a fixed smile on his greedy, weasel face. His hatchet-faced wife was in constant motion, moving around the brightly lighted store, her sharp eyes darting left and right, looking for thieving hands.

Other than her own, Smoke mentally noted.

He walked on, coming to the swinging doors of the saloon. Wild laughter and hammering piano music greeted his ears. It was not an altogether offensive sound. The miners, as a whole, were not bad people. They were here to dig and chip and blast and hammer the rock, looking for gold. In their free time, most would drink and gamble and whore the night away.

Smoke almost stepped inside the saloon, changing his mind just at the very last moment. He stepped back away from the doors and walked on.

He crossed the street and stepped into Louis Longmont's place. The faro and monte and draw and stud poker tables were filled; dice clicked and wheels spun, while those with money in their hands stared and waited for Lady Luck to smile on them.

Most of the time she did not.

Smoke walked to the bar, shoved his way through, and ordered a beer.

He took his beer and crossed the room, dodging drunks as they staggered past. He leaned against a bracing and watched the action.

"Smoke." The voice came from his left.

Smoke turned and looked into the face of Louis Longmont. "Louis," he acknowledged. "Another year, another boom town, hey?"

"They never change. I don't know why I stay with it. I certainly don't need the money."

Smoke knew that was no exaggeration on the gambler's part. The gambler owned a large ranch up in Wyoming Territory. He owed several businesses in San Francisco, and he owned a hefty chunk of a railroad. It was a mystery to many why Louis stayed with the hard life he had chosen.

"Then get out of it, Louis," Smoke suggested.

"But of course," Louis responded with a smile. His eyes drifted to Smoke's twin Colts. "Just as you got out of gunfighting."

Smoke smiled. "I put them away for several years, Louis. Had gold not been found, or had I chosen a different part of the country to settle, I probably would never have picked them up again."

"Lying to others is bad enough, my young friend. But lying to one's self is unconscionable. Can you look at me and tell me you never, during those stale years, missed the dry-mouthed moment before the draw? The challenge of facing and besting those miscreants who would kill you or others who seek a better and more peaceful way? The so-called loneliness of the hoot-owl trail? I think not, Mister Jensen. I think not."

There was nothing for Smoke to say, for Louis was right. He had missed those death-close moments. And Sally knew it too. Smoke had often caught her watching him, silently looking at him as he would stand and gaze toward the mountains, or as his eyes would follow the high flight of an eagle.

"Your silence tells all, my friend," Louis said. "I know only too well."

"Yeah," Smoke said, looking down into his beer mug. "I guess I'd better finish my beer and ride. I don't want to be the cause of any trouble in your place, Louis."

"Trouble, my friend, is something I have never shied away from. You're safer here than in any other place in this woe-begotten town. If I can help it, you will not be backshot in my place."

And again, Smoke knew the gambler was telling the truth. Smoke and Louis had crossed trails a dozen times over the years. The man had taken a liking to the boy when Smoke was riding with the Mountain Man Preacher. In the quieter moments of his profession, Louis had shown Smoke the tricks of his gambler's trade. Louis had realized that Smoke possessed a keen intelligence, and Louis liked those people who tried to better themselves, as Smoke had always done.

They had become friends.

Hard hoofbeats sounded on the dirt street outside the gambling tent. Smoke looked at Louis.

"About a dozen riders," Smoke said.

"Probably the 'deputies' Tilden Franklin called in from down Durango way. They'll be hardcases, Smoke."

"Is this election legal?"

"Of course not. But it will be months before the state can send anyone in to verify it or void it. By then, Franklin will have gotten his way. Initial reports show the gold, what there is of it, assays high. But the lode is a narrow one. I suspect you already knew that."

"I've known about the vein for a long time, Louis. I never wanted gold."

A quick flash of irritation crossed Louis's face. "It is well and good to shun wealth while one is young, Smoke. But one had best not grow old without some wealth."

"One can have wealth without riches, Louis," Smoke countered.

The gambler smiled. "I believe Preacher's influence was strong on you, young man."

"There could have been no finer teacher in all the world, Louis."

"Is he alive, Smoke?"

"I don't know. If so, he'd be in his eighties. I like to think he's still alive. But I just don't know."

Louis knew, but he elected to remain silent on the subject. At least for the time being.

Boots and jangling spurs sounded on the raw boards in front of Louis's place. And both Louis and Smoke knew the time for idle conversation had passed.

They knew before either man sighted the wearers of those boots and spurs.

The first rider burst into the large tent.

"I don't know him," Louis said. "You?"

"Unfortunately. He's one of Tilden's gunhands. Calls himself Tay. I ran into him when I was riding with Preacher. Back then he was known as Carter. I heard he was wanted for murder back in Arkansas."

"Sounds like a delightful fellow," Louis said drily.

"He's a bully. But don't sell him short. He's hell with a short gun."

Louis smiled. "Better than you, Smoke?" he asked, a touch of humor in the question.

"No one is better than me, Louis," Smoke said, in one of his rare moments of what some would call arrogance; others would call it merely stating a proven fact.

Louis's chuckle held no mirth. "I believe I am better, my friend."

"I hope we never have to test that out of anger, Louis."

"We won't," Louis replied. "But let's do set up some cans and make a small wager someday."

"You're on."

The gunfighter Tay turned slowly, his eyes drifting first to Louis, then to Smoke.

"Hello, punk!" Tay said, his voice silencing the

piano player and hushing the hubbub of voices in the gaming tent.

"Are you speaking to me, you unshaven lout?" Louis asked.

"Naw," Tay said. The leather thongs that secured his guns were off, left and right. "Pretty boy there."

"You're a fool," Smoke said softly, his voice carrying to Tay, overheard by all in the gaming room.

"I'm gonna kill you for that!" Tay said.

Those men and women seated between Tay and Smoke cleared out, moving left and right.

"I hope you have enough in your pockets to bury you," Smoke said.

Tay's face flushed, both hands hovering over the butt of his guns.

He snarled at Smoke.

Smoke laughed at him.

"A hundred dollars on the Circle TF rider," a man seated at a table said.

"You're on," Louis said taking the wager. "Gentlemen," he said to Smoke and Tay. "Bets are down."

Tay's eyes were shiny, but his hands were steady over his guns.

Smoke held his beer mug in his left hand.

"Draw, goddamn you!" Tay shouted.

"After you," Smoke replied. "I always give a sucker a break whenever possible."

Tay grabbed for his guns.

Chapter Nine

"Your behavior the other day was disgusting!" Ralph Morrow would not let up on his wife. "Those men are dead because of you. You do realize that, don't you?"

Bountiful tossed her head, her blond curls bouncing around her beautiful face. Her lips were set in a pout. "I did nothing," she said defending her actions.

"My God, I married an animal!" Ralph said, disgust in his voice. "Can't you see you're a minister's wife?"

"I'm beginning to see a lot of things, Ralph. One of which is I made a mistake."

"In coming out West? Did we have a choice, Bountiful? After your disgraceful behavior in Ohio, I'm very lucky the church even gave me another chance."

She waved that off. "No, Ralph, not that. In my marrying such a pompous wee-wee!"

Ralph flushed and balled his fists. "You take that back!" he yelled at her.

"You take that back!" she repeated mimicking him scornfully. "My God, Ralph! You're such a flummox!"

Man and wife were several miles from the town of

Fontana. They were on the banks of a small creek. Ralph sat down on the bank and refused to look at her. A short distance away at their camp, the others tried without much success not to listen to their friends quarrel.

"They certainly are engaged in a plethora of flap-doodle," Haywood observed.

"I feel sorry for him," Dana said.

"I don't," Ed said. "It's his own fault he's such a sissy-pants."

All present looked at Ed in the dancing flames of the fire. If there was a wimp among them, it was Ed. Ed had found a June bug in his blankets on the way West and, from his behavior one might have thought he'd discovered a nest of rattlers. It had taken his wife a full fifteen minutes to calm him down.

Haywood sat on a log and puffed his Meerschaum. Of them all, Haywood was the only person who knew the true story about Ralph Morrow. And if the others wanted to think him a sissy-pants . . . well, that was their mistake. But Haywood had to admit that, from all indications, when Ralph had fully accepted Christ into his life, he had gone a tad overboard.

If anyone had taken the time to just look at Ralph, they would have noticed the rippling boxer's muscles; the broad, hard, flat-knuckled fists; the slightly crooked nose. It had always amazed Haywood how so many people could look at something, but never see it.

Haywood suppressed a giggle. Come to think of it, he mused, Ralph *did* sort of act a big milquetoast.

But it should be interesting when Ralph finally got a belly full of it.

Smoke cleared leather before Tay got his pistols free of their holsters. Smoke drew with such blinding speed, drawing, cocking, firing, not one human eye in the huge tent could follow the motion.

The single slug struck Tay in the center of the chest and knocked him backward. He struggled up on one elbow and looked at Smoke through eyes that were already glazing over. He tried to lift his free empty hand; the hand was so heavy he thought his gun was in it. He began squeezing his trigger finger. He was curious about the lack of noise and recoil.

Then he fell back onto the raw, rough-hewn board floor and was curious no more.

"Maybe we won't set up those tin cans," Louis muttered, just loud enough for Smoke to hear it.

"Tie him across a saddle and take him back to Tilden Franklin," Smoke said, his voice husky due to the low-hanging cigarette and cigar smoke in the crowded gaming tent. "Unless some of you boys want to pick up where Tay left off."

The riders appeared to be in a mild state of shock. They were all, to a man, used to violence; that was their chosen way of life. They had all, to a man, been either witnesses to or participants in stand-up gunfights, backshoots, and ambushes. And they had all heard of the young gunslick Smoke Jensen. But since none had ever seen the man in action, they had tended to dismiss much of what they had heard as so much pumped-up hoopla.

Until this early evening in the boom town of Fontana, in Louis Longmont's gaming tent.

"Yes, sir, Mister Jensen," one young TF rider said. "I mean," he quickly corrected himself, "I'll sure tie him across his saddle."

Until this evening, the young TF rider had fancied himself a gunhawk. Now he just wanted to get on his pony and ride clear out of the area. But he was afraid the others would laugh at him if he did that.

Smoke eased the hammer down with his thumb. A very audible sigh went up inside the tent with that action. There was visible relaxing of stomach muscles when Smoke holstered the deadly Colt.

Smoke looked at the young puncher who had spoken. "Come here," he said.

The young man, perhaps twenty at the most, quickly crossed the room to face Smoke. He was scared, and looked it.

"What's your name?" Smoke asked.

"Pearlie."

"You're on the wrong side, Pearlie. You know that?"

"Mister Smoke," Pearlie said in a low tone, so only Smoke and Louis could hear. "The TF brand can throw two hundred or more men at you. And I ain't kiddin'. Now, you're tough as hell and snake-quick, but even you can't fight that many men."

"You want to bet your life, Pearlie?" Louis asked him. The man's voice was low-pitched and his lips appeared not to move at all.

Pearlie cut his eyes at the gambler. "I ain't got no choice, Mister Longmont."

"Yes, you do," Smoke said.

"I'm listenin'."

"I need a hand I can trust. I think that's you, Pearlie."

The young man's jaw dropped open. "But I been ridin' for the TF brand!"

"How much is he paying you?"

"Sixty a month."

"I'll give you thirty and found."

Pearlie smiled. "You're serious!"

"Yes, I am. Have you the sand in you to make a turn-around in your life?"

"Give me a chance, Mister Smoke."

"You've got it. Are you quick with that Colt?"

"Yes, sir. But I ain't nearabouts as quick as you."

"Have you ever used it before?"

"Yes, sir."

"Would you stand by me and my wife and friends, Pearlie?"

"Till I soak up so much lead I can't stand, Mister Smoke."

Smoke cut his eyes at Louis. The man smiled and nodded his head slightly.

"You're hired, Pearlie."

"Pearlie did *what?*" Tilden screamed.

Clint repeated his statement, standing firm in front of the boss. Clint was no gunhawk. He was as good as or better with a short gun than most men, but had never fancied himself a gunfighter. He knew horses, he knew cattle, and he could work and manage men. There was no backup in Clint. He had fought Indians, outlaws, nesters, and other ranchers during his years with Tilden Franklin, and while he didn't always approve of everything Tilden did, Clint rode for the brand. And that was that.

"Goddamned, no-good little pup!" Tilden spat out the words. He lifted his eyes and stared into his foreman's eyes. "This can't be tolerated, Clint."

Clint felt a slight sick feeling in his stomach. He knew what was coming next. "No, sir. You're right."

"Drag him!" Tilden spat the horrible words.

"Yes, sir." Clint turned away and walked out of the room. He stood on the porch for a long moment, breathing deeply. He appeared to be deep in thought.

Louis shut the gaming room down early that evening. And with Louis Longmont, no one uttered any words of protest. They simply got up and left. And neither did anyone take any undue umbrage, for all knew Louis's games were straight-arrow honest.

He closed the wooden door to his gaming-room tent, extinguished most of the front lights, and set a bottle of fine scotch on the table.

"I know you're not normally a hard-drinking man, my young friend," Louis said, as he poured two tumblers full of the liquid. "But savor the taste of the Glenlivet. It's the finest made."

Smoke picked up the bottle and read the label. "Was this stuff made in 1824?"

Louis smiled. "Oh, no. That's when the distillery was founded. Old George Smith knew his business, all right."

"Knew?"

"Yes. He died six—no, seven years ago. I was on the Continent at the time."

Smoke sipped the light scotch. It was delicate, yet mellow. It had a lightness that was quite pleasing.

"I had been to a rather obscure place called Monte Carlo." Louis sniffed his tumbler before sipping.

"I never heard of that place."

"I own part of the casino," Louis said softly.

"Make lots of money?"

Louis's reply was a smile.

It silently spoke volumes.

"Prior to that, I was enjoying the theater in Warsaw. It was there I was introduced to Madame Modjeska. It was quite the honor. She is one of the truly fine actresses in the world today."

"You're talking over my head, Louis."

"Madame Mudrzejeweski."

"Did you just swallow a bug, Louis?"

Louis laughed. "No. She shortened her name to Modjeska. She is here in America now. Performing Shakespeare in New York, I believe. She also tours."

Smoke sipped his scotch and kept his mouth shut.

"When I finally retire, I believe I shall move to New York City. It's quite a place, Smoke. Do you have any desires at all to see it?"

"No," Smoke said gently.

"Pity," the gambler said. "It is really a fascinating place. Smoke?"

The young rancher-farmer-gunfighter lifted his eyes to meet Louis's.

"You should travel, Smoke. Educate yourself. Your wife is, I believe, an educated woman. Is she not?"

"Schoolteacher."

"Ah . . . yes. I thought your grammar, most of the time, had improved since last we spoke. Smoke . . . get out while you have the time and opportunity to do so."

"No."

"Pearlie was right, Smoke. There are too many against you."

Smoke took a small sip of his scotch. "I am not alone in this, Louis. There are others."

"Many of whom will not stand beside you when it gets bad. But I think you know that."

"But some of them will, Louis. And bear this in mind: we control the high country."

"Yes, there is that. Tell me, your wife has money, correct?"

"Yes. I think she's wealthy."

"You *think?*"

"I told you, Louis. I'm not that interested in great wealth. My father is lying atop thousands and thousands of dollars of gold."

Louis smiled. "And there are those who would desecrate his grave for a tenth of it," he reminded the young man.

"I'm not one of them."

Louis sighed and drained his tumbler, refilling it from the bottle of scotch. "Smoke, it's 1878. The West is changing. The day of the gunfighter, men like you and me, is coming to a close. There is still a great rowdy element moving Westward, but by and large, the people who are now coming here are demanding peace. Soon there will be no place for men like us."

"And? So?"

"What are you going to do then?"

"I'll be right out there on the Sugarloaf, Louis, ranching and farming and raising horses. And," he said with a smile, "probably raising a family of my own."

"Not if you're dead, Smoke." The gambler's words were softly offered.

Smoke drained his tumbler and stood up, tall and straight and heavily muscled. "The Sugarloaf is my home, Louis. Sally's and mine. And here is where we'll stay. Peacefully working the land, or buried in it."

He walked out the door.

Chapter Ten

Smoke made his spartan camp some five miles outside of Fontana. With Drifter acting as guard, Smoke slept soundly. He had sent Pearlie to his ranch earlier that night, carrying a handwritten note introducing him to Sally. One of the older ranchers in the area, a man who was aligned on neither side, had told Smoke that Pearlie was a good boy who had just fallen in with the wrong crowd, that Pearlie had spoken with him a couple of times about leaving the Circle TF.

Smoke did not worry about Pearlie making any ungentlemanly advances toward Sally, for she would shoot him stone dead if he tried.

Across the yard from the cabin, Smoke and Sally had built a small bunkhouse, thinking of the day when they would need extra hands. Pearlie would sleep there.

Smoke bathed—very quickly—in a small, rushing creek and changed clothes: a gray shirt, dark trousers. He drank the last of his pot of coffee, extinguished the small fire, and saddled Drifter.

He turned Drifter's head toward Fontana, but angling slightly north of the town, planning on coming in from a different direction.

It would give those people he knew would be watching him something to think about.

About half a mile from Fontana, Smoke came up on a small series of just-begun buildings; tents lay behind the construction site. He sat his horse and looked at Preacher Morrow swinging an axe. The preacher had removed his shirt and was clad only in his short-sleeve undershirt. Smoke's eyes took in the man's heavy musculature and the fluid way he handled the axe.

A lot more to him than meets the eyes, Smoke thought. A whole lot more.

Then Smoke's eyes began to inspect the building site. Not bad, he thought. Jackson's big store across the road, and the offices of the others in one long building on the opposite side of the road. The cabins would be behind the offices, while Jackson and his wife and brother would live in quarters behind but connected to the store.

Smoke's eyes caught movement to his left.

"Everything meet with your approval, Mister Jensen?"

Smoke turned Drifter toward the voice. Ed Jackson. "Looks good. The preacher's a pretty good hand with an axe, wouldn't you say?"

"Oh . . . him? 'Bout the only thing he's good at. He's a sissy."

Smoke smiled, thinking: Shopkeeper, I hope you

never push that preacher too hard, 'cause he'll damn sure break you like a matchstick.

Hunt, Colton, Haywood, and their wives walked out to where Smoke sat on Drifter. He greeted the men and took his hat off to the ladies. Bountiful was not with the group and Smoke was grateful for that. The woman was trouble.

Then he wondered where the shopkeeper's brother was. He wondered if Bountiful and Paul might be . . .

He sighed and put his hat back on, pushing those thoughts from him. He dismounted and ground-reined Drifter.

"Going into town to vote, Mister Jensen?" Hunt asked.

"No point in it. One-sided race from what I hear."

"Oh, no!" Colton told him. "We have several running for mayor, half a dozen running for sheriff, and two running for city judge."

"Tilden Franklin's men will win, believe me."

"Mister Franklin seems like a very nice person to me," Ed said, adding, "not that I've ever met the gentleman, of course. Just from what I've heard about him."

"Yeah, he's a real prince of a fellow," Smoke said, with enough sarcasm in his voice to cover hotcakes thicker than molasses. "Why just a few days ago he was nice enough to send his boys up into the high country to burn out a small rancher-farmer named Wilbur Mason. Shot Wilbur and scattered his wife and kids. He's made his boast that he'll either run me out or kill me, and then he'll have my wife. Yeah, Tilden is a sweet fellow, all right."

"I don't believe that!" Ed said, puffing up.

Smoke's eyes narrowed and his face hardened. Haywood looked at the young man and both saw and felt danger emanating from him. He instinctively put an arm around his wife's shoulders and drew her to him.

Smoke said, his eyes boring into Ed's eyes, "Shopkeeper, I'll let that slide this one time. But let me give you a friendly piece of advice." He cut his eyes, taking in, one at a time, all the newcomers to the West. "You folks came here from the East. You do things differently back East. I didn't say better, just different. Out here, you call a man a liar, you'd better be ready to do one of two things: either stand and slug it out with him or go strap on iron.

"Now you all think about that, and you'll see both the right and wrong in it. I live here. Me and my wife been here for better than three years. We hacked a home out of the wilderness and made it nice. We fought the hard winters, Indians a few times, and we know the folks in this area. You people, on the other hand, just come in here. You don't know nobody, yet you're going to call me a liar. See what I mean, Shopkeeper?

"Now the wrong of it is this: there are bullies who take advantage of the code, so to speak. Those types of trash will prod a fellow into a fight, just because they think that to fight is manly, or some such crap as that. Excuse my language, ladies. But the point is, you got to watch your mouth out here. The graveyards are full of people ignorant of the ways of the West."

Ed Jackson blustered and sweated, but he did not offer to apologize.

He won't make it, Smoke thought. *Someone will*

either run him out or kill him. And mankind will have lost nothing by his passing.

"Why is Franklin doing these things, Mister Jensen?" Haywood asked.

"Smoke. Call me Smoke. Why? Because he wants to be king. Perhaps he's a bit mad. I don't know. I do know he hates farmers and small ranchers. As for me, well, I have the Sugarloaf and he wants it."

"The Sugarloaf?" Hunt asked.

"My valley. Part of it, that is."

"Are you suggesting the election is rigged?" Haywood inquired.

"No. I'm just saying that Tilden's people will win, that's all."

"Has Mister Franklin offered to buy any of the farmers' or ranchers' holdings?" Hunt asked.

Smoke laughed. "Buy? Lawyer, men like Tilden don't offer to buy. They just run people out. Did cruel kings offer to buy lands they desired? No, they just took it, by force."

Preacher Morrow had ceased his work with the axe and had joined the group. His eyes searched for his wife and, not finding her present, glowered at Ed Jackson.

Maybe I was right, Smoke thought.

"Are you a Christian, Mister Jensen?" he asked, finally taking his eyes from the shopkeeper.

Bad blood between those two, Smoke thought. "I been to church a few times over the years. Sally and me was married in a proper church."

"Have you been baptized, sir?"

"In a little crick back in Missouri, yes, sir, I was."

"Ah, wonderful! Perhaps you and your wife will attend services just as soon as I get my church completed?"

"I knew a lay preacher back in Missouri preached on a stump, Preacher Morrow. Look around you, sir. You ever in all your life seen a more beautiful cathedral? Look at them mountains yonder. Got snow on 'em year-round. See them flowers scattered around, those blue and purple ones? Those are columbines. Some folks call them Dove Flowers. See the trees? Pine and fir and aspen and spruce and red cedar. What's wrong with preaching right in the middle of what God created?"

"You're right, of course, sir. I'm humbled. You're a strange man, Mister Jensen. And I don't mean that in any ugly way."

"I didn't take it in such a way. I know what you mean. The West is a melting pot of people, Preacher. Right there in that town of Fontana, there's a man named Louis Longmont. He's got degrees from places over in Europe, I think. He owns ranches, pieces of railroads, and lots of other businesses. But he follows the boom towns as a gambler. He's been decorated by kings and queens. But he's a gambler, and a gunfighter. My wife lives in a cabin up in the mountains. But she's worth as much money as Tilden Franklin, probably more. She's got two or three degrees from fancy colleges back East, and she's traveled in Europe and other places. Yet she married me.

"I know scouts for the Army who used to be college professors. I know cowboys who work for thirty and found who can stand and quote William Shakespeare for hours. And them that listen, most of them, can't even read or write. I know Negroes who fought for the North and white men who wore the Gray who now work side by side and who would die for each other. Believe it."

"And you, Smoke?" Hunt asked. "What about you?"

"What about me? I raise cattle and horses and farm. I mind my own business, if people will let me. And I'll harm no man who isn't set on hurting me or mine. We need people like you folks out here. We need some stability. Me and Sally are gonna have kids one day, and I'd like for them to grow up around folks like you." He cut his eyes to Ed Jackson. "Most of you, that is." The store owner caught the verbal cut broadside and flushed. "But for a while yet, it's gonna be rough and rowdy out here." Smoke pointed. "Ya'll see that hill yonder? That's Boot Hill. The graveyard. See that fancy black wagon with them people walking along behind it, going up that hill? That wagon is totin' a gunhawk name of Tay. He braced me last night in Louis's place. He was a mite slow."

"You killed yet *another* man?" Ed blurted out.

"I've killed about a hundred men," Smoke said. "Not counting Indians. I killed twenty, I think, one day up on the Uncompahgre. That was back in '74, I think. A year later I put lead into another twenty or so over in Idaho, town name of Bury. Bury don't exist no more. I burned it down.*

---

*Return of the Mountain Man

"People, listen to me. Don't leave this area. We got to have some people like you to put down roots, to stay when the gold plays out. And it will, a lot sooner than most folks realize. And," Smoke said with a sigh, "we're gonna need a doctor and nurse and preacher around here . . . the preacher for them that the doc can't patch up."

The newcomers were looking at Smoke, a mixture of emotions in their eyes. They all wanted for him to speak again.

"Now I'm heading into town, people," Smoke said. "And I'm not going in looking for trouble. But I assure you all, it will come to me. If you doubt that, come with me for an hour. Put aside your axes and saws and ride in with me. See for yourself."

"I'll go with you," Preacher Morrow said. "Just let me bathe in the creek first."

All the men agreed to go.

Should be interesting, Smoke thought. For he planned to take Preacher Morrow into Louis's place. Not that Smoke thought the man would see anything he hadn't already seen . . . several times before, in his past.

THE FIRST MOUNTAIN MAN SERIES BY
WILLIAM W. JOHNSTONE